FAMILY
TREES

FAMILY TREES

KERSTIN MARCH

Bayfield, WI.
Best wishes!
Kerstin March

KENSINGTON BOOKS
www.kensingtonbooks.com

This book is a work of fiction. Names, characters, places, and incidents either are products of the author's imagination or are used fictitiously. Any resemblance to actual persons, living or dead, events, or locales is entirely coincidental.

KENSINGTON BOOKS are published by

Kensington Publishing Corp.
119 West 40th Street
New York, NY 10018

Copyright © 2015 by Kerstin E. March

All rights reserved. No part of this book may be reproduced in any form or by any means without the prior written consent of the Publisher, excepting brief quotes used in reviews.

All Kensington titles, imprints, and distributed lines are available at special quantity discounts for bulk purchases for sales promotion, premiums, fundraising, educational, or institutional use.

Special book excerpts or customized printings can also be created to fit specific needs. For details, write or phone the office of the Kensington Special Sales Manager: Kensington Publishing Corp., 119 West 40th Street, New York, NY 10018. Attn. Special Sales Department. Phone: 1-800-221-2647.

Kensington and the K logo Reg. U.S. Pat. & TM Off.

eISBN-13: 978-1-61773-525-7
eISBN-10: 1-61773-525-6
First Kensington Electronic Edition: June 2015

ISBN-13: 978-1-61773-524-0
ISBN-10: 1-61773-524-8
First Kensington Trade Paperback Printing: June 2015

10 9 8 7 6 5 4 3 2 1

Printed in the United States of America

For David, with love

This saying good-bye on the edge of the dark
And cold to an orchard so young in the bark
Reminds me of all that can happen to harm
An orchard away at the end of the farm.

—"Good-bye and Keep Cold," Robert Frost

CHAPTER 1

HOOKY

A letter with familiar handwriting scrawled erratically in purple ink sat atop the entryway table. It taunted Shelby Meyers as she reached for her keys. She hesitated, and then picked up the white envelope with its crooked stamp. Running her finger over its sharp corners, she considered dropping it into the trash bin and walking out the door of her grandparents' farmhouse.

Over time, corresponding with her mother had become a game. Experience taught Shelby to stop lobbing heartfelt words across the country to whichever city her mother called home. Thoughtless words were slammed back in reply. Her mother's comments were too forceful, and too well positioned, for Shelby to volley back. She learned at a young age to swing lightly, to never challenge, and to accept the fact that she had an opponent rather than a parent. Love–40. Game. Set. Match. Jackie Meyers racks up another win over her only child.

"That you, Shelby?" Her grandmother's voice wafted down the hallway along with the heavy aroma of fried bacon.

Even on a Saturday morning in August, the activities in their household were in full swing before the sun rose.

"In here, Gran."

Although Shelby knew the letter in her hand would contain nothing but more disappointment, she slipped it into her backpack with a pang of expectancy. Maybe this time her mother had put down her racquet and was ready to greet her daughter peacefully at the net. Maybe this time she had written with affection.

"A piece of mail came for you. From your mother." Ginny Meyers walked toward Shelby, wiping her wet hands against a faded paisley apron that was tied snugly around her waist. Ginny believed in hard work and modesty, gratitude and honesty. Her body was still slender and toned from years of working in the outdoors, but her cheeks were round and flushed pink with an abundance of nurturing kindness. Her heavy-lidded eyes were as brown as the earth, warmed with grace, and sparkled with more than a hint of mischief.

"Yep, I found it," Shelby said.

"Fair enough." Ginny looked at the empty space on the table where she had set Jackie's letter the evening before. "She means well."

Shelby gave her grandmother a knowing glance. They both knew the truth.

"You know how busy she is. It's nice that she keeps in touch." Ginny nodded her head, as if willing Shelby to agree with her.

"I suppose."

"Right. Well. She'll come around. I'm sure of it." Ginny's shoulders dropped with a heavy sigh. She reached out to Shelby and gave her a motherly kiss on the cheek. "It's just a matter of time."

Shelby closed her eyes while in her grandmother's embrace and she, too, relaxed. "I should get going."

"No breakfast?"

"Sorry—can't. I want to catch the first ferry."

"Yes, of course. Now scoot!" Ginny opened the front door and affectionately pushed Shelby out of the house that had been her home since birth. "*Promise* me you'll have some fun this weekend."

"Don't I always?" Shelby called over her shoulder.

"Do you really want me to answer that?"

"Love you!"

Shelby heard the front door shut gently behind her as she stepped off the front porch and into the early morning light. She inhaled deeply, taking in the healing powers of Lake Superior's South Shore air. Crisp and clean, she welcomed the familiar scent of balsam, wildflower, white pine, and the damp soil of her grandparents' apple orchard. It was an aroma that always made her feel connected to this place atop the bluffs of Bayfield, Wisconsin.

All was quiet aside from the sound of her footsteps. She sensed a shift occurring in the nearby woods, a changing of the guards, of nocturnal creatures heading for their burrows while the sun-loving animals were just beginning to stir.

Shelby opened the door to her '84 Chevy pickup with a grinding creak, its white paint dulled by rusty edges and a faint layer of dust. She hoisted herself into the cab with ease, pulled a seat belt across her chest, and started up the engine. With the truck in gear, gravel rolled and crunched under the tires' weight as she passed groves of gnarled apple trees, the processing barn, and a hand-painted sign that welcomed customers to Meyers Orchard.

The road leading down the hills into Bayfield Township took her past acres of robust orchards, a few remnants of rusting machinery discarded on the roadside, and a long-retired fishing boat sitting lopsided in a hay field. Knowing the sun would cast a rosy hue on the lake at this time of day, she anticipated the view at her favorite point in the drive. The spot where, for just a moment, she would see Chequamegon Bay sprawled out at the foot of town. It was never a conscious decision to slow down, but somehow her foot always lifted slightly off the gas pedal so she could hold the view for just a moment longer.

The lake never disappointed her. Continuing her drive into town, Shelby marveled at the expanse of water that spanned across the horizon and was adorned by the Apostle Islands archipelago. She watched seagulls circle above a departing fishing boat that motored steadily through the calm, sunrise-reflecting waters.

Her truck coasted around the bend before descending down the sloped road toward town. The marina stood at the water's edge and was wakening with day sailors washing down decks and checking lines. Some were already heading out zigzagging their way across the steel blue bay that separated her historic hometown from the islands.

Bayfield was populated with an eclectic blend of artists, craftsmen, and mariners. It was a place where the Chippewa culture ran as deep as the lake. A town where whitewashed clapboard houses and picket fences were reminiscent of immigrants who made their living fishing, lumbering, and quarrying for brownstone. It was the home to families who loved the land, their children, and the lives they built. This was a community that buttoned up in the wintertime, braving barren isolation, ice road lake crossings, and bitter cold temperatures. In reward, they basked in the glorious summer sun amidst lavender lupine, shimmering poplars, and fragrant apple trees.

And the grand force of it all was the lake herself. As lovely and temperamental as a woman, Lake Superior could dazzle admirers one moment and then, without warning, lash out in fury. When gentle, she would allow a kayak to lightly caress her sparkling surface. And when wicked, she could take a man's breath away and swallow him whole into her icy belly.

This was home. Shelby couldn't imagine living anywhere else.

Shelby drove past the marina and continued on to Main Street. She knew there would be ample street parking at this time in the morning, for the town was like a teen who lazily rises in the mid-morning hours. She spotted a familiar old flatbed truck parked beneath the outstretched branches of a maple tree and pulled in behind it.

"Hey, Gloria!" Shelby hopped out of her truck and called out to the woman who was organizing pint-sized cartons of blueberries into a makeshift fruit stand in the back of her truck. It was a wonder Gloria's truck still ran. Rusted parts dangled precariously from its body, which seemed to be held together with nothing more than yards of chicken wire and silver duct tape.

"Mornin'," Gloria replied, looking up briefly and flashing a broken-tooth smile. She was a tattered woman who looked twice her age due to hard living.

"You don't waste any time setting up, do you?" With her backpack slung over her shoulder, Shelby pressed down the door lock and pushed the door shut.

"You know, early bird and all that."

"Need help?"

"You buyin' berries?" Gloria lived just outside of town in a neglected cabin that sat on ten acres. Although her home was located just off of the main road, very few knew of its existence because it was carefully hidden away among the pines. The land had been passed down through her family and was once the site of a nineteenth-century brickyard. When she wasn't tending to her garden, Gloria regularly scoured her property and the quiet creek that ran through it, searching for remnants of old bricks, pottery, and artifacts in the ground. She used whatever the land provided to make a living, whether dirty remnants of Bayfield's history, twig baskets and honey in the fall, or holiday wreaths made from delicate ground moss and pine.

"You read my mind," Shelby said, walking over to Gloria's humble display. "I'm heading over to the island today. These will be perfect."

Gloria eyed Shelby's backpack. "Playin' hooky?"

"Something like that," Shelby said, picking up two pints and laying down a five. "My grandfather rarely gets the house to himself. Whenever I'm away, Gran likes to visit friends in town, which gives him a chance to have the guys over for poker. He said something about wanting to win back the money he lost in the last game."

After stuffing the bill into her pocket, Gloria ended the conversation with an abrupt nod to Shelby and returned to unloading berries.

Typical Gloria, Shelby thought, smiling in amusement as she began her walk down Main Street. As usual, she was dressed in tune with the outdoors rather than fashion. Her wardrobe mainly consisted of faded jeans, neutral-colored T-shirts, worn boots, sandals, and a turquoise pendant necklace that was a gift from her grandfather. She did little to accentuate her brown eyes, naturally bright skin, and long waves of brunette hair that was often pulled back into a lose ponytail. However, while casual, she always appeared polished. Most of all, Shelby carried herself with confident ease and a warm disposition that drew people to her like seagulls to the water.

"Look at you!" Lou Olson emerged from the grocery store next door, a cheese Danish in his mouth and a newspaper folded under his arm. With his barrel chest, thick upper arms, and a beard that stood out around his face as thick and gray as the fur on a timber wolf, her grandparents' friend always reminded her more of a lumberjack than the town dentist. Lou would have retired years ago, except that even after eleven years, he still didn't have enough faith in his "rookie assistant" to let her take over the practice.

"Hey, Lou! Funny running into you. Were your ears burning?" Shelby stopped to ask. "I was just talking about you."

"About tonight's game? Can't wait to sit Olen's ass down at the poker table—pardon my French." He grinned, rubbing his thick hands together and scrunching up his face in anticipation. "Gotta win back the cash he snaked away from me at the last game. The old bastard."

"But I thought . . ."

"No disrespect, but that grandfather of yours is a real sneaky son of a bitch. Has been as long as I've known him."

"So, you're . . ."

"What's that?" Lou leaned toward Shelby with his good ear. "A sore loser? Is that what he called me?"

"No!" She laughed, swinging her backpack to the other shoulder. "I'd say he's as eager for the game as you are."

"I see. Good. That's good." He hesitated, readjusting the paper tucked under his arm. "Say, while I have you here, I want to say that I still feel real bad about, you know . . . what happened a while back. Can't seem to get it out of my mind. Especially when I run into you like this."

"Oh." She looked down at the sidewalk and shuffled her feet.

"I just . . ." he stumbled. "We all hope you find someone as good as he was. You know? You deserve that."

"That's nice of you to say." She looked past him, toward the lake, biting her lip and suddenly eager to leave.

"You know, my nephew and his son are visiting this summer. A real nice guy, his son. Works in banking. Maybe you two—" he began to offer, before she cut him off.

"I appreciate it, but, you know . . ." She looked back at Lou and offered a slight smile. "I'm doing fine."

"Right."

"But thanks."

"So," he wrapped up, leaning down to look her in the eye. "You take care."

"You, too. Good luck tonight."

Lou wasn't the first to offer up an eligible bachelor. Walking away, she thought of the men she had been fixed up with in the past three years since Jeff's accident the summer before their senior year in college. While there hadn't been many guys, those she had agreed to see were all good people. Men who would be ideal for other women, but to her were best suited as friends.

By now, she had her share of friends.

Shelby was content in knowing what her future held. The years ahead would simply be variations of her past and present. Same place. Same routine. Same people. The only thing she expected to change was the calendar year and the people who would wander in and out of her life. She no longer dreamed of a slow walk down the aisle to become someone's wife. She wasn't looking for a man to feel complete. She had her grandparents, the orchards, a few close friends, and of course, the lake. It was enough.

Once Shelby reached the end of Main Street, she had just enough time to duck into West Bay Outfitters, which was across the street from the town marina and ferry landing. It was an unpretentious shop down by the lake that offered outdoor gear, kayak rentals, and adventure guide services. Even though Shelby had little time for outdoor adventure, she was one of the shop's favorite patrons. And that had everything to do with the shop's owner, John Karlsson.

"Hey, gorgeous," John called out as she approached his

work counter, which was laden with open nautical charts and stacks of hiking maps and travel brochures. Whenever Shelby looked at John's face, she saw beyond the handsome, rugged man he had become and beheld the soft, endearing face of her towheaded elementary school friend. And she was still caught off guard, at times, that the gangly teenager with braces who ran through the orchards with her on summer evenings now owned his own home and business. "How's my girl?"

"The ever-charming John Karlsson." She leaned across the counter to kiss him on the scruff of his cheek.

"Only for you, Meyers." He turned his cheek at the last moment and her lips settled on his for a brief kiss.

"Fiend!" she scolded.

"You want me. You just don't know it yet." He flashed his most magnetic smile.

She set her backpack on the counter, unzipped the top, and pulled out John's black Windbreaker. Shelby looked at her old friend with a twisted smirk and raised eyebrows.

"So you're not here to get your hands on me?" he asked.

"Oh, I'll put my hands on you all right." She raised a clenched fist. "You're the most forgetful person I know. I swear you do this on purpose just to have Gran send me down here."

"Guilty. But come on. Admit it. You love it," he replied, walking around to her side of the counter and pulling her into a one-armed hug before taking the jacket. "So, what are you up to today? Work . . . or more work?"

"No, no," she said, wiggling out of his embrace. "I'm going to hang out with Nic."

"The boss actually gave you a reprieve?"

"Something like that. Nic and I are just heading over to the Island for an overnight at the Gordons'."

"Perfect day for it. And how is Miss Nicole today? Dark and brooding as usual?"

"Be nice." She walked over to a stacked kayak display and ran her hand over the smooth orange exterior of a new model.

"Remind me again why you're such good friends with her."

"Stop. That question is getting old. Just because you don't like her doesn't mean she can't mean something to me."

"That tells me nothing." John walked up beside her and put his hand on the kayak she was admiring.

"I never know what she's going to do or say, and I like that. She challenges me. She's fun and crazy and tough. What can I say, she keeps things interesting."

"I still don't get it."

"Well, there. That's something you two have in common. She doesn't get you, either."

"Ouch!" He grabbed his chest, feigning injury.

She shook her head and walked around to the other side of the kayak without taking her hands off its sleek surface. "I love this one. How much?"

"Twenty-seven hundred," he replied. "We just got it in this week. Fantastic, isn't it?"

"Beautiful."

"You should buy it."

"Right. On my salary. Besides, I know a great guy who lets me use the demos for free."

"No! Who is it? I'll have him fired!"

"Shoot! John, I'm sorry—I have to run," she blurted out, looking at her watch and rushing to the counter to grab her bag. "Ferry's here—love you!"

"Love you, too," he said softly, taking a step forward as she rushed away. They had been connected since childhood, with John always seeming to follow one step behind.

Rushing out of the shop's front entrance, Shelby took a last look over her shoulder toward John, then she slammed squarely into another man's chest. She made an audible "Oomph!"

upon impact, before collecting herself and seeing that she was in the company of three surprised, but amused men.

"Oh! Sorry! I didn't see you." Scanning their faces and recognizing no one, Shelby easily pegged them as tourists. She smiled and made her way through the narrow entrance as they parted to make room. When Shelby came to the third man, the one holding the door, she paused. Although a stranger to her, he seemed familiar somehow. Standing just over six feet tall, he was lean with a muscular build, broad shoulders, and a sun-kissed face. Dark brown hair that curled playfully around his ears. A slightly upturned smile. Striking green eyes.

Shelby held his gaze for a moment, and when she couldn't place him, she simply thanked him and continued out the door. She jogged down the grassy embankment, her focus on the ferry landing across the street, when she heard a familiar, precious voice.

"Shee-bie!" a child squealed, pulling his tiny hand free from his father's grasp and toddling toward her with as much speed as a three-year-old could muster. She dropped to one knee and held her arms open, just in time for Benjamin to jump full-body into her embrace. Holding him tightly, she stood and twirled Benjamin around. His legs rose into the air as if he was on a ride at the fair. Their giggles intertwined. She smothered his neck with kisses and took in the graham-cracker-milk scent of him.

CHAPTER 2

ANONYMITY

When Ryan Chambers entered West Bay Outfitters, his two travel companions were behaving like boys. Although the group was seven years out of Columbia University, they tended to revert back to their sophomoric pranks during these trips. Brad Thorson gave Pete Whitfield a shove to the left, which was returned by a punch to the shoulder. Pete then reached behind him and gave Ryan a quick shove. Their antics stopped the moment a slender brunette smacked right into Brad's chest with a thump.

"Oh! Sorry!" she gasped, a look of surprise on her face. "I didn't see you guys."

"Hey—no! It was our fault," Pete replied with a broad grin. Pete was the kind of self-deprecating guy who joked about being the typical tall, dark, and handsome type—depending on your definition of tall, dark, and handsome. He stood just under six feet, had hair the color of brown ale, and limbs that were brawny from years of playing rugby.

"Gentlemen, let the lady pass." Pete used his arm to move

Brad's body out of her way while Ryan held the door open for her.

She squeezed past the first two before reaching Ryan. Her eyebrows crinkled slightly as if puzzled by the sight of him. Ryan readied himself for what would come next. It was a situation that had played out countless times before. A woman would recognize him from the media as the son of William and Charlotte Chambers, the successful and highly public couple from Chicago whose media empire put them in the social circles—and headlines—along with some of the country's most notable figures.

First would come the woman's recognition. Then her coquettish overture. Flirtation with fame. And his inevitable, yet polite decline. During their college years, Ryan's friends enjoyed the attention he drew from women, as it had been an undeniable boost to their dating escapades. However, now that they had wives waiting for them in Chicago, Brad and Pete had little interest in Ryan's encounter with this woman. They retreated inside the shop.

Ryan dropped his eyes from her gaze, ready for her clever line. Her flirtatious smile. But it never came. Not a word. Not a glimmer of recognition. She simply thanked him and brushed past as she hurried off toward the ferry.

And that was it.

The tension in his shoulders relaxed. Her reaction, or lack thereof, reassured Ryan that this was the perfect place to escape. In this town, he could get the one thing his money couldn't buy back home. Priceless anonymity.

He was about to turn back into the shop when he heard the overjoyed squeal of a child's voice. Ryan watched as the woman pulled a small boy into her arms and spun him around, drew him close, and kissed his neck. The look on their faces took Ryan's breath away. Unconditional love. A love that every child deserves. A tenderness that epitomizes motherhood. Something he had seen many times in scenes from projects his father's company had produced, but never observed in his own home. Growing up as heir to one of the country's most successful media conglomerates, he was raised in the hollow adoration of the public, amid lights and cameras, when what he craved most was the attention of his parents.

The young woman, who had caused a sense of relief in him by giving him little regard, now had his full attention. Seeing her through the child's eyes, and then his own, Ryan realized how unaware he had been a moment earlier. He had been too focused on himself and preserving that precious sense of privacy. How could he have missed it? She was absolutely beautiful.

"Hey, earth to Ryan," Pete called over. "Are you with us?" In public, Ryan was known as William Chambers Jr. or Will. But to his closest friends, he went by his middle name of Ryan.

"Coming!" The sound of Pete's voice made him realize he had been standing there, lost in his thoughts, watching her until she said good-bye to the child and his father. Her husband? Ryan closed the door behind him and walked across the shop to rejoin his friends.

"See something interesting?" Pete asked with one eye raised.

"Just watching them load the ferry," Ryan answered flatly. He paid little attention to Pete while extending his hand across the counter to the man wearing an Outfitters T-shirt and smoothing out the curl of a scrolled nautical chart. "You must be John."

"Hey, Mr. Chambers."

"I'm not much for formalities," Ryan insisted, reaching out his hand. "Ryan."

"Good to meet you." John returned the handshake.

"Likewise." Ryan smiled. "You have a great operation here."

"What can I say? Life's not bad when a day at the office is a day on the lake."

"I can imagine," Ryan agreed. He looked down at the chart. "Were you guys mapping out our route?"

"Yep," Pete replied. "Instead of a four-day trip, John recommends we do a short overnight on Madeline and return to Bayfield sometime tomorrow afternoon."

"Head out again when the weather clears," Brad added.

Ryan leaned in to get a better look at the course John had plotted out in pencil. "Storm from the southwest?"

"'Fraid so." John looked out the window to his left and squinted toward the rising sun reflecting off the water. "Unless the storm shifts, it'll reach us by around six tomorrow night."

"When I checked the weather before we left Chicago, I saw there was a chance of it hitting this area. How reliable is the forecast?" Ryan asked.

"It's coming," John answered. "And believe me. The last place you'll want to be when it hits is in the middle of this lake with your ass stuck in a kayak."

"Agreed." Ryan looked at his friends for consensus. "Besides, we're pretty good at changing plans at the last minute." A shared zest for spontaneity was what had helped forge their friendship in college. But the truth was, Ryan knew his friends were becoming less willing to participate in his impulsive breaks from reality. They were building careers and establishing homes with the women they loved, while he was no more grounded now than he'd been in college. His parents had grown impatient with him. It was time to step up, they lectured. It was imperative that he embrace his responsibilities, take initiative, roll up his sleeves, and help grow the family business.

Pete nodded.

"No problem." Brad was one of the first friends that Ryan made in college, back when both of the young men were eager to break away from their families, but had very few life skills that would enable their success. While Ryan's mother hired others to handle domestic chores in the home and help raise her son, Mrs. Thorson was a doting mother who did virtually everything for her Brad. As a result, Brad and Ryan were equally ill-equipped for the real world. Once on campus, navigating the Laundromat and making ramen noodles in a coffeepot became a bonding experience for the two freshmen. Then, when Brad and Ryan demonstrated mutual loyalty and stupid courage during a frat party altercation—one that involved a stolen keg of beer, a varsity wrestling trophy, and a taxidermied armadillo—a lasting friendship was born.

"One more thing. There's a sailing regatta today. And, in addition to the sailboats, there will be a number of powerboats out there, so you'll have to keep an eye out as you cross the bay. And you'll want to stay clear of the ferry routes, which run back and forth across the bay right here," John instructed, pointing to the blue dotted line on the chart that linked Bayfield and the historic town of La Pointe on Madeline Island. "Be careful as you round the southern tip of Madeline. The water can get pretty choppy in the south channel as you make your way into the bay. You'll come across brownstone cliffs along the eastern side of Madeline, right here. I'm sure it goes without saying to stay clear of those cliffs if you hit any whitecaps."

"We appreciate all of this, John, but we're experienced on the water," Pete assured him.

"We have our certifications with us," Brad added.

John put both hands squarely on the counter and leaned toward the men. "With all due respect, I don't care if you're Captain Ahab. This is your first time on *this* lake. It's my job to make sure you have a plan. You need to wear your wet suits and respect the water. And by all means, gentlemen, keep your eye on the sky. Conditions here can change on a dime. I have no interest in pulling kayakers off the lake," John said point-blank. "Even the experienced ones."

"All right! All right!" Pete put his hands up.

"Jesus," Brad muttered under his breath.

"We get it, John," Ryan said calmly. Ryan respected John because he didn't give him any special treatment. In fact, he didn't seem to give a damn who he was. "We appreciate the advice. What the guys mean to say is that we've kayaked in the ocean, in cold weather conditions, in remote locations."

"Suit yourself," John said, turning toward the side door that opened to the lake.

John led them outside and down to the shore, where three kayaks sat in the sand, packed and ready for launch. As they walked, Brad casually asked, "Hey, John, do you know who that woman was?"

"Who?" John dropped his cell phone in the sand. "Damn it!" he uttered under his breath while reaching down and brushing the sand from his device.

"You know, the brunette who was leaving as we walked in?"

John hesitated, shoving the phone into his back pocket. "Can't say that I do."

"Huh. It seemed like she knew you."

"No." John shook his head. "Nope."

Brad eyed John as they neared the lake's edge, but his look wasn't returned. "You sure?" he asked again.

"Okay, all set," John announced, slapping his hand down on the nearest kayak. The sound echoed within the vessel's hollow chamber. "Time to get you guys on the water."

"It seems we have a mystery on our hands," Brad taunted

as each man chose a kayak and shoved his day pack into the deck hatches. "And no one likes a good mystery better than you, Chambers."

"That's enough. Now let's hit the water." Ryan was the first to put his kayak in the shallow. He settled into the narrow cockpit and took a firm hold of his paddle. Before taking the first stroke, he looked over his shoulder and saw John standing on the beach. John's arms were crossed, his jaw clenched. He stood silently, feet firmly planted in the sand, almost as if he were waiting for some kind of threat to cast off and disappear into the deep. Ryan turned back to the lake and took his first couple of strokes. He then set his rudder and kept on paddling, enjoying the sound of water lapping against the kayak's hull as he glided out toward open water.

CHAPTER 3

ROCK

Seeing that the ferry was already full and preparing for departure, Shelby raced down between the two lines of cars waiting for the next ferry, and then hurried up the boarding ramp and onto the boat. As expected, Nicole "Nic" Simone was waiting for her.

"Cutting it close this morning?" Nic commented as Shelby joined her on the ferry deck.

"I know! I got a bit sidetracked," Shelby said, catching her breath and setting her bag down at her feet. She turned her head to glance back toward shore, but Benjamin and his father were gone.

"I'd say," Nic mumbled with a raised eyebrow. She followed Shelby's gaze. "Looking for someone?"

"Hmm? Oh, I just saw Benjamin. He was with his dad."

"I saw them, too. Anyone else?"

"No." Shelby's attention turned to the crewman who was loosening the ferry's stern lines.

"Really." Nic ran her hands through her bottle-blond,

pixie-cut hair. What she lacked in stature, she made up for in estrogen-fueled bravado. Nic could talk down the mangiest character with just a few well-honed words. While most people did their best to stay on Nic's good side, Shelby saw something special in her from the day they met in the eighth grade. Shelby broke through Nic's rough façade and appealed to the softer side of her personality, which surprised no one more than Nic herself. In return, Nic gave Shelby a shot of spontaneity during the most unlikely moments.

Shelby shrugged her shoulders. "Come on, we're shoving off." She took a few steps away from the boarding ramp, with Nic in tow.

"Then I guess you don't know anything about that tall guy who was standing in the doorway? The one who watched you run all the way over here?" Nic challenged, gesturing toward West Bay Outfitters with a tilt of her head and raised eyebrows.

"Who?" Shelby watched the crewman work the hydraulics to haul up the stern ramp.

"Are you serious?" Nic exhaled with impatience before taking hold of Shelby's shoulder to get her full attention. "Good God. You really don't know."

"You mean the guys at John's shop?"

"You tell me."

Shelby shrugged out of Nic's hold to allow a family of four to emerge from their car and shuffle toward the topside viewing deck. "I ran into some tourists when I was leaving. I mean *literally*. Slammed right into them." She pointed to one of the crewmen, who appeared to be having difficulty untangling the last bowline. "Nic, maybe you should go help that guy."

"Nah, he'll get it soon enough." Having worked on the Madeline Island Ferry Line since high school, Nic handled herself on ferries better than most men three times her size. "I love you, Shel, but sometimes you really don't have a clue. It's okay to flirt back once in a while. To accept a little attention. Hell, to even *notice* the attention would be a step in the right direction." She cupped her hands and yelled out to whomever was in earshot, "Hey—who here thinks my friend is gorgeous?" Shelby cringed upon hearing a few meager whoops and whistles coming out of a rusted-out van with open windows. Pitiful.

"I don't know what you think you saw. Really. It was nothing." The man at West Bay Outfitters was a tourist. Another guy passing through town. Someone like that was the very last thing she needed. She had seen it far too many times. Visitor who spent short vacations or extended summer stays in town, sparking summer romances that burned out by autumn. Or, in the case of her mother, Jackie, a brief encounter that resulted in pregnancy. When her mother's future skidded to a catastrophic stop, just weeks into her freshman year at a California college, Shelby's life was forming. From the moment of Shelby's birth, though she had played no part in sealing her mother's fate, Jackie mothered her daughter with a resentful heart and regarded her as little more than a reminder of her sordid mistake.

The idea of catching a tourist's eye? Shelby would have no part in it. If Nic was right, then he'd set his sights on the wrong local.

The ferry's engine powered up, churning water into a powerful boil beneath the hull. Shelby could feel the vibration beneath her feet. The sound intensified as sturdy metal chains clanked and lifted the stern lift gate. The crewman, recognizable in his casual khaki pants and blue Madeline Island Ferry Line shirt, returned to set the gate locks. "Morning, Nic!" he called over.

"Hey, Derrick! You on all day?"

"Yep. The *Island Queen* today. *Nichevo* tomorrow. You?" He joined the women, the ferry now in motion.

"I'm off for a few days," Nic replied. "Remember Shelby?"

He wiped his hands on the sides of his khaki pants and then, as if unaware of what to do with them, crossed his arms awkwardly across his chest. "Yea, of course—hey, Shelby!"

"Hey." Shelby smiled back, noticing a smudge of ketchup on the collar of his short-sleeved, blue uniform.

Derrick then returned his attention to Nic, rocking back and forth on his heels as the ferry forged effortlessly into open water. "So, when are you gonna take me up on my offer to grab a beer?"

"Listen, Romeo, you know that won't happen anytime soon."

"Still with Hank?"

"Still with Hank," Nic confirmed.

He turned to Shelby with a boyish grin. "So, Shelby, how 'bout you? You wanna grab a beer one of these nights?"

"You'll get nowhere fast with this one. She doesn't get out much," Nic teased.

Despite the truth in Nic's statement, Shelby still felt its sting. "Ignore this one, Derrick, you're better off without her," Shelby countered. "It was good to see you."

"You, too." He left to collect passenger tickets.

"Catch'ya later!" Nic called out. Derrick waved his hand over his head before ducking down to the passenger window of a silver sedan.

Shelby turned to look out upon the lake. Watching bubbles of white water churn behind the ferry, her thoughts flowed back to her encounter with Benjamin before boarding the ferry. The way the child's eyes squinted when he smiled.

The faint peppering of freckles that crossed over the bridge of his round nose. Blond hair as fine and wispy as dandelion fluff. A contagious, wonderful laugh. Benjamin's resemblance to his uncle Jeff was undeniable—and a bittersweet reminder of what she and his family had lost.

"Coming?" Nic motioned for Shelby to follow. They wove through the parked cars before climbing an iron stairway, as narrow and steep as a ladder, which led to the outdoor upper deck. Each step rang out with a metallic clang.

Shelby found an open seat on one of the paint-chipped red benches near the back of the deck, while Nic ducked into the wheelhouse, as she always did, to greet the captain. Shelby didn't mind. With the *Island Queen* running at top speed, she settled in for a quiet twenty-minute ride across the bay to La Pointe.

Shelby enjoyed the sun's warmth on her face, cooled by the wind that blew across the lake. She watched a regatta in the distance that was racing parallel to the ferry route. While the boats looked serene and graceful, she knew the level of energy aboard them was highly charged. The race was surely exhilarating, with clamorous commands to adjust the mainsails and tighten the jibs, waves crashing against the bows of the speeding vessels, and wind slapping against the billowing sails every time they came about.

But here, from her perch atop the ferry, it looked like a watercolor painting in motion. Bold strokes of color darted across the blue canvas. A feathering of mist that hovered just above the water's surface softened the edges of the landscape. She became lost in it. The lake had a way of taking away her worries. Concerns about the orchard and her grandparents' ability to continue managing it as they aged. The suppressed resentment she felt for her mother. Her enduring grief over

Jeff. And perhaps most of all, her inner compass that had lost its direction. The arrow kept spinning between a decision to stay in Bayfield out of family loyalty—or to branch out on her own.

As the regatta moved on, Shelby imagined herself racing away with the sails, the wind, and the spray, and never looking back.

The *Island Queen* was barely secured to the ferry dock in La Pointe's harbor when Nic grabbed Shelby's hand and pulled her to her feet. "Oh yeah, it's the weekend, baby!" she cheered, rousing her into a livelier mood.

As Shelby made her way down the stairs to the ferry dock, she looked up and noticed Nic's boyfriend, Hank Palmer, right away. It was hard to miss him, sitting in his car at the end of the dock, waiting for their arrival. Nic's boyfriend was a burly man who regularly wore a black knit cap pulled tightly over a tangle of black hair that was as unruly as his beard. He looked like a longshoreman, except instead of traveling aboard an ironclad ship, Hank drove a yellow VW Bug that hardly seemed big enough to contain him.

The women stepped off the ferry and walked down the dock amid a small throng of pedestrians, bikers, and cars, who were disembarking together at this quirky island town. For as long as she had lived in the area, Shelby never ceased to marvel at how time seemed to slow down to a stroll on Madeline Island, and how the days passed as easily as a lazy afternoon on the beach.

"Hey, babe!" Hank called out through the open window of his car as they approached. While the women threw their overnight bags into the trunk, Hank remained seated, rapidly tapping the steering wheel as if it were a snare drum. Shelby was reminded that chivalry was not one of Hank's strong points. Settling herself into the backseat, she watched as Nic slid into the seat beside Hank and he pulled her close for a gentle kiss. "I missed you," he said, nuzzling in her ear.

"Thanks for picking us up," Shelby said, leaning her head back and looking out the window.

"No problem. I'm glad you two are finally here. I don't know how much more I could take being alone with the Gordons. It was a rough night." As he drove, Hank kept one hand on the wheel and held the other one out his car window. The rush of wind streamed off of his open palm and blew into the backseat, whipping wisps of Shelby's hair about her face.

"I'm sure it was *real* difficult," Nic said in a deadpan tone.

"I'm telling you, Nic! They threw ribs on the grill, broke out a few cold beers . . ."

"A few?" Nic eyed the overgrown man at her side.

Shelby enjoyed their banter. They were an unlikely pair who ended up being perfectly suited for one another, like a bear and a precarious beehive laden with honey.

"What else did you guys do? You know, that made the night so difficult," Nic asked.

"They made me sit by the fire and play Scrabble." The image triggered hearty laughter as the yellow Bug sped down Big Bay Road away from the harbor.

Meals at Abby and Luke Gordon's house were always memorable, and the breakfast they prepared the following morning was no different. Poached eggs, roasted potatoes with peppers, blueberry muffins, and dark roast coffee. Although still newlyweds, the couple worked together in the kitchen as if they had been entertaining together for years. They always appeared in synch, whether cooking together in the compact kitchen, or throwing and firing pots in the studio behind their modest cottage. Even in appearance, the Gordons were a perfect match—caramel brown hair streaked blond from the summer sun; Birkenstocks in the summer and Sorels in the winter; blue eyes, square jawlines, and lanky legs. Best of all, they had infectious laughs that made even the most resolute curmudgeon smile.

"Who's up for a walk?" Abby asked after the group had finished their meal. Her wooden chair scraped against the floorboards as she pulled away from the table. "I don't know about you guys, but if I don't get outside after a big breakfast, I'll be napping by noon."

"Sounds good to me." Hank yawned, rubbing his hands over the faded Rolling Stones T-shirt that was stretched tightly across his barrel chest.

"You want to exercise?" Nic asked in surprise.

"What? Hell, no." He ran his finger around the edge of his plate and then sucked off the remaining bits. "I was leaning toward a nap around noon."

"What do you have in mind?" Luke called out to his wife from where he stood in front of the kitchen sink, filling the basin with warm, soapy water. "Where do you think you'll go?"

"State Park?" Abby suggested as she retrieved her shoes from the front hall closet.

"I'm on to you, Abby," Nic said knowingly. "I know your idea of a walk. I'll go, but I'm not jogging over there, then hiking, and then jogging all the way back."

"Don't worry. I'm not feeling that ambitious today," Abby replied. "I thought we'd drive."

"Hey, better yet—let's moped!" Nic jumped up with sudden interest. Then, almost in the same instant, she tempered her enthusiasm and looked directly at Abby. "That is, of course, if it's okay with you. I don't want to assume—"

"But you're so good at it, Nic," Abby teased, rousing a chuckle among the friends. She walked over to Nic and set her arm around her shoulder. "Of course we can. It's a great idea!"

"Great! So which one of you two wants a buck on the back of mine," Nic said, resuming her enthusiasm. Abby shook her head. "Shel?"

Shelby knew better. "Right. I'd rather arrive there in one piece. Abby, I'll ride with you."

"Coward," Nic muttered.

Before heading out, Abby popped back into the kitchen. "Last chance—sure you don't want to come?"

"You go ahead. Hank and I will clean up and then head down to the dock," Luke replied while scrubbing a frying pan in the suds, leaning sideways to kiss his wife without getting her wet.

"And watch the game this afternoon," Hank added, still comfortably seated at the table and nursing a lukewarm cup of coffee.

"What a surprise." Nic reached over to brush a few crumbs off his beard. "Come on, you lug. Get up and make yourself useful. You can't expect Luke to do all of the work."

"Nap later?" He winked and gave her bottom a pat. "You and me?"

"In your dreams, lover boy." Nic pulled on his arm to coax him out of the chair. He surprised her by jumping up suddenly, taking her in his arms, and burrowing his face in her neck, delighting in her giddy shriek.

At the Madeline Island State Park, Abby, Nic, and Shelby parked the pair of mopeds near the trailhead entrance. Although it was nearly noon, there were surprisingly few cars at the park, which ensured the women would enjoy a quiet hike. They set out on a trek that snaked through a serene forest of aging red and white pine, aspen, and maple. The trail itself was well maintained and easy to navigate, aside from a scattering of rocks along the path and fallen trees that lay crumbling and covered in patches of green lichen. Splintered sunbeams shone through the tangled branches overhead, casting pinpoints of light onto the most diminutive plants that carpeted the forest floor—tufts of silver moss, the delicate fringe of blue-petaled wildflowers, and the tangerine pop of shy mushrooms.

Continuing farther down the trail, the forest scents blended with the cool lake breeze and became even more aromatic. Shelby could hear the rhythmic crash of waves sloshing against massive rocks that walled the shore. Sounding like a resting giant who breathed a powerful inhale and exhale of water, Lake Superior waited for them just beyond the forest's edge.

The women reached the point in the trail where the trees parted to reveal the lake's vast expanse of water. To their right, the trail meandered back into the trees. And to their left, it continued along the jagged shoreline, gradually descending to a mile-long strip of beach and calmer waters. Directly ahead of them, a split-rail fence discouraged visitors from climbing onto a broad ledge of tiered rock flats and narrow, deep crevices. The ledge ended with a steep drop to the water.

"Keep walking?" Abby gestured her hand toward the beach.

"Can I just meet you guys back here? I'd like to sit out on the rocks for a bit," Shelby replied.

Abby glanced at Nic and then back at Shelby. "Everything okay?" she asked.

"Of course," Shelby assured her friends. "You guys go ahead. I'll be here when you get back."

Nic stood with her hands firmly on her hips, her head tilted slightly to the side as if she were trying to see through Shelby. "All right. But don't get too close. . . ."

"To the edge, I know." She smiled. "No worries."

As Abby and Nic proceeded down the trail, Shelby climbed

over the fence and made her way onto the rocks. Wide clefts in the sandstone formed an uneven stairway to the edge. With careful footing, she walked out onto the rock ledge, stopping just short of the cliff's edge. She found a spot bathed in sunlight and sat down, pulling her knees up to her chest and wrapping her arms around her legs. It didn't take long before Shelby reached behind her and slid a folded envelope out of her back pocket. She carefully smoothed out the crease that divided the envelope in half and pressed it flat against her thigh.

In a world that communicated in real time with e-mails, instant messages, and texting, Shelby preferred the intimacy of a hand-written note. A phone call. And best yet, a face-to-face encounter. Nic chided her for being decidedly outdated and hard to reach, but Shelby wasn't ready to give in to cell phones and portable computers, when landline phones and the daily paper were still working just fine for her.

Unlike pixels that formed letters on a brightly lit computer screen, she had always appreciated hand-written script because it captured a piece of the writer's personality. Even as a child, she was comforted by the image of her mother taking a moment out of her day to sit down and write to her daughter. The slant of the *S* or the curl on the *Q* was distinctly her mother's. The words at the beginning and end of each letter meant so much more than the words in between. "Dear" and "love." Of course she always wanted more. But it was all her mother was able—or willing—to give.

Looking at the envelope in her hand, Shelby noticed the return address still listed the same street in Alhambra, California. Thinking back on the past several letters she'd received, Shelby figured her mother must have been living in the same place for nearly two years. What an accomplishment.

She pried the envelope open with her finger, being careful

to tear it evenly across the top, before reaching in and pulling out a folded sheet of college-lined paper with fringed edges that had been ripped from a spiral notebook. She took in a slow, deliberate breath upon seeing "Dear Shelby" written in her mother's hand.

"They're only words," she exhaled into the wind that blew up over the edge of the rocks. *She's thousands of miles away. She doesn't know me well enough to hurt me. They're only words.*

> *Dear Shelby,*
>
> *I haven't heard from you in a while. Not that you asked in your last letter, but everything is perfect here in California. I'm living the dream, baby! Do you remember Calvin the broker? Well, it's over. That got very old very fast. He's a serious one, and I got tired of playing the role of his dolled-up mistress.*
>
> *But here's the great news. I'm now completely & totally enamored with Simon LaFonde. You'd love him. Everyone does. He's French. French-Canadian actually, but he knows some French and sounds just like Gérard Depardieu when he orders food. Crème brûlée. Fondue. Chardonnay. Très sexy, if you know what I mean. He works in Hollywood. Knows all the big-name actors. Pitt. Clooney. Streep. Hasselhoff. It's just a matter of time before I start going to their swanky parties. You'll probably see me in some of those paparazzi photos— that is, if you kept up on tabloid news. You're always so serious. Just like Calvin. A little celebrity gossip would do wonders to lighten you up.*
>
> *So, when are you going to step foot off that godforsaken orchard? Aren't you bored to death, stuck up there in the boondocks? Maybe you're just cowardly. I swear, I don't know how you do it. Day after day. After day. I'm depressed just thinking about it. If you*

*ask me, I think they should just sell the place. God
knows, we could all use the money—and it would do
you good to grow up, get a man, and finally move out.*

*Plenty of great catches in California, if you ever get
the nerve to leave Wisconsin. (Who am I kidding,
right?)*

Love, Mom

Shelby looked up from the letter and stared blankly ahead.
Her eyes welled with tears. *Damn her. Damn her letters.* She
wadded the paper in her hands until she had squeezed her
mother's insensitivity out of it. She had the urge to hurl it toward the water and watch it drop over the cliff. Closing her
eyes tightly, she visualized it hitting a rock before being pulled
under by a frigid, merciless wave. Her mother's letter would
gloriously disappear as the paper dissolved into pulp.

She could feel the emotions buried deep within her rising
to the surface. The familiar heartache of loving someone who
didn't love in return. The agony of abandonment. Shelby
pulled her legs closer to her chest and curled inward, pressing
her eyes hard against her knees, trying in vain to stop the tears.

Laughter broke into her thoughts. A man's voice called, but
Shelby was unable to make out his words. A different voice
seemed to respond. She lifted her head from her knees, squinting into the sun toward the muffled conversation that skipped
across the water. Moving closer, the boisterous sound bounced
down the shore. She wiped the tears from her cheeks with the
back of her hand and then raised her arm to shield her eyes
from the glare off of the lake.

Eventually, she made out a red kayak nosing its way around
the jagged point, followed by two others. The agile kayakers
cut through the chop and were now making their way directly
toward her perch on the rocks.

Turning her gaze from the men, she closed her eyes and let the sun's warmth bathe over her. She let the men's voices drown out her mother's words. With a healing sigh, Shelby willed the image of her mother away. It was replaced by a sweeter memory of walking through a fruit-laden orchard with her grandparents as a young girl. Walking between them, her tiny hands held tenderly in theirs, arms swinging, she knew at a young age that they were her safe haven.

Shelby was a child born out of a foolish night spent between her mother and a young man who spent a few carefree August days in Bayfield. There were last calls and first names. Skinny-dipping and breaking curfew. On a break from her school in California that summer, Jackie felt invincible. She would finish her degree and leave her small hometown for good.

Jackie's plans were thwarted a few months later. Pregnant and considering her options, Jackie chose independence over motherhood. Ginny and Olen chose their granddaughter, Shelby. Without hesitation and with full hearts, they adopted her into their home.

Shelby pushed away the thoughts of her mother and opened her eyes to find the men now paddling past her place on the rocks. She smiled, knowing they were likely unaware that she had overheard most of their conversation as they traveled down the shoreline. She could see "West Bay Outfitter" markings on the side of their kayaks. John's customers. It was a fit group of men, particularly the last one in the nautical caravan. Taking a closer look at his profile, she noticed something familiar about him. *It could be the guy from . . .* she thought, just as he turned to look at her, tilting his head to the side as if recognizing her, as well. He raised his paddle slightly to gesture hello. Without thinking, she raised her hand slightly to return his greeting. Holding the man's gaze wasn't uncomfortable or unwelcome. It was as if she knew him somehow.

And then, just as she felt a directional shift in the breeze, the moment was over.

He dipped his paddle back into the water and moved quickly through the glistening waters to catch up to his companions.

CHAPTER 4

CLICK

Hours earlier, Ryan and his friends had packed up their campsite at a secluded spot on the island and then paddled their way through the South Channel. They navigated around a particularly jagged point that resembled the profile of a bear peeking its head out of the forest. Noticing a pair of hikers threading in and out of the trees that jutted out precariously close to the edge of the cliff, they knew they had reached the State Park. The men were careful not to float too close to the waves that crashed and then receded away from the cracks and cavernous holes in the sandstone.

Pete kept a steady, swift pace as he led the way. Brad followed next with Ryan lagging slightly behind, stopping on occasion to take photographs. "Take your time," Brad shouted back to Ryan. Once he and Pete were in calmer water, they set down their paddles and waited for Ryan to catch up.

Ryan watched as the waves rolled into a low overhang in the cliff and sprayed out like a geyser through a crevice above. Just as he was about to reach back into the bulkhead to retrieve his camera, he saw something move out of the corner of his eye. Looking farther down shore, his eyes settled on a young woman seated atop one of the rock formations. Her arm was raised and she appeared to be watching Brad and Pete. Intrigued, he dipped his paddle back into the water and moved closer. She turned her head away from his friends and looked out toward the horizon, her silhouette highlighted by the sun. Although he wasn't close enough to see the details of her face, he imagined her eyes were closed and she was enjoying the gentle wind coming off the lake.

Inspired by the serenity of the scene, Ryan secured his paddle atop his kayak and removed his camera from the waterproof pouch in the bulkhead behind him. He lifted his Nikon to his face, adjusted the zoom to a wide shot, gently turned the polarized lens just enough to brighten the colors of the lake and soften the light that was reflecting upward to the woman on the rocks.

Click.

He then manipulated the zoom to take a second photograph, this time a tighter shot that pulled the woman into sharper focus and turned the background outside the depth of field into a soft blur of green and blue light. As she came into view, intimately close in the eye of his lens, he saw a loose tangle of brunette hair pulled back into a ponytail. Full lips. Her eyes closed and her head tilted up toward the sun. With keen creative instinct, he knew it was a stunning shot. And then it hit him.

Click.

He slowly lowered his camera, held it against his chest, and sat motionless. The waves gently rocked him. He listened to the glugging sound of water as it lapped against the hollow shell of his kayak. He was certain she was the woman he saw the day before. A chance meeting twice in two days? He felt compelled to paddle closer to her. To say something.

"Ryan, we're losing you again!" Brad shouted over his shoulder, some distance away now.

Ryan replaced the lens cap and returned his camera to the bulkhead, then took a firm hold of his paddle, dipped it in the water, and pulled hard. With steady strokes, he eventually rejoined his friends out in deeper water.

It didn't take long before Ryan was close enough to see her clearly without the aid of a lens. She opened her eyes and watched as the men paddled across her view. The woman raised her hand to block the sun and smiled, seemingly amused.

He wanted to call out to her. To make a connection somehow. What was it about her? First, walking past him at the entrance of West Bay Outfitters with no recognition whatsoever. Then holding a child with more love than his mother had ever shown to him. And now, alone on the rocks, looking as though she belonged there.

She turned her focus on him and he locked eyes with her. Without thinking, Ryan lifted his paddle to gesture "hello." The woman. The lake. The photographs. The combination was inspiring. An idea was coming together and he embraced the possibilities. Instead of joining his father at Chambers Media, to finally assume the role in his family's business that was always expected of him, was it time to pursue something he loved to do instead? Was he prepared to leave Chicago, even temporarily? Make a change. Take a risk. It was something he had only dreamed of doing, never knowing when or where or how. Until now.

Ryan was so lost in thought that he didn't notice his friends had paddled ahead again. He didn't feel the wind shift direction, or sense that the weather behind him was beginning to change. He didn't hear his friends calling out to him, eager to make their way back across the bay to Bayfield's mainland.

And he didn't notice when a crumpled letter, stained with scribbles of washed-out purple ink, floated toward his kayak like a child's paper boat and tapped against its bow.

In that moment, the only thing on his mind was a notion she had inspired. It was the spark he needed.

The idea simply . . . *clicked*.

CHAPTER 5

PIE

John Karlsson from West Bay Outfitters had been right about the weather. As he had predicted, the early evening winds had picked up significantly, just as Ryan, Brad, and Pete were pulling their kayaks out of the water back in Bayfield. A summer storm followed closely behind the winds, breaking just as the men arrived at their rental cottage. Though the dwelling's windows rattled through the night, and thunder clapped loudly through the thin walls, it wasn't enough to keep the men from falling into an exhausted sleep.

The next morning, the sun peeked over Lake Superior's horizon and cast golden light between the trunks of pine and poplar trees along the shore and onto the cottage that sat nestled in tall grass and wild field daisies. Residual drops of rain water clung to its peeling white paint, dripping, glistening. A screen door squeaked open and then banged shut as Ryan stepped barefoot onto a lichen-covered porch. Dressed in a fitted black tee and khaki hiking shorts, he found a resting spot on the creaking front steps that led to a grassy path to the water. He sat with his elbows resting on his knees and leaned forward, a mug of hot black coffee held in his hands.

Though the temperature was expected to warm to the low nineties that day, there was just enough chill in the morning air to be refreshing. Looking out onto the water, Ryan marveled at the lake's ability to wash away his stress. The flashing lights. Impatient horns. Angry commuters. Rumbling subways. Screeching tires. Ruthless paparazzi. Life in Chicago seemed a million miles away from this small clearing on the shore. And that was just far enough to allow Ryan to breathe easy.

Ryan had found the cottage online and, after seeing a single photograph of the place, he knew the seventy-year-old rental property would be private and perfect. He rented it under the assumed name of Charlie Bucket, which was the alias he used most often. Ever since he was a child, he had been captivated by the story of Willy Wonka and young Charlie, the boy who had plucked a golden ticket out of a foil-wrapped chocolate bar and saved his family from poverty. Ryan never envied Charlie's good fortune at the end of the book. It was the *beginning* of Charlie's story that he loved most. How wonderful it would be, Ryan thought, to be tucked away in a tiny room, covered protectively in warm blankets, surrounded by parents and grandparents who loved him unconditionally.

"Like hell you will!" The imagined rage of his father's voice exploded into Ryan's thoughts like a thunderclap. Ryan put down his coffee and ran his fingers through his hair, as if by doing so he could drive out the image of his father. William Chambers, CEO, the one man who would certainly take issue with his decision to decline his newly created position with Chambers Media. It was a job that had been offered out of nepotism rather than merit, to work for the family business that had thrust him unwillingly into the public eye.

Ryan would have to sort out his plans carefully before confronting his father. Shut down the Chicago apartment. Pack up his photography equipment, clothes, and a few incidentals. He would happily leave the meaningless luxuries behind. If he moved to a place like Bayfield, he could escape his public life. He could escape the familiar, uneasy sensation of being watched. He could separate himself from the scrutiny of being William and Charlotte Chambers's only son and heir apparent to Chambers Media. His sister, Martha, had managed to move away and start a family of her own in South Carolina. He still didn't understand why she was praised for making a life of her own, while the ties of duty were bound so tightly around his wrists.

It was time he deviated from the family plan that had been laid out before him. This time, he would follow his own dreams. But first, there was the matter of the woman from the rocks. It seemed crazy, even to him, to think that this new plan of his was somehow connected to her. A complete stranger. He felt compelled to find her again before he returned home.

Hearing the sound of his friends beginning to shuffle about the kitchen, rummaging for coffee cups and whatever they could pull together that resembled breakfast, Ryan picked up his mug, stood, and called through the screen door, "I'm heading into town. You guys need anything?"

"Food," they grunted in unison. Ryan shook his head and smiled to himself. Some things never changed. The outdoors, beer, and food. It didn't take much to tame the lions.

After a short drive from the cottage into town, Ryan rounded the corner onto Main Street, which ran uphill from the marina and ferry landing. The street was flanked by turn-of-the-century brick and wood-paneled buildings that once served as a union bank and trade businesses and now housed small businesses such as a small wine shop, gift stores, and boutiques. His jet-black Mercedes turned the heads of two middle-aged men who were walking dutifully behind their window-shopping wives. *Note to self,* Ryan thought, *swap out the Mercedes for something less conspicuous on the next trip.* There weren't many people out at that hour. He drove past a tourist with a camera slung over her shoulder, a couple pushing a stroller, and a pair of teenagers walking with their arms around one another's waists.

Ryan pulled his car to the side of the road and parked in front of the local grocery store. Unbuckling his seat belt, he noticed that he was under the observation of an elderly couple seated on the sidewalk bench, quietly sharing a breakfast pastry. They licked icing off their fingers and held Styrofoam cups of coffee gingerly between their legs.

As he stepped out of his car, Ryan saw the shapely, tanned legs of a woman carrying a stack of white pastry boxes that obstructed her face. She made her way to the grocery store entrance and, with the boxes teetering in her arms, tried to push the door open with her foot.

"Hey, hey! Hold up!" He rushed over to offer assistance. "Let me get that for you."

"Thanks!" came the woman's voice from beneath the sweet-smelling boxes. "I don't know what I was thinking!"

"Here, let me take a couple of these for you." He lifted several boxes from her load. When her face was revealed, his breath caught in his chest. What were the chances? He pressed against the door to hold it open for her.

"Thanks!" she said with relief, easing her way past him. She wore a loose pair of cuffed jean shorts, which appeared softened from wear and were cinched at the waist with a woven belt. Her complexion looked smooth and radiant against the crisp white of her T-shirt.

"Say, didn't we . . ." he began, looking for a glimmer of recognition in her eyes.

"Hmm?" She blew a wisp of hair out of her eyes with a puff.

"I mean—where to?" he asked, following her into the store. It was a simple grocery store that seemed to offer just enough of everything. A small, but well-stocked dairy case. Dry goods. Meat cooler. A bank of freezer doors. A single cashier station. And, throughout the store, the enticing aroma of fresh bread baking. Yeasty, toasty, and tempting enough to lure customers right off the street.

"Just over there." She pointed with her chin. "On the bakery counter."

"Whatever you have in here smells incredible!" Ryan said. "Strawberry?"

"Yes, you have a good nose," she replied, leading him hastily toward the back of the store. "A couple of blueberry, too."

"Did you bake them?" *How did he find her so easily?* he wondered. Nothing worthwhile was ever that easy.

"Did I bake them?" She paused, gently biting her lower lip. "I did. Yes." She set the boxes down gently and peered over the counter that separated the bakery kitchen from the rest of the store. "Thanks again for your help." She appeared distracted, now looking past Ryan and over his shoulder.

"Ryan," he added, placing his boxes next to hers.

She barely glanced back at Ryan. "Excuse me?"

"My name. It's Ryan."

"Well, Ryan. Have a nice stay in Bayfield." She looked at him with eyes that creased with smile lines. "And thanks for coming to my rescue." Aside from her nose—rosy from the sun and slightly peeling—there was softness to her skin.

"How do you know I'm visiting?" God, he thought, how long had it been since someone saw him for *him,* rather than for the man they recognized from the media?

She was behind the counter now, still looking for whoever was to receive the pies and standing beside a cooling rack filled with trays of sourdough and Scandinavian specialty breads. She turned, taking a few steps backward, and answered, "I guess you just have the look." And with that, she disappeared into the warm kitchen.

Ryan ran his hand through his thick tangle of hair and rubbed the back of his neck. He stood there, feeling rather foolish. Should he wait for her? And if he did, what else could he possibly say? That his father built the family business into a thriving media conglomerate that now handled some of the most successful film and television projects in the country? That his family was based out of Chicago, but also had homes in California and New York? That his parents lived an extravagant lifestyle and socialized regularly with high-profile people?

"Excuse me, are you waiting?" asked a young woman who walked up beside him, a sleeping infant harnessed to her chest. She held one hand gently upon her baby's head, and carried a gallon of milk in the other.

"No, not at all," Ryan answered, stepping aside so she could move up front and set her milk upon the counter. "Do you need help?"

With tired, drooping eyes, she looked for someone else's assistance. "I'm good, thanks," she answered. "Just picking up some wine bread."

"Heather!" The cashier waved to her from the end of the aisle. "I have your order up front." The young mother walked away, leaving Ryan alone with his thoughts once more.

Here, in this small town, he wasn't interested in talking about how, for reasons he would never understand, people seemed fixated on his life. And how his face recently appeared in a national magazine under the ridiculous moniker of one of

"America's Most Eligible Bachelors." He couldn't tell someone he had just met how he wished the spotlight would dim
so he could step out of the public eye.

And most of all, he couldn't confess that the sight of her
on Madeline Island had inspired him to alter the trajectory of
his life.

"You making deliveries for Ginny now?" A tall, angular,
white-haired man with a full beard and eyes the color of faded
denim suddenly appeared next to Ryan. He began reading the
flavors hand-written on the side of each box.

"Is that her name?"

"Rhubarb. You've got to try her rhubarb." The man tapped
his finger against one of the boxes.

"I'll be sure to do that, thanks," Ryan said. "So, the woman
who made this delivery—her name is Ginny?"

"Yep, Ginny comes in a couple of times a week with the
pies. Usually picks up a few things for herself, too. You say she's
driving today?" The man looked around.

"I'm not sure. I just helped her in," Ryan said, shrugging
his shoulders and crossing his arms.

"Good Lord, she's somethin' else. I thought she was supposed to be takin' it easy."

"Why?"

"Pneumonia, poor thing. Damn near landed her in the
hospital. I'm surprised she's already working again," the older
man replied.

"Pneumonia? I'm surprised. I mean, I only just met her,
but she looked healthy."

"Well, good. She's a strong woman. Good Norwegian
stock. So I guess I'm not surprised she's back at it." He paused,
putting his hands on his hips. "Huh. Guess I thought her husband would make the delivery."

"Husband?" *Of course she's married,* Ryan thought, surprised by his disappointment.

"Yep. Olen. Great couple, those two. Just great. Hard workers, too." The man chatted away freely. "Too bad about their daughter, though. Kind of a rotten egg, if you ask me."

A rotten egg? What kind of man is this who would say something like that about a young child? Just as Ryan was about to speak in defense of a child he didn't know and a woman he had just met, she returned.

"Well, hey there, Shelby." The man wrapped his wiry arm around Shelby's narrow shoulders and gave a squeeze.

"Shelby?" Ryan was surprised to hear the sound of his own voice, feeling relief and confusion in a singular moment. She raised an eyebrow in Ryan's direction, as if to ask why he was still there. He wasn't sure himself, so he offered her a slight nod and grinned sheepishly. If only there was something he could do to appear useful.

"Hey, Boots, I was looking for you," she said to the other man. "Sorry for bringing these in late. Forgive me?"

"Don't mention it. Don't you know I keep a couple back in the freezer as backup?" Boots said. "But more importantly, shouldn't Ginny still be resting?"

"She is—Gran's at home. And she's feeling much better. Practically back to her old self. In fact, she was already frying doughnuts when I left the house."

"Huh. A bit of a misunderstanding then," Boots said, looking Ryan in the eye and then turning his attention back to Shelby. "Your friend here was asking some questions about you, and here I thought he was talking about your grandmother."

"My friend?"

"Ryan," Ryan said, offering his name to her again and feeling more uncomfortable by the minute.

"Right." She pulled herself away from Boots's embrace and introduced the two men. "Actually, we just met. Ryan—Boots. Boots—this is Ryan."

Now Boots was the one who appeared baffled, as he looked back and forth from Ryan to Shelby. "Well, it's really none of my business. Tell your grandmother ol' Boots says hello, would'ja?" Without another word, Boots took some of the boxes to the kitchen. In the same instant, Shelby left Ryan to make her way out of the store.

"Wait! I'll walk you out." He rushed to catch up.

"No need." She threw up her hand and walked faster.

"Hold on," he urged, hurrying up beside her. "Can I walk you to your car? I'm heading out, too."

Shelby scanned the front of the store, perhaps searching for a diversion, then turned on her heel to face him straight-on. Arms crossed, she looked up at him and blew a wisp of hair out of her face with exasperation. "All right, but I'm in a bit of a hurry." Before he could reply, she was heading for the door once more.

"So . . . you work with your grandmother?" *She's clearly amazed by your conversation skills, Chambers,* Ryan chided himself.

"Yep."

"What do you do? You know, besides baking," he asked as they made their way across the street.

"A little bit of everything, I suppose," she replied, her voice polite but distracted. "And what do you do, besides hang out in grocery stores while on vacation? I would imagine a guy like you would have a lot more fun being out on the water."

"Oh, a little bit of everything," he teased. With that she gave him a sidelong glance and the hint of a smile. "So tell me. What gave me away?"

"Hmm?"

"The tourist comment."

"Oh, that. Well, for starters, I've lived here all of my life and this is a very small town. You're new. Two, you don't know Boots. Everyone around here knows Boots. And three, you have the look of a weekend outdoorsman." She tapped her wrist in reference to his Yacht Master Rolex watch. "No offense."

"No, no. It's okay. You're right. We arrived from Chicago a few days ago and we're staying through Sunday."

Shelby stopped beside her parked truck and quickly fished keys out of her pocket. "Wonderful. I hope you and your . . . girlfriend? Wife?"

"College friends."

"Nice," she said, holding her keys. "I hope you all have a great time."

"Do you want to do something?" As soon as he blurted it out, he cringed. He sounded less confident than an awkward teen. He wiped perspiration from his brow and wasn't sure if it was brought on by the sun or his nerves. What was it about this woman that caused him to fumble for words?

"Excuse me?"

"Grab a bite to eat? You know, so I could learn a thing or two about Bayfield from one of its finest residents?" His attempt to cajole her fell flat.

"Thanks, no. I mean, don't get me wrong. It's a nice offer. But I actually need to get back to work." When Shelby opened the door to her truck, the hinges creaked with age.

"Of course." He shoved his hands into his pockets. "Some other time then?"

"Listen, Brian . . ."

"Ryan."

"Ryan. I'm in a relationship. But I'm sure there are plenty of other girls around town who would be interested in having 'lunch' with you," Shelby said, emphasizing "lunch" with sarcasm. She pulled herself into the cab with ease and pulled the door shut. She was buckling her seat belt when Ryan put his hand on the rim of the open driver's side window.

"Hang on, I think you have the wrong idea here. Despite

the way you twisted my words just now, I actually was interested in *just lunch*. And even if I had known that you were involved—which I didn't—it wouldn't have mattered because it
still would have been *just lunch*. But I'll forgive your assump-
tions about my character because I have one very big weakness
and you're the only one who can satisfy it."

"I can imagine . . ." she said under her breath while fumbling to jam a key into the ignition.

"Pie."

"Sorry?" Shelby's hand dropped to her lap and he could
hear the *clink* of keys hitting the floorboard. Good. He'd
caught her off guard. He had one more shot at a good impression.

"I'm crazy for pie. When I ran into you earlier, I was actually on a mission to buy pie. And then, after meeting you at the
store, and becoming overwhelmed with the desire to have
'lunch,' I completely forgot about the pie."

Ryan watched as Shelby raised her hand over her mouth
to suppress a laugh. He had successfully put his foot in the
proverbial door before she slammed it in his face and drove
away.

"I could always go track down Boots again," Ryan continued. "But I figure, if you have any more on hand, it would be
easier just to buy one from you right here. Besides, now that
I've met Boots, I wouldn't be surprised if he'd just sell me one
of the old ones he keeps stashed away in the freezer." He could
plainly see she had another half-dozen pie boxes stacked on
the floor of the passenger seat.

"How about two?" she replied with a hint of challenge.

"Why not make it three?" And with that, she let out a robust, contagious laugh that immediately hit a chord with him.
The sound made him feel alive, like that new song on the
radio that you can't wait to hear again.

"Okay. Three it is . . ." She paused. Would she remember? "Ryan."

And just like that, she was gone. Ryan was alone, standing on the sidewalk and looking uphill toward the white truck that had turned at the first intersection and disappeared. As he stood there, three pie boxes in his arms, he wondered how he would explain it to his friends. Certainly they'd wonder why, instead of the usual provisions of salami, cheese, chips, and beer, he would bring nothing but pie back to the cottage. But he wasn't interested in heading back into the grocery store to shop and running into Boots again.

"Did you get her number?" A bearded man snuck up beside Ryan and startled him.

"Boots!" Ryan said with a jolt, taking a step back and nearly slipping off the curb. "Jesus," he muttered.

"I said, did you get her number?" Boots stood beside Ryan while twisting his spindly index finger into his left ear to snub out an itch. The men didn't look at each other. Instead, Boots stared up the road.

"Um, no."

"Come on. A good-lookin' fella like you and you couldn't even manage to get her number?"

"No, I . . . I didn't ask," Ryan said, adjusting his grip on the pie boxes. "It appears she has a boyfriend."

"Does she?" Puzzled, Ryan studied the man's expressions carefully. "That's news to me," Boots continued. "In case you're wondering—and judging from the sorry expression on your face, I gather you do—I think she's intrigued." Boots ran his tongue along the inside of his cheek and then used the fingernail of his pinkie finger to pick something out of his teeth. "Looks like you blew it."

"What do you mean?"

"Young, handsome, and dumb as a rock." Boots shook his head slowly and turned to look Ryan in the eye. "Now, listen. Shelby generally doesn't give men the time of day. And guys like you, who come and go all summer long and try to flirt with the pretty gals in town? Forget it. You're barkin' up the wrong tree." He paused to chew whatever tiny bit of food he was able to pry from his teeth. "But I will tell you this . . . she saw somethin' in you right off the bat."

"I don't think so. She shot me down cold." A few days ago, he would never have believed that he would be standing on the sidewalk in a small town, holding three boxes of strawberry-rhubarb pie, and getting advice about women from a guy named Boots.

"Of course she did. That's how she was raised. She's not going to go off with any young city slicker who rolls through town, 'cuz you weren't the first and you won't be the last. But what makes this situation different is not what she *did* do, it's what she *didn't* do."

"I'm not following you."

"She didn't turn down your offer to help. That girl prides herself on not needing a man's help for *anything*. Help to carry pies into the shop? Hogwash." Boots chuckled and then coughed, thumping his chest with a closed fist, then turning his head to spit a wad of phlegm into the street. "I've seen her kick in the door to my store with one boot, during a snow-storm, carrying a much larger load, without needing a single bit of help." Boots looked squarely at Ryan. "Your little act of chivalry? Please."

Ryan moved the pies from one arm to the other and looked up the empty road again. If Boots was right, Ryan would be a fool not to give it one more shot.

"As I walked out of the shop just now, I saw her drive off in a huff. Not sure what you said or did, but I'll tell ya, pal— you blew it." Boots shook his head.

"There isn't a boyfriend?" Ryan asked with raised eyebrows.

Boots shook his head. "Hasn't had one for years."

"And the child?" Ryan added, thinking back to the sight of her twirling a small boy in her arms.

"Nope."

When he turned back to ask Boots where he could find Shelby, he realized the white-haired man had disappeared as quietly as he had approached. Boots was already meandering down the sidewalk as if the conversation had never taken place.

Ryan was about to cross the street and return to his car, when he noticed a sparkle of light bounce off of a delicate piece of metal on the sidewalk. It lay in the precise spot where Shelby had been standing beside her truck. He bent one knee down to the sidewalk, set the boxes on the ground, and picked up the ice-blue stone pendant that looped onto a delicate silver chain.

CHAPTER 6

SERENDIPITY

Back at the cottage, Ryan leaned against the kitchen counter, his fingernails clicking against the Formica in a rapid drumroll rhythm. He had never been one to believe in fate, and yet he had this unwavering feeling that running into Shelby again was serendipitous. He also realized that the interest was likely one-sided, despite the opinion of one bearded grocer named Boots. And yet, like an osprey feeling the internal pull of an impending migration, Ryan was restless to return to her. He stopped the drumming and laid his hand flat against the countertop. Who was he kidding? When it came to Shelby, it seemed he was less like a creature on a migratory track—and more like the dim-witted bird that abandons its flock and ends up flying directly into a windowpane, flapping its wings against the glass without realizing he's going nowhere.

Brad and Pete were sitting at the table, hovering over two open pie boxes. The tongs of their forks tore into the pies like the teeth of ravenous wolves. Ryan wondered what his friends' wives would say if they saw their husbands now, two grown men reduced to grunting boys who ate right off the pie plate—breaking the rules and enjoying every minute of it.

"Did you want any of this?" Pete called out to Ryan, a smudge of strawberry filling smeared across his unshaven chin.

"I'm good." Ryan smiled.

How difficult could it be to find her again? The easiest thing, of course, would be to simply return to the grocery store and ask Boots. But he sensed that Boots wouldn't have much more to say to him. Ryan knew she had a grandmother named Ginny. It couldn't be too difficult in a town like this, could it? On the other hand, people could be more like John from West Bay Outfitters—protective over their neighbors— and not as forthcoming as Boots. Particularly when dealing with a stranger.

"Ryan, these pies are killer! Where'd you say you found them?" Pete asked.

"At the grocery store in town."

"The grocery? But that's not what the label on the box says."

The label?

Ryan moved to the table and closed the lid of one of the boxes. Funny, he hadn't noticed it. But there it was. Clearly embossed in the lower right-hand corner of the lid was the answer he needed:

MEYERS ORCHARD

BAYFIELD, WISCONSIN

FAMILY-OWNED SINCE 1963

Leaving his friends and what little remained of the pie, Ryan drove off to find Meyers Orchard. After driving several miles up a wooded county road, he arrived atop the bluffs that overlooked Lake Superior. It was there that Ryan came upon a fork in the road that was marked by a curious signpost. Nearly a dozen signs, each painted a different color, were nailed haphazardly to a single post. Lake View Orchard. Chequamegon Apple Company. Dormer Farms. He scanned them until he spotted the one that he was looking for, positioned near the bottom. "Meyers Orchard" was lettered carefully in white paint upon a berry red arrow that pointed left. Filled with a rush of anticipation, Ryan put the car in Drive and proceeded onto a gravel road, kicking up a cloud of dust until he reached the farm.

Ryan slowly turned into the driveway and pulled up next to the only other car in the visitor parking area. He opened the car door and stretched out his long legs while taking a look around. Surrounded by acres of orchard land, the well-tended farm included three structures. One appeared to be a modest whitewashed home that featured a wraparound porch, porch swing, and black shutters. A simple garden of golden marigolds cheerfully adorned the stone paver walkway that led to the front porch.

The second structure was a wood-paneled barn with worn red paint and white trim that resembled the roadside sign. There was a copper weather vane, greened by patina, posted atop the copula. Its design depicted a galloping horse with waves of tail and mane that trailed off its body like ribbons. The barn's double-wide sliding doors were pulled open to reveal a rustic living space inside, complete with a sunken couch, large apple crates that seemed to serve as tables, some camping lamps, and a television sitting atop an overturned barrel. It looked as though a bent wire hanger was serving as a TV antenna.

Finally, he turned his attention to the building that stood directly in front of him. A "Welcome" sign, with small apples stenciled across the bottom, hung above the entrance. He approached the store just as a middle-aged couple opened the door. One of the men was carrying a gift bag, while his partner held on to his arm, laughing.

The scent of cinnamon and cedar greeted Ryan as he entered the store. In contrast to the stifling heat outdoors, the spice-infused, air-conditioned space conjured thoughts of October on the hot August day. He meandered around the displays of handcrafted baskets, jams, and apple-themed gift items. And then, in the back corner area of the store, working behind a bakery case that showcased streusel-topped berry pies, applesauce muffins, and sugared doughnuts, he found a petite woman putting the finishing touches on a lattice pie. *Ginny.*

"Hello," Ryan offered easily as he approached.

Ginny Meyers turned around, wiped her hands on her flour-smudged, oil-stained apron, and smiled. "Well, hello," she acknowledged him before politely coughing into the crook of her arm. Her hair was winter white and full, cut into a short bob that swung like the skirt of a dancer when she moved her head.

"It smells like heaven in here." He bent down to peruse the pastry case. "I haven't eaten all day. Any recommendations?"

"Here," she offered, reaching into the case to pull out an apple cider doughnut hole that had been generously rolled in cinnamon sugar. "Give this a try."

He popped the warm pastry into his mouth, enjoying the crunch of its fried outer edge and the delicate spice cake within. Brushing bits of sugar from his lips, he gushed, "Now *that* is good."

Ginny cleared her throat and nodded. "It is, isn't it?"

He couldn't help but notice that Ginny had the same brown eye color that he had admired on Shelby. "I will definitely be taking those back with me. A dozen, please," he said, and then remembered the appetites of the lions back at the cottage. "Actually, better make that two dozen."

"Well, you'll certainly make someone happy when you return home with these," she said confidently, filling up two paper bags with the baked goods.

He pointed over her shoulder to a back table. "What are those? Behind you . . ."

She followed his gaze. "Oh, those are strictly off-menu, I'm afraid. They're just the bits of dough that float off of the doughnuts in the fryer. They're overcooked and not to my taste, but Lord love him, they're my husband's favorites."

"You don't say."

"The man has had a handful of those doughnut dribbles and a glass of milk for his afternoon snack nearly every day for God knows how many years. Can you imagine? He never tires of the damn things." She passed two doughnut bags across to Ryan and then grabbed a towel to wipe down the counter. "If you ask me, I think it's his secret. He's as healthy as they come!"

"He may be on to something."

"Are you visiting long?" she asked, again covering her mouth with her sleeve to stifle a slight cough. He'd been pegged as a tourist once again.

"I'm here for the rest of the week. But you never know, I may have to return someday for more of these doughnuts!" He spoke easily with her, enjoying the way she smiled with her entire face, rosy and round.

"Be careful now. You may fall in love with the area and

never want to leave." She moved out from behind the bakery counter and waved to two women entering the shop. "Hello, ladies! Let me know if you need any help," she sang out kindly.

"I can see how that could happen," Ryan said, reaching into one of his bags to grab another doughnut hole. "If you don't mind my asking, how long have you been here?"

"In Bayfield?"

He nodded while chewing.

While the other two customers browsed leisurely in the homey shop, Ginny appeared relaxed and interested in continuing her conversation with Ryan. "Oh my," she began, looking past him. "1960? No—1961. That was my first visit. But we moved here permanently in '63." She led Ryan to a small seating area in the shop where customers could sit with a cup of coffee and a baked good. One wall in the space was adorned with family photographs of varying sizes, in an assortment of mismatched frames.

"My husband and I came to Bayfield on our honeymoon and, later on, when we were deciding where to settle down, we decided to make a go of it up here," Ginny continued. "It was a bit of a whim. We were just kids. We knew nothing— absolutely *nothing!*—about what it takes to live this far north, let alone how to grow apples or run a farm." She shook her head, obviously still in disbelief after all of those years.

"I never would have guessed that. It's a beautiful property, Mrs.—"

"Meyers. Ginny Meyers." She appeared to be the type of grandmother that everyone deserves, but few are fortunate to have.

"Mrs. Meyers."

"Heavens no!" She placed her hand firmly on his arm. "Call me Ginny. Everyone does."

"All right. Thank you, Ginny." He turned to a shelved jam

display at his side and ran his finger along the shelf, noticing how each glass Ball Mason jar was carefully hand-labeled and capped with a calico fabric lid. Finally, he said, "I believe I met your granddaughter this morning."

"Did you?" she replied slowly, tipping her head to the side with raised eyebrows.

"I ran into her when she was making a delivery for Boots." He read the labels. Raspberry. Apple Butter. Blueberry Marmalade.

"My, my. For a visitor, you certainly are getting to know some of Bayfield's finest. First you mention Shelby, then Boots," she said in good humor while taking a closer look at his profile. "Funny, she didn't mention it to me."

"Truth is, I didn't make much of an impression on either one of them. She probably didn't consider it noteworthy." Black Cherry, his favorite. He grabbed a couple to add to his purchase.

"Really? I find that hard to believe." Ginny changed her stance and placed a hand to the side of her face. "She didn't recognize you?" Her forehead pulled up in a wrinkle of disbelief.

"Excuse me?" He turned to face her.

"I mean, she didn't recognize your obvious *charm?* She must have been preoccupied," she recovered, and then reached across Ryan to grab a third jar to add to his purchase. "Trust me. You have to try this blueberry marmalade. It happens to be my granddaughter's favorite."

Chatting a bit longer about the farm, Ginny radiated a warmth and openness that Ryan hadn't come across much in his daily life. As Ginny spoke, she gestured toward the wall of photographs adjacent to the jam shelves. He approached to take a closer look and noticed one photograph in particular. It was of a young girl, perhaps ten years old, with round brown eyes and a cascade of brunette hair that curled up around her shoulders. While she was a lovely child with a sweet expression, something seemed to be missing from her smile. It was probably nothing, but he couldn't help but notice a hint of sadness.

Ginny pointed to another photograph of the same child. She was a few years younger, dressed in red overalls and sprawled out in a mountainous pile of fall leaves. This time, she was laughing with an open, gap-toothed grin.

"That's Shelby. Not only is she beautiful, but she's loyal, smart as a whip, and works harder than anyone I know." She continued to point out a few other photographs on the wall. "Here's one of my husband and me celebrating our first harvest. God, we were young. And this is a photograph of Shelby as a baby. My sweet girl," she sighed and moved on to other photographs. "This here is another special picture. It's the day Olen and I opened the farm for business. You can see from the size of the trees behind us that a lot has changed over the years. The orchard was so immature at that time that we hardly made enough money to live on. We had to supplement our income with garden produce, and Olen took part-time jobs around town. Those were difficult times."

"Is this your granddaughter, too?" Ryan asked, pointing to a photograph of a child riding a bicycle down a tree-lined path.

"No, that's our daughter, Jackie," Ginny said, giving the frame a gentle tap. "She and Shelby do look a bit alike. But they couldn't be more different."

"Does she live in Bayfield, too?" He suddenly remembered the "rotten egg daughter" comment from Boots earlier that day.

"No. She's out in California." The manner in which Ginny turned away from the photographs made it clear to Ryan that the family show-and-tell was over.

"My goodness, you have a way of getting people to talk," Ginny said over her shoulder as she led Ryan to the cash register near the front door.

After paying for his items, Ryan had one last question for Ginny. "I was wondering . . ." he said, shoving his wallet into his back pocket and trying to sound casual. "Is she here, by any chance?"

"Hmm?"

"Your granddaughter?"

"Well, I wondered how long you were going to stand here talking to an old lady before you came around to that question." Ginny straightened her posture and set her hands on her hips. "Since I'm a sucker for good-looking men, I'll tell you what. If you walk out behind the store and head to the eastern side of the orchard, you'll find Shelby. She's out working this afternoon."

"Thank you." He reached out his hand. "It was a pleasure meeting you."

Instead of a handshake, Ginny took his hand, held it in the warmth of her soft palm, and gave it a nurturing pat. "And if you ever visit Bayfield again, do it in early October when the apples are at their peak. We have an apple festival that is quite a hoot."

"I'll remember that." He smiled, released her hand, and headed out the door.

"One more thing . . . ?" Ginny called out.

He held the door open and looked back.

"When you find her, tell her that I'd like her to wrap it up. My husband is having some produce buyers from the Twin Cities up this afternoon and he'll need to use the truck. I'm sure she can find something else to do during the remainder of the day." She either winked at him or blinked away something in her right eye. Considering the way her eyes nearly creased shut when she smiled, it was difficult to know for sure.

"Of course." Ryan thanked her and walked outside with a boost of optimism.

After stashing his purchases in the car, he headed off in the direction Ginny had instructed. He passed a "Pick Your Own Apples" sign and wished it was October. That would have given him an excuse for showing up unannounced in the orchard. As he walked between the rows of apple trees, he thought it would probably end poorly, but it felt right—and exciting—and real. It could be a huge mistake, but he was willing to give it a second shot.

It didn't take long before Ryan spotted Shelby. Compared to how she looked earlier, her jean shorts were now scuffed with dirt and her T-shirt clung to her skin, which glistened with perspiration. She looked endearing with her hair pulled up in a ponytail that looped through the back of a red baseball cap. Instead of bounding up to her, he paused under the cool shade of a tree to consider the best way to introduce himself. Again.

Standing on a ladder that leaned against the tree trunk, she appeared to be checking the condition of the apples. There was a large bucket on the ground beside her ladder where she seemed to be collecting damaged fruit and shoots that must have been pulled from the tree. Shelby moved effortlessly. While it was obviously a strenuous task, particularly in the rising heat, she hardly appeared out of breath. There was rhythm to her movements, as if she were in synch with the trees.

He knew very little about apple farming, but from what he could observe, it seemed the Meyers family would have an abundant crop. The tree branches were heavy with fruit. The apples grew in clusters throughout the tree, even hanging down from the branch tips like grapes from a vine. The apples were young, pale green and blushed with pink, with only a few displaying a touch of red.

When Shelby paused to wipe the sweat from her brow with her work-gloved hand and readjust her hat, Ryan saw his opportunity. He took a deep breath and slowly stepped out from behind the tree.

CHAPTER 7

BLUSH

"Hello?" came a man's voice from the orchard shadows. Shelby gripped the ladder to steady herself and looked wide-eyed toward the sound. With the sun directly behind the man, she couldn't make out the details of his face.

"We aren't picking apples yet. It's too early in the season," she called out, raising her free hand above her eyes to try to block the sun and get a better look. "But you can find berries on the south side of the barn."

"Yes," he said, making his slow approach. "I know."

"Someone at the store can help you."

The appearance of this stranger put her on guard. People rarely wandered into this section of the orchard, let alone men on their own. In fact, she doubted if she had *ever* seen a man come out alone. Men on dates, yes. Men with families, definitely. But alone? Never. So why was this one here? She instinctively looked around to see if anyone else was nearby, in case she needed help. Seeing no one, Shelby stepped down from the ladder.

"You should head out to the other part of the farm," she

said again, with more insistence, while pointing in the direction he had come.

He raised his hand in greeting. "I came out to see you."

"That's far enough!" she said sternly, walking toward her truck without taking her eyes off of the man. She swallowed hard. "You need to back the hell—" Just then a cloud blocked out the sun and, in its shadow, the man's face came into view. It was him. The tourist who had helped her with the pies. She sighed with relief. As the tension in her arms and shoulders relaxed, her fear turned into bewilderment. It still didn't make sense why any man would be in the orchards, let alone this one, who certainly must have had more interesting things to do on his vacation.

"I'm sorry if I startled you."

"That's an understatement."

He shoved his hands into the front pockets of his khaki shorts and shrugged. "Should I go?"

"Yes—I mean, no," she faltered. Shelby rubbed the side of her neck while considering the man standing before her, unaware that in doing so she left a smear of dirt across her skin. "You don't have to go. I didn't realize it was you." The cloud passed overhead and the orchard was bathed in sunlight once again. She pulled the brim of her hat lower over her eyes to block out the glare. "Brian, was it?" She knew it was Ryan.

"It's Ryan, actually." A smile settled on his face as he took a few more cautious steps toward her.

"Yes, Ryan. Sorry. I'm terrible with names."

"And you're Shelby. I remember." He was now standing a few feet away.

She remembered him being attractive, but out here in the afternoon sun, he was stunning. "What are you doing out here?"

"Your grandmother told me where to find you."

"Gran?" The thought of her grandmother's involvement was somewhat reassuring, only because Shelby knew she was an excellent judge of character. He must have said or done something right for Ginny to send him into the orchard to find her. Shelby set the branch cutter down on the ground and crossed her arms over her chest, curious to hear what he had to say.

"I hope you don't mind," he answered, now standing in front of her. "But earlier—back in town—you drove away so quickly. I didn't have time to give you something."

"Give me what?"

He pushed his hands deeper into the khakis that hung loosely over his narrow hips. She averted her eyes until he found what he was looking for and extended his hand toward her. When Shelby looked up, she saw her turquoise pendant necklace dangling from his fingers. She removed one of her work gloves and set her hand upon her collarbone. Her neck was bare. The necklace swayed back and forth from his fingers, like a clock slowly ticking off the seconds until she found her voice.

"I don't know what to say. I guess . . . I didn't realize I had lost it." Shelby reached out, touching Ryan's hand lightly as he slipped the delicate silver chain from his fingers to hers. A warm blush rose up and spread across her cheeks. *It's your apple blush, Shel,* Jeff had said after he kissed her for the first time, so many years ago. She withdrew her hand and pushed back the memory.

"Thanks. It was nice of you to come all the way out here to return this." She removed her other work glove and held them between her knees while she secured the necklace around her neck. "It's sentimental to me. It was a gift from my grandfather and I honestly don't know what I would have done if I'd lost it."

"It was no trouble," he said, his face lit up in a smile.

"Where did you find it? And how did you know it was mine?"

"I saw it on the sidewalk, right where you had been standing before you got into your truck. I had a hunch that it might be yours."

"Pretty good hunch." She heard a soft rustling through the orchard as a breeze passed through and cooled the back of her neck.

"Guess you could say it was a bit of a Cinderella moment," he said. "You know—pretty girl drops something as she rushes off, only to be found by the charming prince . . ."

"Charming prince?" *Come on—is this guy for real?* she thought in disbelief. *Tourist.*

"Your grandmother called me charming earlier, so I'm going with it," he joked, displaying a boyish dimple in his left cheek that she hadn't noticed before. "And before they have a chance to get to know each other better, she notices the time and drives off. . . ."

". . . in an old pickup?" she interjected, appreciative that he'd gone out of his way to help her—again—but not about to succumb to his charms.

"Yes. In your case, a truck. And the poor guy is left with nothing more than the glass slipper."

"The necklace."

"Precisely."

"Well, I'll have to agree with Gran. You *are* charming. And thoughtful to come all the way here, especially when you could have just given it to Boots."

"That would have been far less interesting."

"Perhaps." She laughed in spite of herself. "So. Thanks again. First this morning. And now this. But I should be getting back to work." Shelby slipped the gloves back on her hands as Ryan retrieved her bucket of tree shoots and damaged apples.

"Right, of course," he said. "But let me ask you a question first."

"Sure."

"What's your boyfriend's name?"

"Excuse me?" She couldn't have heard him correctly. He extended the bucket to her with an amused smirk on his face. Like a chess player who casually challenges his rook to her queen and whispers, "checkmate," Ryan knew her game was over.

"Simple enough question," he continued. "Does he live nearby?"

I'm not playing, she thought, putting up her guard again. She took the bucket from him and asked, "Aren't your friends going to wonder where you are?"

"Nope. They'll hardly notice I'm gone," he said with confidence. "Is the guy a Badgers fan?"

"What?"

He pointed to her hat with the white *W* for Wisconsin embroidered on its front. "Your boyfriend. Did he go to Madison?"

She raised her other hand to touch its frayed brim. "I went to Madison." She placed the bucket in the flatbed of her truck with a heavy *thud* and turned back to the tree to retrieve the ladder. As she folded the ladder, its joints stiff from age and its metal rungs warm from the summer heat, she blocked out the sound of Ryan's prying questions and recalled a happier time.

It was fall and football and new beginnings. For the first time in her life she was away from home and the possibilities for her life seemed endless. Shelby and Jeff were freshmen dressed in red and white along with a stadium of cheering Badger fans. Jeff had put his cap on her head and kissed her cold nose that October night, as they huddled under the stadium lights, wrapped in a bleacher blanket, waving college pennants. She had never felt happier.

"I'm sorry," she heard Ryan finally say. "I can see you don't want to talk about this."

The memory of Jeff's face faded as she turned her attention back to the man standing before her. "You seem like a nice guy, but I hardly know you and I really do need to finish up here."

He insisted on helping her load the ladder into her truck. "I know I'm keeping you, but here's the thing. And I know it's going to sound crazy," he said with a pause.

"Yes?" she asked, shifting her weight to the other leg as she waited.

"It simply comes down to this—I'd love your company, I mean, I'd like to spend a little time with you," he finally said, grimacing a bit at the awkwardness of his own words.

Shelby slammed the tailgate shut, brushed off her hands, and faced him squarely. The soft blush in her cheeks was replaced with a flush of rising irritation. "Listen, Ryan. That's nice, and, like I said before, I'm sure there are plenty of girls who would love to keep you company while you're in town. But I'm not—"

"You're not one of them. I get that," he said gently while resting his arm on the tailgate. "I don't know what kind of men you've spent time with in the past, but I think you're getting the wrong impression. I mean, you have to admit it's unusual that we have literally run into each other several times in the short time that I've been in Bayfield."

"It's a small town."

"Okay, maybe it's something. Or nothing at all," he continued. "But if you were Cinderella and I came to you with the glass slipper, would you tell me to take off? Or would you agree to another dance?"

He's charming, and those dimples are irresistible, but he's exactly the kind of guy Mom would go for, she thought, standing firmly with a clenched jaw.

"I'm going to The Inn's rooftop for a drink tonight at around eight, and your grandmother said she'd like you to call it a day. Something about needing that truck of yours," he suggested. "So what do you say—join me?"

Before walking away from him and climbing into the driver's seat to head back to the barn, Shelby put on a polite Midwestern smile and said simply, "Sorry, but I'm no Cinderella."

CHAPTER 8

WATER

At 8:45 that evening, The Inn's rooftop bar was busier than Ryan had anticipated for a weekday. People congregated around plastic tables and chairs, drinking from bottles and disposable cups as the sun set over the waterfront park and marina below. Even at this hour, the day's heat had only dropped by a few degrees. Men wiped perspiration from their brows and necks while women pulled at their blouses and fanned themselves with laminated bar menus. Ryan knew Brad and Pete were keeping cool back at the cottage with beers in hand and their feet in the water. Now, looking down at the ice melting in his second gin and tonic, certain she wouldn't come, he regretted abandoning his friends.

"What do you mean, you're going into town for drinks?" Pete had asked earlier that evening while manning a black Weber grill in the backyard of the cottage, a plume of gray smoke billowing up around him as he flipped steaks over a mound of ashen charcoal briquets that gave off a slight red glow.

"I'm meeting someone," Ryan had answered nonchalantly

from where he sat on the back porch steps, a safe distance away from Pete and the smoke. "Actually, to be honest, I'm not sure if she'll show. I could be back early."

"You're meeting up with someone tonight?" Holding three cold beers in his hands, Brad pushed the screen door open with his foot to join the others. The door shut behind him with a spring-loaded slam.

"How's Holly?" Ryan asked, knowing that Brad had spent the last half hour on the phone with his pregnant wife.

"She's great. Five months along now, if you can believe it. Her sister is visiting right now. But hang on—don't change the subject. Who are you meeting?" Brad sat down next to Ryan and handed him a beer. "I don't remember you meeting anyone. Was it that blonde from the coffee shop?"

"No." Ryan took a sip from the chilled bottle.

"So give it up," Pete said from behind the smoke. "This is supposed to be a guys' trip. Which *you* planned, by the way. And now you're going off with someone else, leaving us high and dry? We're not letting you off so easily without getting some details."

"Shit, Pete—are you burning our dinner again?" Brad stood up to check on the steaks, which were now engulfed by angry, spitting flames.

"Get outta here!" Pete snapped at Brad with his blackened BBQ tongs. "Step away from the grill and let the master create."

"Yeah, we know what you create. You're the master of char on the outside and raw in the middle." Brad shook his head and returned to sit back down next to Ryan. "Seriously, what's goin' on?"

"Do you remember that woman we ran into at the outfitter shop?" Ryan began. "The day we picked up our gear?"

"At the door?" Pete asked.

Ryan lifted his bottle in Pete's direction. "That's the one. Her name is Shelby."

"You know her name?" Brad asked with surprise, looking from Ryan to Pete. "Hang on a second. Is that what you were doing today, tracking her down? You weren't looking at boat charters?"

"Not exactly." Ryan picked at the paper label that was peeling off his bottle, wet with condensation.

"I'll bet she was surprised to see you again," Pete said, stepping over to grab the unclaimed bottle at Brad's side.

"Just the opposite," Ryan replied, turning the bottle around in his hands, remembering the episode with Boots and the pies. "She didn't know me from Adam."

"Is that right?" Pete coughed, back at the Weber and fanning smoke away from his face as he moved the steaks to a cooler section on the grill.

"I like her already," Brad said.

Ryan took a pull from his beer and considered how to put his thoughts into words without sounding like he'd lost his mind. "I know next to nothing about this woman, but there's something about her. I can't put my finger on it. When she talks to me I feel like she's really talking to *me*—not some guy she's read about." He laughed to himself while rolling a piece of the torn label into a small ball between his fingers. "Not only does she see me as just some guy on a summer vacation—it's clear that she doesn't like me much."

"So she has great instincts, too!" Pete hooted.

"She must have picked up on the fact that you never commit and you can be a real pain in the ass," Brad agreed, as the friends laughed at Ryan's expense.

When the laughter quieted, Brad turned to Ryan with some concern. "Okay, seriously—let's say she actually shows up tonight."

"Unlikely," Pete added.

"But let's say she does. You have a few drinks. Blow off some steam. That's all well and good," he said. "But if you spend any real time with her this week, you can't hide who you are. I mean, I know you always like to downplay it, but you gotta keep it real."

"I don't know," added Pete as he gave the steaks one last flip. The heavy aroma of charcoal smoke and seared beef billowed around them. "I agree with Ryan. Think of it this way—what's honest about some of the things people say about him? What's honest about people who want to meet him just because they recognized him from the media? Or because of his money?"

"That's true, and believe me, Ryan, we know what you've gone through." Brad reached his hand over and gripped Ryan's shoulder. Ryan still wasn't accustomed to the sensitive side of Brad that had come out after he married Holly. Previously known as a man of few words, the guy now loved to talk. "We know how you've been burned by women in the past. But if she really thinks of you as an ordinary guy, you're being dishonest."

"I hear you. But I can't tell you how . . ." Ryan searched for the right word. "How *freeing* it is to talk to a woman without being loaded down with all of the baggage that comes along with being a Chambers."

"So let's say she shows up tonight. And let's say you see her again. What happens when we head back to Chicago?" Brad asked before finishing off his beer.

"Nothing happens. We go home." Ryan flicked the paper ball into the center of Pete's grill and watched as it disappeared into the coals. Although he trusted them implicitly, he wasn't ready to admit how intrigued he was by this woman and the notion of breaking away from his family ties. Even if just for a while. He needed time to think it through.

"Time to eat!" Pete announced, loading the charred steaks onto a plate and shutting down the grill.

Brad shook his head at Ryan and stood up. "One of these days, you're going to finish what you start."

"It's just drinks." Ryan rose from the steps and held the door open for the men to go inside to dish up.

As best as he could tell, Ryan sat unnoticed at a corner table of The Inn's rooftop venue, tucked behind a bar awning that was draped in strands of lights that resembled miniature red chili peppers. If anyone recognized him, they were politely keeping it to themselves. Just as he was preparing to abandon his hopes for the evening, he looked toward the entrance once more. Then Shelby appeared at the top of stairs. She paused, one hand placed atop the wood banister while the other fidgeted with the folds in her gray linen skirt. Ryan watched as she scanned the faces of those on the deck. He didn't move. The glow from a streetlight backlit her hair and the silhouette of her body, which he could faintly make out through the light fabric. Her hair was pulled up casually with a single clip. A few strands of hair curled down upon her bare shoulders, which were a golden tan against the crisp white of her camisole.

Once Shelby spotted Ryan, she offered the hint of a smile and a discreet nod of her head, gesturing for him to follow. Without waiting for a response, she turned and disappeared back down the stairs. He had invited her out for the evening, but she clearly had the upper hand.

The flimsy plastic chair that Ryan was sitting on caught on the deck flooring and nearly tipped over as he hastily pulled away from the table. He left a generous tip beside his glass of melting ice before rushing after her.

"I didn't think you'd join me," he said with quickened breath once he joined her under the streetlight on Main.

"That makes two of us." Standing next to The Inn, they could hear an Eagles melody stream from the bar. Shelby glanced up toward the sound of the music and then stepped into the darkness. "Come on, let's walk."

Walking away from The Inn and toward the lake, Don Henley's voice became an inaudible muffle backed by the hum of his band and a low bass beat. With the sun nearly set, the sky turned twilight blue with a splash of red along the horizon. The first stars were making their appearance and a waxing moon was on the rise. Ryan wasn't sure why she was leading him to the water, but he didn't ask. She embodied grace and strength. Effortless beauty. And also trepidation, as if at any moment she would turn and disappear. He decided it best just to follow.

"Thanks for coming," he said simply. "I was beginning to think up excuses to give my friends about why you stood me up."

"You could thank my grandparents."

"Your grandparents?" That was unexpected.

"It seems you made quite an impression on Gran today. She must have said something to my grandfather because they just kept staring at me throughout dinner. I could tell they were anxious for me to say something about you—and why you stopped by the farm." She glanced at him briefly.

Ryan would have loved to reach out to her, but instead he walked with his hands in his pockets. "Come on. I'm sure I'm not the first guy to stop by."

"You're the first unexpected, unknown, out-of-town guy to stop by, I'll give you that."

Nice to be an unknown, he thought. "Did you tell them you couldn't wait to see me again, or did you tell them the truth?"

Before she could reply, they were interrupted by the approaching flapping sound of sandals hitting the pavement. A man wearing a short-sleeved jersey and cargo shorts was about to pass them on the sidewalk when he suddenly stopped to stare at Ryan. The man then extended his hand and looked poised to say something.

Back home, Ryan always took time to say hello to people who approached him. But here, in a place where he was enjoying his anonymity in the company of an alluring woman, he didn't want to spoil the night. Acting against his nature, Ryan turned his head and quickly brushed past the man. Ryan hoped Shelby hadn't noticed.

"Do you know him?" Shelby asked as they continued down the sidewalk.

"No, did you?"

"No, but it looked like he needed to ask you something."

"Really? I guess I didn't notice." He didn't look back. "Now, weren't you about to say something about your grandparents?"

She glanced over her shoulder and must not have seen anything unusual, for she picked up the conversation easily. "I was about to say that Gran asked if I was going to see you again. When I mentioned The Inn and cocktails, they practically jumped out of their chairs. I swear they were hovering over me until I finally agreed to come down here."

"Huh. Your grandparents . . . And here I thought it was my irresistible personality that lured you out tonight," he teased, hoping she would begin to relax. "They didn't pay you, did they? That would really add insult to injury." He caught a smile at the corner of her mouth. It was a start.

They crossed through the lakeside town park and stopped at a spot along the shore, beside a solitary iron bench with ornamental armrests that curled like scrolls.

"Let's go down to the rocks." Shelby slipped off her sandals and placed them beside the bench before walking barefoot down the rocky embankment. He watched in the dim light as she lifted the hem of her skirt and climbed effortlessly over a round boulder. "Coming?" she called out.

"Right behind you!"

Ryan tossed his shoes beside hers and then made his way to the rocks—maneuvering over them with much less finesse—and joined her at the water's edge. They stood in silence, looking out onto the moon, which perched low in the sky and reflected across a dark expanse of lazy waves.

"It's beautiful here." He turned to her, wanting to feel the touch of her hand. He was drawn to her in the way that waves were drawn to the shore.

"It's one of my favorite spots, particularly on a night like this. Just wait. It won't be long before the sky will be filled with a million stars."

"You're not concerned about being out here in the dark with some guy you hardly know?"

She tilted her head in Ryan's direction. "Why, should I be concerned?"

"Of course not."

"Good. After all, haven't you heard what they say about small-town girls?"

"What do they say?"

She answered mischievously, "We don't lock our car doors, we sleep with the windows open, we drink straight from the bottle, and we're not afraid of the dark."

As twilight faded into a starlit evening, their conversation took on a relaxed rhythm.

"Where is home for you?" Shelby asked.

"Chicago." *Did it feel like home?* he wondered.

"I imagine it must be crowded. And loud." Sitting on a partially submerged rock with her skirt gathered above her knees, Shelby dangled her feet in the cool lake water. "I've never been."

"You'd like it," he said from his spot on the flat-topped rock beside her.

"I would probably like the anonymity of being one of a million, rather than one of a few hundred. Like I am here."

He felt just the opposite, enjoying a greater sense of anonymity in rural towns like hers. "I know how you feel."

"Do you? Hmm," she pondered. "You don't strike me as a private guy."

"Very."

"I'm not sure I believe you."

"Really?" Ryan set his bare feet in the water and immediately pulled them out again. He wondered if he'd ever get used to Superior's frigid temperature, even during an August heat wave. "Think you have me pegged?"

"Maybe." Shelby, on the other hand, seemed completely at ease in the water.

"All right. Give me your best shot." There was still a distinct possibility that Shelby had recognized him all along and was about to call him out on it. He hoped that wasn't the case.

She lifted her feet out of the water and turned to face him. "Your watch is worth more than my truck and you drive a luxury car. But you're young. And since you have time to vacation, I'm guessing that you're not an entrepreneur who found success at an early age. I don't recognize you as an actor or entertainer, although you could pass for one."

"Is that a compliment?"

She ignored the question and continued with her assessment. "My guess is that you come from a wealthy family. You're an Ivy Leaguer. Well educated. You said you're from Chicago, so I'd guess you're working your way into finance or banking. Maybe investments . . ." She reached into the lake to collect some water to cool the back of her neck. Ryan couldn't help but notice the way the water trailed down the shallow between her shoulder blades and caught a shimmer of moonlight on her skin.

"I have a feeling that you could travel just about anywhere you wanted to," she continued. "So, based on the fact that you're here, I'd say you either have a great appreciation for the outdoors—or you're hiding from the cops."

Ah, a joke, he thought. Ryan put his hands on the rock behind him and leaned back, relieved that she was warming up to him. "I'm impressed," he said. "You're pretty close, except the part about the cops and working in finance. I'm lousy with numbers."

She let out a soft, low chuckle. He wanted to hear it again.

"And you don't think I'm a private person?" His question was followed by the lilting call of a solitary loon floating past, hidden in the dark.

"I get the sense that people are naturally drawn to you," she said.

"Is that why you're here?"

"What do you mean?"

"I don't know." He leaned forward, resting his hands on his knees. "Just wondering if you're here just because your family pushed you out the door, or because you feel drawn to me."

Shelby sat up straight and crossed her arms. Ryan prepared for her comeback when a heart-wrenching scream shattered the moment.

"Lucas!" a woman cried out in distress. "Oh God! Help!" The desperation in her voice sent a chill down Ryan's spine. Instinctively, he jumped up and scrambled over the rocks to the grass embankment. "Stay here!" he shouted to Shelby before taking off in the direction of the woman's screams.

CHAPTER 9

RESCUE

Stay here? I don't think so! Shelby thought to herself the instant Ryan ran off toward the sound of the screams.

No sooner had he left than Shelby was chasing after him, holding up her skirt and feeling its light fabric flutter about her legs. During the time when she and Ryan had been sitting on the shore, clouds had crept across the moon and shrouded the park in darkness. Now, Shelby could scarcely see Ryan until he darted through a circle of light beneath a lamppost at the marina entrance and disappeared again down the boat dock.

Shelby ran blindly toward the woman's voice and winced whenever her bare feet landed on something hard and sharp in the grass. Though her heart pounded wildly with adrenaline, she focused on the rhythm of her breathing to keep calm. *Please God, don't let this lake take a life tonight,* she prayed. Once on the dock, the pads of her feet slapped against the splintered wood planks and echoed off the water beneath her.

She finally reached a middle-aged couple dressed in bath-

robes and standing on a transient slip where a thirty-foot sailboat was docked. She wasn't sure if Ryan had been the first to
arrive at the scene, but he was the first to dive into the coal-
black water without a moment of hesitation.

"Over there!" Shelby heard the man shout. She knelt
down at the edge of the dock as Ryan resurfaced in the next
slip over with a child in his grasp. Holding the boy's head
above water with one arm and making broad strokes with the
other, he started swimming back to the dock. The child was
coughing and clinging to Ryan.

At the same time, the couple worked together to hoist a
woman out of the lake. She clung to their hands and pleaded
frantically, "Who has Lucas? Where's my son?!"

It didn't take long before Ryan reached the dock. "He's
here!" Shelby called out, as she reached down to take hold of
Lucas's outstretched hands. Below her, Ryan worked to keep
the boy's head above water.

"Do you have him?" Ryan's voice cracked. He didn't re-
lease his grip on the child until Shelby had a firm hold. The
dripping wet boy, blond and roughly seven years old, was
dressed in striped pajama pants and a short-sleeved *Star Wars*
shirt that dripped and clung to his shivering body. Someone
threw a blanket around the child just as his mother fell to her
knees beside him and enveloped him in a full embrace, her
voice crying words of gratitude.

Shelby looked back at Ryan, who was now using the py-
lons under the dock for footing. He didn't accept Shelby's
hand as he pulled himself up over the edge of the dock and
collapsed onto his back, laid a hand across his chest, and struggled to catch his breath.

"My God, you must be freezing!" Shelby placed her hand
on his shoulder and called out to the others, "Hurry! Does
anyone have another blanket?"

The bathrobed woman rushed into the adjacent sailboat and returned with a yellow fleece blanket to wrap around Ryan. "You were amazing, the way you came out of nowhere and jumped in after him," she said with admiration. "You're a godsend. Thank you."

He sat up and tightened the blanket around his shoulders. Shelby rubbed his back with both hands to help bring some warmth to his body. "Are you sure you're okay?"

"Yeah," Ryan said with chattering teeth. His shoulders were hunched up against the cold and his hands were tucked tightly under his armpits to keep warm. A shiver shook his shoulders as he asked how the boy was doing.

"Looks like he'll be okay," Shelby assured him.

They looked over to see the child being warmed and comforted in his mother's arms. Without a word, Ryan stood and walked over to the frightened child. He then knelt before him, and with the mother's nod of approval, carefully reached for the boy's hand. Shelby couldn't hear what he whispered in the child's ear, but his lips stopped quivering and his face seemed to brighten. The child then wrapped his arms around Ryan's neck. Ryan laid his other hand on the back of the boy's head and closed his eyes.

"Thank God you were here," the mother said, her chin quivering. "When he fell overboard, I just grabbed a life jacket and jumped in after him. But I'm not a good swimmer." She began to cry, stammering out her words. "I can't swim well. I couldn't get us both out of the water. Dear God. If you hadn't . . ."

"You saved your son. It was *you*," he reassured her. "You were the one who called for help. You kept him afloat."

"How can I thank you?" the mother asked, too tired to wipe the tears that were trailing down the sides of her face.

"You obviously love your son. That's thanks enough." He

removed the blanket from his shoulders and wrapped it around the mother and child. After another reassuring smile to the boy, Ryan turned to Shelby. "Come on, we should go," he said quietly.

Neither of them spoke as they left the scene. But once they stepped out of the lamppost's circle of light at the dock's entrance and their feet touched the grass, Shelby took Ryan's arm and walked him back to the rocky beach under the stars.

"Are you sure you don't want to call it a night so you can go back to your place . . ." Shelby started to ask as Ryan removed his soaked shirt and hung it over the back of the park bench. The sight of his broad chest and taut abdomen caught her off guard. She cleared her throat and continued, ". . . to put on something dry?"

"I'm fine."

"I think I have a beach towel in the truck." Her hand gestured toward the road. "I could get it and . . ."

"Really. I'm okay." He looked out on the water. The clouds pulled away from the moon like a curtain to let the moon's light reflect once more on gentle waves. He turned to her with tired eyes and a tender smile before making his way over the rocks to where they sat earlier.

"You were amazing tonight," she said, following him. "Heroic, even."

"Anyone would have done it."

"I saw you jump in. You didn't even hesitate," she said with admiration. She tried to read his face as he sat on the flat-topped boulder, so much quieter now than before the rescue.

"What did you say to that little boy? You know, before we left. You whispered something in his ear?" She adjusted her skirt and sat down beside him.

"Can we talk about something else?"

She noticed vulnerability in him. She couldn't deny that the sight of his bare skin, tan and smooth over well-defined muscles, was a pleasant distraction.

"I'm not ready to leave, but I also don't want to dwell on what happened tonight. You know what I mean?" he asked, staring straight ahead.

"Yes. Of course." But in fact, she had no idea what he meant. "What would you rather talk about?"

"You could tell me about your family."

"My family," she answered slowly, "is complicated."

He ran his fingers through his wet hair to push it off his face. "There you go. Now we have something in common."

"Okay. Let's see. My family. I'll try to give you the abridged version," she began, raising the hem of her skirt before dipping her feet into the water. "My mother's name is Jackie. Like me, she grew up in Bayfield as an only child. Her parents, my grandparents, are Ginny and Olen—but you already know that."

"Yep, I saw the honeymoon photos."

"You did?"

He nodded.

"That's funny. Gran hates showing people those old photos. It's my grandfather who insists on keeping them on the wall at our store," she said. "Anyway, they wanted to have a large family, but after my mother was born, Gran wasn't able to have more children. They always say life was good until Mom hit her teens. I guess she grew to resent the isolation of this town, particularly during the winter. No one was surprised when she hightailed it to California to study at Scripps after graduation." She paused and looked down at her submerged feet. "God, why am I telling you all this?"

"Everyone has a story. That's what makes life interesting," he encouraged her gently. "Go ahead. I'm listening."

She watched as languid waves washed up against the rock, curled around her ankles, and then retreated again with slow repetition. The evening was still—the only sound was a soft *shush* of water breaking along the shoreline. Loose beach stones rattled like marbles in a rolling jar.

"A few months into Mom's freshman year—surprise!" Shelby pointed to herself, trying to make light of it. "She was pregnant. The problem was, the only thing she knew about my father was that he had been living on a sailboat for a couple of weeks with an older brother that summer. His name was Chad."

Ryan pressed his lips together and nodded slowly. "Let me guess. A tourist," he said.

"Yep." Shelby dropped her hands into her lap and continued, "She didn't have a relationship with him. And she didn't want a relationship with me."

"I'm sorry," Ryan said, and she believed him. She wondered how her impression of this man could change so quickly in a single evening. Her grandparents might have been right about him. He just might be one of the good guys. She knew she might never see him again, but tonight, after what happened in the marina and the tranquility of the lake, Shelby felt safe in sharing thoughts that were usually kept hidden.

"My grandparents refused to let her put me up for adoption."

"And they raised you." Ryan picked up a stone and attempted to skip it across the water. It sank with a *plunk*.

"Yes." She thought it was endearing the way he reached for another stone with a look of boyish determination.

"Do you visit her?" Ryan gave the second stone a sideways toss across the water. This time it bounced gracefully across the moonlight.

"No—I don't . . ." she admitted. "I mean, I'm not interested in going to California. I don't really travel anywhere, for that matter. Even if I wanted to, I don't have the time. My friends would tell you that they practically have to drag me out of the house, even for a weekend," she admitted while picking up a stone of her own and moving it back and forth between her hands, feeling its cool, smooth surface.

"Why is that?"

"My grandparents. They mean everything to me. They're the only family I have, really. And they're getting older. I feel I should be here to help them with the farm, the house. Whatever they need."

"So she visits you here?" He pulled up one of his long legs and leaned against it, turning to look at her.

"During the holidays once in a while, but she prefers to come up in the summer. When it's warm. But she never stays long."

"Why not?"

"I've spent a lifetime asking why." Shelby rubbed her thumb across the stone in her hand. "Why do you abandon your baby? Or provoke your parents and run away from your responsibilities?" Seeing him cringe at her mention of running away made her wonder if she had hit a chord with him.

"So what's it like—you know, when she visits?"

Shelby bit her lip and tossed her stone across the water, watching it gracefully skip four times before sinking.

"I'm sorry," he apologized. "Too personal?"

Shelby looked down, then pressed her hands over the folds in her skirt. "No, it's all right." She considered her words carefully before answering. "My mother is like a cold draft in a warm room. Just when you're feeling comfortable and relaxed, her presence causes a chill—you want to pull your feet up and wrap a blanket around your shoulders." Shelby shifted her position and tucked one leg beneath her.

"That's a lot for anyone, but especially for a child," he said. "How did you manage it?"

"I started writing," she said, her mind traveling back to her childhood. She began to tell Ryan a story about how her grandparents had shielded her from the truth when she was very young. It was easy. Ginny and Olen were the only parents she had ever known, so she regarded her mother only as that relative who visited over the holidays or for extended stays in the summer. It wasn't until years later, when she was old enough to notice her grandparents' hushed conversations behind closed doors and long-distance phone calls that were taken in the other room, that she began to suspect her grandparents kept secrets. It never occurred to Shelby that those secrets revolved around her.

At least, not until Shelby's sixth Christmas. Her grandparents were cleaning dishes in the kitchen and Shelby was alone, sitting beneath the Christmas tree, amid a pile of crumpled wrapping paper and tangles of ribbons. She held a new doll in her arms. It was a beautiful blue-eyed girl, with long lashes and eyelids that closed when Shelby laid her down to sleep. The moment Shelby pulled the doll from its box, she named her Polly and confessed her love for her.

"It doesn't always happen like that, you know," Jackie said when she entered the room and found Shelby playing with the doll. The young woman fell back into Olen's oversized chair, looking disheveled in flannel pajama pants and an oversized sweatshirt, her hair piled up on the top of her head like a bird's nest. Even with a rainbow of Christmas tree lights reflecting in her eyes, Jackie was sullen.

"What?" Shelby asked.

"Feeling like a mother right away," Jackie said flatly. "Like you did, with that doll this morning."

"Yes, you do," Shelby said assuredly. *All mommies do,* she had believed.

"No, sometimes it takes a while. Not everyone is ready to be a parent right away." Jackie pulled her knees up to her chest and hugged them, as Shelby was hugging Polly. "Sometimes, babies are raised by people who are better at being parents."

"But you're not a mommy." Shelby had laughed weakly.

"Gran and Grandpa haven't been honest with you, Shelby."

"What?" She looked toward the kitchen, willing her grandparents to return. Sensing that she'd need protection from the secret that was about to be revealed to her.

"I'm talking about me. I'm not just a family friend, Shelby," she said, dropping her feet back onto the floor and leaning forward. "I'm your mother."

Jackie reached out to Shelby, but she recoiled and hugged Polly tighter, instinctively protecting the doll from someone she thought she could trust.

"Come here, Shelby." Jackie's attempt at a motherly smile came across, instead, as a contemptuous sneer. Shelby shuddered. "Give your mom a hug."

Instead, she scrambled to her feet and ran into the kitchen with a trembling chin and eyes brimming with tears. Shelby found her grandmother standing at the kitchen sink and flung her arms around Ginny's leg until Olen reached down to lift her up. With her arms wrapped tightly around her grandfather's neck, her tears wetting his shirt, and her grandmother speaking softly into her ear, Shelby listened as the two people she loved most reluctantly told her the truth.

Later that morning, Shelby retreated into her room and climbed up onto her bed with Polly and another gift she had received. This one from her grandfather. It was a diary with a smooth red cover, gold-edged pages that she thought were beautiful, and gold lettering that spelled out *My Diary* in a delicate script. The diary's best feature was a lock and key that she felt certain would be strong enough to keep Jackie from knowing her innermost thoughts.

In her best printing, and using what few words she knew how to spell at the time, Shelby began to write. About her questions. Her fears. Dreams. She poured her truth onto those pages.

As the years went on, Shelby never forgot the sound of her mother's words or the pain they incited. Shelby learned that her best defense was to keep her mother's voice at bay. If Jackie wanted to communicate, she could do it in letters.

"Despite everything, she's still my mom," Shelby finally told Ryan. "And she's my grandparent's daughter. I don't think they'll ever stop worrying about her and the decisions she makes. And I don't think I'll ever wonder what my life would have been like with parents in it."

"Do you still write?" he asked.

"I used to—" she began, realizing it had been a long time since anyone other than her grandparents had asked about her writing. "I was actually studying journalism at Madison. Something happened a while back and I," she said with some apprehension. *Too much, too soon,* she thought. *What is it about this guy? We just met and here I am telling him everything.*

He looked at her curiously. "You quit?"

"No, not exactly. I had to come back to help out on the farm," she lied. "I'm sure I'll go back and finish out my last year. Eventually." *Or never,* she thought.

"I don't know. It seems to me that they'd want you to finish that degree," he said. "Pursue your own dreams regardless of what anyone else thinks. Particularly your mother."

"I wish it was that easy. I mean, I wouldn't expect you to understand, coming from a city like Chicago. It's just that they're getting older and the farm is a huge responsibility and"—she said, perhaps to reassure herself more than Ryan—"they just need me."

"Maybe so," he offered. "But it seems to me that you have

two people who love you unconditionally. With that kind of support, anything's possible."

"Is it?" Shelby reached down to pick up one last stone and threw it into the lake. Gentle ripples circled away from the diminutive splash and, like childhood memories, caught the moon's glow as they traveled back to her.

CHAPTER 10

LIGHTS

"Your table is ready," Ryan said, sweeping his arm over a picnic blanket. Their first evening in the park, which hardly qualified as an actual date, had been eventful. Once he had dried off from his lake plunge and Shelby's guard started to come down, ever so slightly, they spent the night talking. And by the time they parted ways, they were even laughing. She had agreed to see him again.

That was a few days and several dates ago and on this evening, Ryan had driven Shelby to a small beach outside of town that offered privacy, sand dunes, and a view of Madeline Island across the bay. The week was passing quickly and Ryan would be leaving for Chicago in two days.

"I hope you're hungry because I went a bit overboard," he told her, referring to the assortment of cheeses, salami, bread, and smoked whitefish wrapped in newspaper. Kneeling beside her on a plaid blanket, he held up two cardboard containers of strawberries and blueberries. "I didn't know which one you liked better, so I grabbed both."

"Strawberries, hands down." She reached for one of the crimson berries, plucked off its fringed green top, and took a bite. "I'm impressed—you thought of everything."

"You don't mind eating outside?" Once again, he had managed to plan a date with Shelby that kept them out of the public eye, such as it was in Bayfield.

"The restaurants will always be there, but it's not often that I have dinner on the beach. In fact, I'm actually surprised you picked *this* beach—you know, considering the bears and all," she said, removing the pungent, smoke-infused fish from its oil-stained paper wrapping.

Ryan was slicing a wedge of softened Brie, its insides melting away from the white outer skin and onto the picnic cutting board, when he held the knife still and looked up. "Bears?"

"You didn't know?"

His eyes started darting about the deserted beach.

"Huh, I'm surprised. I thought you would have read about it in a travel guide or something." Shelby tilted her head and looked at him with a quizzical expression. "This is the most popular place for bear watching. In fact, people often sit in their cars on the side of the road over there, and wait to spot them," she explained casually, pointing in the direction of Ryan's parked car.

"I've never really thought of bears on the beach. . . ." His voice trailed off as he glanced over his shoulder.

"No, I suppose not. But we're talking about Wisconsin black bears. They love to forage on these dunes," she continued without concern, removing the skin from the smoked fish and pulling away a flake of its tender meat. "Berries, smoked fish . . . and sometimes, they even enjoy a good pinot." Shelby popped the piece of fish into her mouth and gave a nod to the unopened wine bottle at his side. She then covered her mouth, chewing and laughing.

"Bears," he chuckled, reaching into his bag for a corkscrew. "You didn't fool me for a minute."

"I don't know . . . you had that look on your face . . ." she teased. "Do bears make you nervous?"

"You make me nervous."

"For a visitor, you seem quite at home." Shelby lay on her side, propped up on her elbow and unable to eat another morsel of their picnic dinner.

"I love it up here."

"Do you realize you've done more in one week than I probably do in an entire summer?"

"Come on, that can't be true."

"I'm serious," she said, taking another sip of wine. "Let's take yesterday. I've lived here all my life and I never kayaked into the sea caves until I went with you and your friends. Or this picnic—I can't tell you the number of times I've been to this beach, but never once did I think to come in the evening. And look at what I've been missing—it's so peaceful."

"Beautiful," he said, admiring Shelby more than the scenery. "In fact, do you mind if I take a picture of you, while there's still a little light?"

"I'm too stuffed to pose."

"Don't move."

As he reached into his camera bag to retrieve his equipment, Ryan was taken by Shelby's confidence and ease. There were no pretenses with her. She was naturally beautiful and unconcerned about impressing others, including him.

He stepped away from the blanket and raised the camera to his eye. His attraction for her grew as she smiled at him through the camera's lens. *Click.* He took more shots from different angles and distances while she became playful in her expressions—sometimes serious and contemplative, sometimes cross-eyed with puckered lips—and sometimes just herself. *Click.* When he knelt at the foot of the blanket to take one last shot of Shelby in the fading violet light, Ryan realized how much the photographs summed up their brief time together. It was a balance between respect and attraction. Enjoying the day without regard for tomorrow.

"I've noticed, over these past few days, that you really seem to know your way around that camera. When did you pick it up?" Shelby asked.

"In college," he said, replacing the lens cap. "Before that, I was mainly into drawing. I spent a lot of time sketching cars when I was a kid." He reached for his camera bag and packed up his equipment while she watched.

"Do you still draw?"

"A bit."

"I'd love to see your sketches someday."

They hadn't talked about what would happen between them once he left for Chicago. Ryan hadn't mentioned the distinct possibility that he'd return. She brushed her hands back and forth across the blanket before bringing up the topic he had hoped to avoid. "You haven't talked much about your family this week—they must enjoy seeing your photographs."

"My dad treats it like a hobby." He snapped the camera case shut and moved to sit beside her. "He'd rather see me behind a desk than behind a lens."

"And your mom?"

"She's more supportive. In fact, she gave me my first camera when I was thirteen. It was one of those handheld cameras. Blue." He smiled at the memory. "I think it was her way of encouraging me to put down the pencil and try to connect with my father. Since his work involves video and film, so to speak, she probably thought he would relate more to me through photography."

"You've obviously moved on from that little blue camera."

"That's true. I hadn't really thought much of photography as art until I was in college. Have you ever heard of Vivian Maier?" Ryan wasn't interested in discussing photography at that moment. In fact, it was taking everything he had not to lean over to Shelby and kiss her for the first time. The only thing holding him back was knowing that although they had seen each other every day since that first night in the park, she was firmly against becoming attached to someone who was passing through town.

"No, I haven't." Shelby gently bit her lower lip and he wondered if they were sharing the same thoughts.

"I hadn't either, until a friend dragged me to her exhibit on campus. She had an incredible story. You see, she took thousands of photographs that were packed away in boxes and forgotten. Years later, someone found the boxes of negatives in an old storage locker, printed them, and realized how incredible they were. She wasn't discovered by the art world until after her death."

"Great story," Shelby said. "What did she photograph?"

"Black-and-white candids of ordinary people doing ordinary things. And yet, she was able to capture the stories and emotion behind those ordinary moments," he said, trying to take his mind off his attraction to Shelby by reflecting on Maier's work. He had been so moved by the woman's photographs that he returned to her exhibit three more times that week, just staring at the images and trying to figure out what it was that made them so unique. Was it her composition? Lighting? Expression? Because of Vivian Maier, an artist who created images for herself rather than for her public, photography was never the same for him again—and his new aspiration was born.

★ ★ ★

After the sun disappeared beyond the horizon, the only remaining light came from a few votive candles that Ryan placed in the sand, the distant lights from Madeline Island across the bay, and the rising moon. A second bottle of pinot sat off-kilter against a rock, uncorked and half-full. Lying on their backs and looking up at the night sky, Ryan wondered aloud how long it had been since he had felt this relaxed. The soft blanket beneath them, a gentle breeze brushing off the water, the sound of her laugh—the combination was more intoxicating than the wine.

He looked over at Shelby and noticed color rising in her cheeks. First rose toned, then a golden orange, and finally a blazing emerald green. From the corner of his eye he saw a brightening overhead. Looking skyward, he uttered his amazement. He watched in awe as a kaleidoscope of light shifted and blended fluidly above them. It was as if God was orchestrating a silent symphony in the skies. Inspired, Ryan reached across the blanket for Shelby's hand before realizing she'd likely pull away. Instead, she entwined her fingers with his and he felt a rush of desire sweep through him.

Cast in the light of aurora borealis, with Shelby at his side, Ryan was at a loss for words. This woman—this place—had made him feel more alive than ever before. He couldn't rationalize how quickly she had filled his heart any more than he could explain why the sky was now aflame in color. In his head, Ryan knew he was witnessing solar flashes in the night sky—but his heart knew he was taking a glimpse of heaven on earth.

He couldn't let another day pass without expressing through touch what words couldn't convey. How do you describe a bond you feel for someone, when logical thought insists that it couldn't happen so quickly? You don't earn someone's trust in a day. Love doesn't happen in a single evening. At least that's what he had always believed.

Ryan slowly rolled onto his side, so close to her now that they nearly touched. The small space between their bodies felt charged. He raised his hand to touch her cheek, ever so lightly. When Shelby looked at him, her eyes were bright with emotion and reflecting the lights above them. He leaned in close enough to feel her quickening breath on his lips. His nose barely brushed against hers. A playful touch before his lips fell softly on the blush of her cheek. With his lips no more than a whisper away from hers, he smiled with his eyes, touched her chin, and then kissed her lightly.

He pulled away to take it all in. He would hold the image of her in his mind, clearer than any photograph, and remember how lovely she was in that moment. Her bright eyes were dazzling as they reflected the spirited wisps of color that moved across the sky. Ryan then gathered Shelby in his arms and kissed her with more passion. She arched her body against his and kissed him back as the sky continued to cast its transcendent light upon them. They lay atop the blanket on the sand dunes, wrapped in each other's embrace, until the candles burned out and the northern lights faded to black.

"Come on, I want to show you something," Shelby said on their last evening together. As soon as he arrived at the farmhouse, she had met him at his car and took his hand. The sun was disappearing quickly, casting a ribbon of warm light across the horizon. She led Ryan to her favorite spot on the property, the barn. He had noticed it the first time he visited Meyers Orchard and admired its architectural character. It was a gamble-roofed barn, painted apple red with white trim. As they approached, Shelby explained how Ginny had fallen in love with its charm the first time she and Olen had stepped foot on the property. Tonight, silhouetted against the early eve-

ning sky with amber lamplight shining within, it seemed almost magical.

"Would you believe this is the first time I've been inside a
barn?" Ryan asked as they entered.

"You don't get out much, do you?" Shelby gave his hand a
playful squeeze.

"If I were to imagine the quintessential barn, I think this
would be it," he said once they were inside. He dropped her
hand and walked about the space, looking up at the high-
ceiling framework that resembled the inverted skeletal hull of a
ship.

"Quintessential? You *are* a city boy."

Ryan chuckled as he walked past a stack of empty storage
crates.

"Would you believe it if I told you this was a mail-ordered
barn?" she asked, seemingly delighted to show him this place
that she loved.

"Seriously?" He touched some of the antique tools that
hung on a pegboard along the far wall.

"The original owners ordered this barn from a 1911 Sears,
Roebuck catalog for roughly five hundred dollars. You're
standing inside the 'Barn Number Twelve' kit." Shelby made
her way around the crates to join him. "I've always loved the
thought of a gigantic package arriving here with words stamped
across the sides of the crate, 'Some Assembly Required.'" She
laughed. "Can you imagine?"

"Some assembly is right," he agreed with admiration. "It's
still in excellent condition. I'm glad you brought me here—it's
incredible."

She led him past a pile of musty burlap bags and stalls filled
with farming equipment and tools, until they reached a quirky
space near the barn's double-wide doors.

He listened as Shelby talked about what made the barn so

special to her. When Jackie was born, long before "man cave" became part of the modern vernacular, Olen had carved out his own retreat in the barn. Like a makeshift clubhouse for a grown man, the space boasted a secondhand couch, over-turned apple crate tables, camping lanterns, and a television connected by a string of extension cords that snaked up a sup-port beam, across the adjacent wall, and into an electrical out-let. On warm nights, after Olen's work was done and a much younger Jackie was tucked in bed, he would go to the barn to recharge.

When he and Ginny were raising Shelby, however, Shelby said that he no longer felt the need to get away. Instead, he welcomed her into the club, she told Ryan with obvious pride. The two spent countless rainy days and summer eve-nings in the barn with the doors open to the sky. They would watch Packers games with a popcorn bowl between them, play backgammon under the dim light of a camping lantern, read *Little Women* and Judy Blume, and talk about school. The lake. Constellations. Her mother. No topic was ever off-limits.

Ryan took a seat on the lumpy couch while Shelby turned on one of the lanterns. "You talked about everything with your grandfather?" he asked.

"I still do." The lantern cast a warm golden light across her face. She set it down on a crate and walked to the workbench behind the couch where she had placed a bottle of wine and two glasses before his arrival. "When I was younger, he loved to talk about everything. Homework, farming, friends, boys," she said, joining him on the couch.

"Boys?" Ryan raised one eyebrow skeptically. "I can't imagine having conversations like that with my parents, let alone my grandparents."

"Guess I just got lucky," she answered with a laugh. "Wine?"

He accepted a glass and held it out while she gave him a healthy pour.

"Don't you talk to your parents about what's happening in your life?" she asked, pouring a glass for herself before setting the bottle down beside the lantern.

"Not really."

"Why not?" Shelby tucked her legs beneath her, turning sideways on the couch to face him.

"I don't know." He paused, looking down at the armrest while thumbing a firm thread that stuck out of the piping like a stray whisker. "It just wasn't something we did."

"Do you want to talk about it?" Shelby asked, and from the look of concern in her eyes, he realized she was picking up on feelings that he wasn't interested in discussing.

"On my last night here?" he said, trying to sway her away from the topic by setting down his glass and reaching for her hand. "I can think of much better ways to spend this time."

"I look at you and think how fortunate you are to have had your parents."

"You have Ginny and Olen," Ryan said quietly, entwining his fingers with hers. "Besides, parents can be overrated."

Shelby shook her head slightly. "You don't really believe that, do you?"

"You haven't met mine."

Ryan took her glass and set it beside his own, then shifted on the couch to face her. Perhaps it was the wine. The night air that breezed in through the open barn doors. Or the look in her eyes that expressed a longing for something that no one but Jackie could give her. Whatever the reason, his attraction to Shelby was undeniable.

"I'm sorry your mother wasn't there for you," he said, lightly caressing her palms with his thumbs. "But you had two people who loved you." He raised her hands to his lips for a light kiss.

Ryan pulled up on one knee, drawing her to him. They moved closer together, slowly, with wanting, until they were no more than a breath away from one another. Once he brushed her lips with a kiss, his worries fell away. Family obligation. Disappointments. Choices. When his hand slid behind her neck and his fingers buried into her hair, he hoped to smooth away her mother's verbal lashings. Ryan wanted Shelby to feel protected in his embrace, as he felt in hers.

That evening, as gentle kisses became more passionate and they gradually fell back into the cushions, Ryan didn't think about his impending departure the next morning. Or that, once again, she would be deserted—this time, by no one else's fault but his own. There were no promises between them. Only possibilities of what could be, should he dare to take those steps.

"Shelby?" came Olen's protective voice out of the darkness, just beyond the barn's open doors.

She quickly pulled away from Ryan's embrace and straightened her blouse. "Grandpa?"

Shit, Ryan thought to himself, feeling like a sixteen-year-old kid caught in the basement with a girl who was up past her curfew.

"I think it's time for your *friend* to leave, don't you?"

"He was just heading out," she called back, shooting an apologetic look at Ryan. She stood up and reached out to take his hand. "Sorry, I feel like a fool," she whispered. "Here I am, at an age when I should have a place of my own, and Grandpa is calling me out. As if I'm back in high school."

"It's nothing," Ryan assured her while rising from the couch.

"Fair warning—don't say anything to him as you leave." She groaned. "I'd bet good money that he's out there wearing nothing more than a pair of white briefs and his work boots."

Ryan laughed out loud, despite the awkwardness of the situation. And then, knowing Olen was watching, he refrained himself. Ryan gave Shelby a discreet hug and whispered into her ear that he understood. Before they walked out of the barn together, she stopped beside the glowing lantern on the apple crate.

"So, I guess this is good-bye." Shelby looked him in the eyes, offered a slight smile, and turned out the light.

CHAPTER 11

FOOL

It was mid–September, only a few weeks after she and Ryan had parted ways, and Shelby was remorseful. She couldn't believe that she had put herself in a position that, before meeting Ryan, she had successfully avoided. Heartbroken over a tourist. As the days went on, she cared less about how much she enjoyed her time with Ryan and instead, grew more critical of herself for breaking her convictions. *For God's sake, I barely even know him!* she thought. *So why can't I get him out of my mind?*

Fortunately, she had her work. The orchard's early apples were ready for picking and there was enough work on the farm to keep her distracted.

The Lupine Hus Inn hadn't changed much since the boutique hotel opened over a century ago. In fact, the hotel's restored interior was integral to its popularity. Visiting the inn was akin to being whisked away in a time warp. The upstairs guest quarters looked just as they did when the inn opened, except now the crimson carpet, one of the few things that had been replaced several times over the decades, was pink and threadbare. The staircase railing was worn smooth by the hands of countless guests, and the floorboards groaned under each visitor's weighted footstep. The sagging space had the clean, yet aged, scent of lemon and leaves.

On the main level, the walls of the intimate dining room were covered with photographs and memorabilia that had been collected over the years. Diners sat at the simplest of wooden tables and chairs, furniture built for feeding the masses rather than contributing to the room's décor. And every Friday night, from spring to fall, the inn boiled fish outside in a huge pot that hung low and heavy over a tended fire pit.

But today wasn't Friday. Rather than partaking in the fish boil, Shelby and her grandmother were sitting at a corner table enjoying BLT sandwiches and tomato soup when a waitress named Margaret Aikin carried a portrait-sized picture frame into the dining room.

"Now where's Margaret going to find room for that?" Shelby nudged Ginny.

"Lord knows, they don't need anything else on these walls," Ginny agreed, briefly glancing over her shoulder at Margaret and then returning her attention to a piece of bacon that had fallen from her sandwich.

Shelby watched Margaret carefully remove a Frankie Avalon *Bikini Beach* movie poster and replace it with something new. At first, Shelby couldn't see what it was because Margaret blocked her view. Once the frame was centered, Margaret stepped aside to admire her work. That was when Shelby saw a photograph and newspaper article displayed side by side within a cream-colored mat. Shelby dropped her spoon and it hit the table with a *clang,* skipped off the surface, and fell to the floor.

"Ryan?" Shelby blurted out, suddenly pushing her chair back with a loud scrape. She stood up from the table and rushed to the frame as Margaret walked away. It was him. The man she hadn't expected to see again was now staring at her through the other side of the glass.

She put her hand over her chest to calm the nervous energy that pulsed rapidly through her heart. Ryan's image was placed alongside a *Duluth Herald* article that had been published in the Sunday paper. *Two days ago,* she thought. *What was I doing on Sunday? I don't remember reading the paper. Why didn't anyone tell me?*

Stars Light Up the North
by Carl Williams, Staff Reporter

Duluth Herald
Sunday, September 15

Hollywood stars are casting light on remote parts of northern Wisconsin, and local residents aren't surprised. Most people can understand how anyone, famous or not, wouldn't be able to help falling in love with the state's untold beauty and serene lifestyle.

Before Oscar-nominated actor Charles Haven relocated to a sprawling ranch in Colorado, there was speculation that he was looking for real estate just north of Cornucopia. British singer-songwriter Jimmy Phillips and his wife, film producer Ruby Lange Phillips, have owned a secluded home on Geneva Lake for more than a decade. And in the 1990s, actress Brigitte Moreau rented a summer home on Madeline Island for six consecutive years, calling the area "a true oasis."

Most recently, new rumors are being shared in Bayfield's coffee shops and cafés that William Chambers Jr., of Chicago-based Chambers Media and one of the country's most sought-after bachelors, has been spending time in the quaint waterfront town.

He kept to himself during his week there and was only seen on occasion, kayaking on Lake Superior with friends and dining at the Lupine Hus Inn.

Shelby turned to Ginny and mouthed, "It's *him,*" while pointing to the article. Ginny shrugged her shoulders and offered a knowing smile, before taking another bite of her sandwich and licking a dab of mayo from the side of her mouth. Shelby scanned the rest of the article, which described Ryan's interests in outdoor sports, his amiable nature, and his penchant for low-key travel destinations. As he wasn't interviewed for the article, several Bayfield locals were asked to give their impressions of him. It didn't surprise her that their responses were brief. This town wasn't drawn to the limelight. Their quotes offered little more than William Chambers is "an attractive fellow," "appeared friendly enough," "kept to himself," and "seemed pretty normal to me." Shelby read to the end of the article.

"He was interested in trying something distinctly local, so I recommended the whitefish livers," said Margaret Aikin, a waitress at the Lupine Hus Inn. "He was extremely polite, rather quiet, and quite easy on the eyes."

Who knows, residents say, whether he loved Lake Superior's south shore enough to return?

William Chambers. How could she have been so naïve? Did she ever ask for his last name? She couldn't remember asking, but that seemed unlikely. Of course she had asked. People asked those things! Or did he tell her and she simply didn't make the connection? He probably evaded the question altogether, just like he kept all of the important details about his life so vague. Ryan from Chicago. That was how she referred to him. Ryan from Chicago. Staying a week. A tourist. Keep things simple. No last name required. It wasn't like she was going to see him again. So why did he lie about his name?

She stared blankly at the framed display, unaware that Ginny was now standing beside her.

"Well, look what we have here," Ginny said, setting her hand on Shelby's shoulder. "It's a nice photograph of him."

Shelby swiveled sharply to face her grandmother, causing Ginny's hand to drop.

"He's very photogenic, isn't he?" Ginny continued. "Nice strong jaw on that boy."

"Hang on!" Shelby burst out, and then just as suddenly lowered her voice to an agitated whisper. "Hang on—you *knew?*"

"Of course I did—don't be silly," Ginny said matter-of-factly. She leaned in to take a closer look at the article. "Clever headline, don'tchya think?"

"Why didn't you say anything?" Shelby strained to keep her voice down.

"What was there to say? A nice young man comes knocking on your door. Who am I to stir the pot?" Without her bifocals, Ginny had to squint to read the article. "Did you read this, Shel? Did they interview any of our friends? I wonder if this reporter spoke with Mary—I ran into her the other day and she mentioned speaking with Ryan at the Heritage Center while he was here. Did I mention she's doing research on the old brickyard? Anyway, I imagine she talked his ear off."

"Outside," Shelby said through clenched teeth before taking her grandmother's hand and leading her out of the dining room. Once they were outside, standing in the gravel parking lot that spread out beyond the front entrance, the two women turned to face one another.

"This wasn't about stirring the pot! It's about clueing me in to the fact that he was someone—you know . . ."

"Famous?" Ginny stated the obvious without inflection, as if she had been asked something as simple as the color of the sky.

Shelby knew her grandmother was playing it cool just to have fun at Shelby's expense and, God love her, it was working. Ginny had probably been waiting for the day when it would finally dawn on her.

"This is crazy," Shelby said, shaking her head.

"I'll tell you what's crazy—how easy it is to get you riled up," Ginny said, placing her hands squarely on her hips. The joke had run its course and she was ready to get motherly. "If you calm down, you'll realize that it isn't so important *who* he is—it's *what* he is."

"A liar? A manipulator?"

"He's the first young man to get your duff off the farm to have a little fun—something you haven't done since Jeff passed away."

"Please don't bring Jeff into this."

"You were smiling again. And for that, your grandfather and I don't give a damn who he was as long as he treated you well."

"Grandpa knew, too?"

"Of course he knew. In fact, I'm pretty sure most everyone around here recognized him," Ginny said, without hiding her amusement. "Well, except you, that is."

"Everyone except for me. Well, that's just perfect." Shelby threw her arms out at her side. "This changes everything!"

"And why's that?"

"I can't believe I have to explain this to you, of all people . . ." Shelby began to pace like a tiger in a tight cage.

"Has he changed?"

"No. But he—"

"He isn't who you thought he was?"

"Yes, but it's more than that, Gran." Shelby clenched her hands into fists and forced out the words. "Ryan, my ass. He didn't even give me his real name!"

"Nope." Ginny reached out for Shelby's arm to stop her pacing.

"He deceived me," Shelby seethed, now shoving her balled fists under her arms in an attempt to regain control of her emotions.

"And there it is," Ginny said with a sigh. "Yes, I suppose he did. It's a shame, really. Now you have no other recourse but to go back to your usual ways."

"What?"

"It's all right, Shelby. I understand. You have your easy way out. Just put him out of your mind."

"What do you mean, 'easy way out'?"

"Nothing. Let's just get back inside. My lunch is getting cold and this conversation has run its course."

"Gran, he played me. Can't you see how that makes me feel? He must think I'm an idiot," Shelby said. *Oh my God. That's it. He was probably laughing at me the entire time. I'm sure he and his friends had a great time talking about the dimwit who didn't recognize William Chambers. If he ever comes back, I'd love to give him a piece of my mind.*

"I don't think so," Ginny said reassuringly.

Shelby continued to mumble angrily. "A toy to play with and discard."

"You and I both know you're much too smart to be someone's plaything. Come on. We raised you better than that." Ginny chose her next words carefully. "If you want to put him in a box along with the others who have betrayed or left you, then be my guest. That's what I mean by taking the easy way out. But before you cast him aside, consider why he might have kept his identity from you. Think, Shelby. What drew you to him in the first place? Are you forgetting the connection you felt with him? Perhaps that's all you needed this summer. Maybe that's what you both needed."

Shelby unclenched her fists. "I'm not sure what to think," she admitted quietly.

"It will come to you," Ginny offered. "Now, I'm going back inside. Are you coming? Or are you going to continue stewing?"

An easy out? Put him in a box? Reasons?

"One more thing, Shelby," Ginny said, looking carefully at her granddaughter. "Why are you getting so worked up anyway? You told me that everything between the two of you was casual. I know you didn't expect to see him again. So why are you letting this get to you?"

"I'm not sure. It was supposed to be nothing, but then . . ." Shelby said, more to herself than to her grandmother. "Who knows? Maybe I can walk it off. See you back at home?"

Ginny nodded. "Just chalk it up to one of life's little surprises."

Shelby walked off toward Main Street, but before reaching the sidewalk, she stopped to call out thanks to her grandmother.

Ginny paused at the inn's entrance, nodded with a wave, and disappeared back inside.

★ ★ ★

Shelby was blocks away from the inn now, walking heavy-footed with her head down, wondering how she could have been so trusting. How she had put down her guard. And for what? There was no real reason for her to be concerned. No harm was done. In fact, she should be amused. Imagine her—a farm girl from Northern Wisconsin—traipsing about with someone like Will Chambers.

But then again, Shelby thought, *Why not me?* Her mother's words raced to the forefront of her thoughts—*silly girl, home-bound, directionless,* and *afraid.* Words that sent Shelby back to questioning, once more, whether she was worthy of ever having something wonderful.

When Shelby finally stopped walking, she realized where she had been unconsciously heading all along. She was on Broad Street and Washington at the foot of the stairs that led up to the Bayfield Carnegie Library, a handsome brick and brownstone building that had held the community's books, maps, directories, marine data, and history since 1903.

She needed answers.

Shelby climbed the stairs to the library's entrance. She straightened her posture, took a deep breath to steady her nerves, and grabbed the brass doorknob. Giving it a pull, she looked into the historic library and was relieved to see no one in the lobby except for the librarian.

"Hey, Claire, how's it going?" Shelby called out as she entered.

If Pippi Longstocking were a middle-aged woman, she would look like Claire Dollins. The town librarian had unruly red hair that she wore pulled back into a lopsided bun, a peppering of freckles across her full cheeks, one large front tooth that stuck out from the rest in an otherwise lovely smile, and a mischievous laugh that rang out loud and often—and usually at the most inappropriate times.

"No complaints," Claire answered cheerfully, delighted to see Shelby. "Better than you, it appears. You look a bit . . . discombobulated. Everything all right?"

"Not the best day, but I'll be okay."

Claire removed the purple and green polka-dotted glasses from her nose and closed the book she was reading.

"Really. It's nothing," Shelby assured her with a forced smile. "Gran and I have a difference of opinions about something and I thought I'd come here to do a little research on the topic."

"Need to prove you're right?"

"Something like that."

"Is that all?" Claire tapped a pencil against the desktop while keeping a keen eye on Shelby.

"Yep."

"I have a pretty good sense about these things, so I can tell you that I doubt that's the full story." Claire's face took on a dour scowl, and then suddenly brightened into a toothy grin. "I'm joking! I'm joking. Now, what can I help you find?"

"Is your Wi-Fi up?" Shelby tried to sound casual, even though she felt unsettled about the information she would uncover. She could have used the family's outdated home computer, instead of coming to the library, but that would have meant facing her grandparents and dealing with a painstakingly slow Internet service. She wanted to sort this out quickly and privately.

"Sure," Claire said, scurrying out from behind the desk. "Don't tell anyone, but I was actually using the computer to look up recipes on the Food Network site a bit ago. I just love that Bobby Flay. My brother and his wife, Candice, are coming up for a visit tomorrow night from Hayward and I thought I'd make one of Bobby's 'ultimate rib' dinners. But then I remembered that Candice is always complaining about things being too spicy. Too spicy! I can't even sprinkle a little garlic salt on the chicken without her going on and on about her 'delicate palate.' So I don't think ribs will do. Nope. I'll have to stick with something basic. Something flavorless. Something with cream of mushroom soup and a side of white bread. I can't picture Bobby on TV pulling out a loaf of white bread just for Candice, can you?"

"I'm sure whatever you make will be delicious, Claire," Shelby answered, following the librarian to the only computer in the building. Today, she welcomed Claire's knack for dominating a conversation.

"You are a doll," Claire replied. "Now, do you need help with your search, or are you good?"

Shelby took a seat in front of the computer. "I'm good, thanks."

"If you need me, just holler." Claire patted Shelby's shoulder before heading back to her desk. She didn't get more than a few steps away when she turned back, adding, "Our printer has been jamming lately. It's kinda hit or miss. I need to call Al about that—I'm sure he could fix it. That man knows how to fix everything in this town, don'tchya know."

"Okay, Claire. The printer. Got it," Shelby answered vaguely, for she was already distracted by a screen that showed pages of hits for the search: WILLIAM CHAMBERS JR. "Unbelievable," she mumbled. Shelby slumped down in her chair and clicked onto the first entry, "William R. Chambers— (NNS) National News Source," and read what followed:

> **William Ryan Chambers Jr.,** often referred to as Will, is an American businessman and novice adventurer. The son of WILLIAM RYAN SR. and CHARLOTTE MASON CHAMBERS, William Jr. is the younger of two children. His sister, MARTHA CHAMBERS PALMER, is an aspiring poet who resides in South Carolina with

her husband, Joseph Palmer, and a daughter. Chambers is unmarried and has been labeled one of the country's most eligible bachelors.

Perfect, thought Shelby. *He gets crowned "most eligible bachelor" while I'm crowned "village idiot."* No wonder she had let her guard down so easily. Dating women was obviously one of his specialties. *They should have added "recreational adventurer and philanderer" to his bio.* Although she was tempted to shut down the computer and storm out of the library, she couldn't seem to pull herself away from the screen. She wanted to know more about the spider whose web she had fallen into.

EARLY LIFE AND EDUCATION

Chambers attended private school through twelfth grade in Chicago, Ill., before graduating with honors from Columbia University with a degree in communications. After college, he interned in Costa Rica for a team of *National Geographic* photographers documenting the Arenal Volcano and its surrounding rain forest. Back in Chicago, Chambers worked for an urban youth organization, fostering children's programs and participating in the organization's fund-raising efforts.

Chambers earned a master's degree in business from Northwestern University before joining Chambers Media. He is expected to assume control of the company upon William Chambers Sr.'s retirement.

What did Ryan say he did for a living? The only thing she remembered was that he had been evasive whenever she brought up the subject. She knew they both had a stake in their family businesses. Unlike her, however, Ryan considered it a burden. He mentioned communications. Shelby assumed it was something small or midsized. Certainly not an industry leader. Why hadn't she pressed him further? Chambers Media— they were involved in virtually *everything*!

"Finding what you need?" Claire called out from the stacks.

"Yes, thanks!" Shelby replied over her shoulder. "Everything's right here, in black and white."

Emotions hit her like a fast-moving storm on the lake. Anger, self-doubt, admiration, curiosity, dismay. Once again she found herself deeply questioning why this man would be interested in spending time with someone like her. No matter how she looked at it, even when giving herself the benefit of the doubt, it didn't add up.

"How's it going?" Claire suddenly appeared directly behind Shelby, placing a hand on her shoulder and leaning in toward the computer screen.

"God, Claire!" Shelby burst out as she smacked her hands on the desktop. "You scared the crap out of me!"

"William Chambers? Huh," Claire said, oblivious to Shelby's surprise. "He's sexier in person, don'tchya think?"

"Is he?" Shelby looked from Claire to the computer and cringed upon realizing that she had clicked on a photo of Ryan walking across a city street. He looked casual yet polished, even in jeans. A gray wool scarf was wrapped loosely around his neck and tucked into a luxurious black leather jacket. *So out of my league,* she thought.

"Did you see him when he was here?" Claire asked.

"Nope," Shelby quietly lied, running her fingers through her hair.

"So why are you looking him up?"

"Oh, you know, I read it in the *Herald* the other day." Shelby kept her inflection blasé. "I was curious to see if there was any more news about it."

"I saw that article, too. They say he pretty much kept to himself." Claire had no qualms about reaching over Shelby to grab the mouse and scroll through more photographs of Ryan.

"So I heard." Shelby leaned back in her chair, arms crossed, trying to avoid being hit in the nose by Claire's elbow as she took control of the computer.

"I only saw him once, down at the South Point Marina. I think he was checking out sailboat charters." Claire clicked her tongue when she came across a photo of Ryan looking incredible with a surfboard under his arm on some exotic beach.

Shelby's mind flashed back to that first night with Ryan and how she had tried to keep from looking at him as he sat shirtless beside her on the rocks. "Did you talk to him?" she asked Claire.

"No, but I did overhear him ask about charter dates for this fall, so who knows, maybe he'll be back." Claire stepped away from the desk and grinned like the Cheshire Cat, obviously quite pleased with herself for being able to pass along a tasty bit of gossip to a new set of ears.

"I don't know," Shelby said. "Out of all the places in the world, I can't imagine he'd want a repeat vacation in this town." She took hold of the mouse and moved the cursor to the corner of the screen and clicked to close the page. And just like that, Ryan vanished. Shelby let out a long sigh, and when she was ready, pushed herself away from the computer desk and stood to leave.

"I kinda hoped he would," Claire said, somewhat deflated.

"I'm sorry, Claire. As I said, rough day. You're probably right about him." Shelby slid her chair back under the desk. "I'll see you 'round."

Claire's smile returned. "You bet." She then leaned over to straighten a stack of resource books that sat beside the computer. "See ya."

Shelby walked swiftly past the front desk, out the ornate doorway, and into the fresh air. It was incredible to her that a simple news article hanging on the wall of the Lupine Hus Inn had the power to change her perception of someone she was undeniably drawn to, but barely knew.

What did he say before leaving the barn that last night? *"You've made me feel more grounded than anyone I've ever met,"* she recalled. *"I can't give you any promises tonight, and I know you're not asking for them—but I can tell you something that I know for sure. This isn't how our story ends."* The words had held romantic promise that evening. But today, they seemed empty, like scripted lines from a play. Lines that Ryan had probably recited many times before as he charmed his way in and out of women's lives.

She knew there was someone who would help her to feel better. The one person who had always been there for her—whether she felt the pain of her mother's abandonment, or overwhelmed by the stress of helping keep the farm profitable, or grief-stricken over losing Jeff to the lake. Shelby needed to hear his voice. To feel the comfort of his embrace.

Her feet knew the way—continue down Main Street all the way to the shore. She'd find her old friend John at his shop by the marina.

CHAPTER 12

BREAKS

Dressed sharply in charcoal trousers, a black pullover sweater, and a black leather jacket, Ryan walked out of his apartment building on North Lake Shore Drive before most Chicagoans' alarm clocks went off. He wrapped a wool scarf around his neck, flung a pack over his shoulder, and hopped onto his hybrid bike. After a couple of blocks, Ryan wished he'd worn gloves as well because even though the early morning light looked warm—the way it bounced off the skyscraper glass, street puddles, and car chrome—the late September wind and an unexpected cold front gave him a chill. By the time he pulled onto the sidewalk in front of Chambers Media's corporate office, the city streetlights had extinguished like candles on a cake.

The 1920s limestone building on the corner of Michigan and Van Buren had been refurbished on the outside and, aside from its pumpkin orange window casings and a singular *CM* cast in brushed nickel and positioned above the entryway, its architectural integrity remained intact.

Ryan rolled his bike through the entrance, then hoisted it

under his arm and carried it across the freshly waxed lobby. While the Chambers Media office was historic on the outside, it was state of the art within. The design played with the old and the new—dim orange lights that backlit original crown molding, brightly textured modern art hanging above chocolate brown Chesterfield sofas, and a wall of television screens encased in the building's signature brushed nickel.

"Morning, Will," said the uniformed security guard sitting at the front desk, awaiting the end of his shift.

"How's it going, Mike?" Ryan said in greeting, as he had on so many early mornings in the past.

"Oh, you know. Quiet night. Just the way I like it," Mike answered easily with just a hint of a childhood Tennessee drawl. He leaned back in his chair and gave his arms a good stretch.

"Didn't your daughter have a big softball game while I was gone?" Ryan asked, setting down his bike and leaning it against the front desk.

"Sure did. Man, I was proud of her." Mike beamed. "That little girl is the smallest kid on the team but she is *fast*. Whenever she hits the ball, which isn't often—*boom!* She tears across the bases like a jackrabbit. Now, if she could figure out how to catch the ball, well . . . that would be something to see."

Ryan knew it was a challenge for Mike and his wife to work separate shifts, but they were managing. He also knew that as soon as Mike checked out, he would rush home to join his family—Ryan imagined him eating cereal at the counter and helping his wife load school backpacks and lunchboxes. He envied the lifestyle.

"How 'bout you? I haven't seen you in weeks, ever since I switched shifts with McMillian during his leave. Did you know they had a boy?" asked Mike.

"That's great news. His first."

"Yeah. He's back now. Anyway—good trip?"

An image of Shelby and the northern lights came to mind. "It was. I went up north with some friends," Ryan answered without elaborating. "But hey, I don't want to keep you." He readjusted his shoulder pack and lifted his bike.

"Have a good one," Mike said, giving a quick glance at the security door, waiting for his replacement to arrive for the next shift.

"You, too." Ryan gave Mike a nod and then carried his bike to the elevator bay.

While taking the elevator down to the basement level to store his bike, his thoughts returned to Shelby. He wondered what she was doing at that moment. Sharing breakfast with Olen and Ginny. Gearing up for a busy harvest day. Checking on the weather. He thought to call her the night before, to get her assurance that everything he was about to undertake would turn out well. But he didn't call. He had left Bayfield six weeks earlier without telling her anything about his life in Chicago, his determination to change his life, or his plans to leave CM. And it wasn't something he felt he could bring up casually—unexpectedly—over the phone. He'd tell her in person.

First things first. His father. If history was to repeat itself, Ryan expected William Sr. to shoot him down flat. He had been dreading their meeting, but now that it was at hand, Ryan felt strangely empowered by the prospect of breaking away. If Bayfield and its people hadn't inspired him, how long would he have stayed in this building, following in his father's footsteps, solely out of familial obligation? A year? Five? A lifetime?

Ryan never belonged at CM. He was like a dolphin in a shark tank and his father knew it. "Rise above it, son," William Sr. would say. "Chambers Media is in your blood."

From Ryan's perspective, the only trait that had passed from father to son was an interest in film. In fact, his fondest childhood memories were those of watching movies at home with his sister and parents. They would discuss plot and characterization, special effects, and the role music played in heightening the audience's emotions. Lighting. Storytelling. Mounting tensions. Cliff-hangers and comedic relief.

But that was where the similarities ended. Professionally, William Sr. had a passion for moving images, while Ryan preferred stills. The Chambers family had climbed to the upper echelon of the entertainment business because of their innate ability to spot talent, develop quality programming, and produce successful film projects. They also knew how to use public relations to their advantage, even at the cost of their family's privacy.

Ryan had a different gift. He could tell a story in a single photograph. Keep it honest. Capture joy. Engage. Be real. It mirrored the way he tried to live his life.

"I'm leaving, Dad."

"What are you taking about, Will?" Ryan's father asked without particular interest while leafing through an orderly stack of paperwork on his otherwise spotless mahogany desk. Although Ryan stood a few inches taller than his father, he felt small. William Sr. had a presence about him that dwarfed everyone he encountered. A man of money, exquisite taste, and influence, his father was a powerful force. He had high cheekbones and a solid jawline, piercing green eyes that looked out from beneath a dark brow, and raven black hair combed back with a dapper sheen. And even when he was home on a quiet Sunday morning, the man was always impeccably dressed.

"Do you have an appointment uptown today?" his father continued without much interest.

"No," Ryan replied, jamming his left hand into his pocket while the other firmly held an envelope addressed to William Chambers Sr., CEO.

"Excuse me?" His father raised his eyes to look over the tortoiseshell bifocals that were poised on the tip of his nose.

"I'm going back to Bayfield," Ryan replied, echoing his father's emotionless tone. "I'll be taking some time to concentrate on my photography."

"What does that mean exactly, going back to Bayfield?" William Sr. asked, taking off his glasses and setting them atop the paperwork. "Don't tell me you're off on yet another vacation? Jesus, Will, you just returned from—"

"It's not a vacation," Ryan interrupted, taking confident steps toward his father's desk. "Dad, I'm here to respectfully decline the promotion. I know there are others on the executive team who are more qualified for the job than me."

"Is this a joke?" William Sr. laughed condescendingly. He sat up straight in his high-backed leather chair and placed his hands atop the desk, fingers clasped so tightly together they resembled a tightly wound knot.

Ryan continued to outline his plans. "I intend to pursue my photography for a few months—maybe longer. I was inspired by the town and the Apostle Islands area, where—"

"God, you're a fool!" William Sr. hissed through clenched teeth. "Throwing away your education, opportunities, and status, for what? A hobby? You have responsibilities here. As you are *keenly* aware, the board has approved my recommendation to promote you to senior VP of operations. Everything has been finalized. And now, in the eleventh hour you prance in here with your fucking Pollyanna whims to take photographs . . . indefinitely?"

"I haven't signed the new employment contract and you haven't formally announced the organizational change. Hell, you want me to eventually lead operations, but everyone knows Maria Colton is far more qualified to manage that function. I'd be nothing more than a figurehead for CM."

"That's not true. You're needed here and you damn well

know it. This . . . this *fantasy* of yours to be an artist needs to stop once and for all."

"It's not a fantasy."

William Sr. laughed with contempt, his flawlessly veneered teeth exposed behind tightly pressed lips.

"There's a difference between a fantasy and a dream," Ryan continued. "Or have you forgotten that?"

"What the hell is that supposed to mean?"

"You! This!" Ryan opened his arms to gesture widely at the expansive office with its mahogany and leather furniture, imported rugs, wet bar, closet full of spare designer suits, and an eclectic art collection that included the works of Chihuly, Warhol, and Leibovitz. "You did it, Dad. You're living the dream. But this is *your* dream, not mine."

"It's *ours*. This belongs to all of us. Why haven't you ever been able to see that?" Ryan's father slammed his hands on the desk with startling force. "Yes! It was always our plan for you to take ownership of CM. And you're about to throw it all away because of some artistic nonsense!" Like a mounting storm cloud, William Sr. rose from his chair and his powerful presence seemed to darken the room. He turned to the picture windows behind his desk to face a coveted view of Lake Michigan, and stood solidly with his right hand fisted into the left, grinding against his palm like a baseball player conditioning his mitt.

"I never asked for this," Ryan explained, looking at his father's well-tailored form, now bathed in morning light that streamed in through the window. "I've been trying to tell you that for years, but you don't listen. I won't settle for a life that was mapped out by my family. I need to do what's right for me."

Ryan took a few deep breaths before continuing. "I didn't expect you to understand. Or to support me . . . so here," he said, dropping the envelope onto the desk. Upon hearing the soft *pat* of the letter landing, Ryan's father turned around. "It's my resignation," Ryan explained. "I'll be leaving Chicago by the end of the week. Everything's been arranged."

"Just like that. Leave your responsibilities, your apartment, the commitments . . . everything," William Sr. spat, his eyes on the crisp white envelope. "Just so you can take pictures of a goddamned lake."

Ryan nodded. As much as he tried to stifle his emotion, he felt tension in his shoulders and neck and a dull pain beginning to radiate behind his temples. "It's more than that, and you know it." He jammed his hands back into his pockets, this time to dry the perspiration from his palms.

"Believe me, I know exactly what this is," Ryan's father said, slow and stern. Ryan continued to stand tall, even though the child inside of him wanted to cower and disappear. "You're running away again, and I'll be damned if I'm going to stand here and support this behavior!"

"With all due respect, Dad, you didn't support me when I was younger, so I'd hardly expect you to do it now," Ryan said solidly.

"Is that right? Listen, Ryan, I may not have been there for every school event and soccer game, but I supported you," his father said. Unexpectedly, and suddenly, the tone in his voice softened. "I worked hard. I built this business to make sure my family was well taken care of—you had the best schools, the best travel experiences, the best opportunities. I believed—I still believe—that I am a supportive father to you and your sister. I did everything in my power to provide you with a good life."

Perhaps Ryan should have given his father more credit. When the outside world was shut out, and it was just the four of them without any distractions, his family had shared some good times. There simply weren't enough of those moments to amount to a happy childhood for him or his sister.

"And here I was, proud to see you finally step into a role you were born to assume," Ryan's father continued. And then, in a blink, the softer side of his father's personality disappeared and Ryan was back on guard. "But it turns out that you're not ready to be a man, are you? You're still following childish pursuits rather than an ambitious career path," William Sr. growled, having perfected the ability to shout without raising the volume of his voice. "You want to quit?" He grabbed the envelope and a red felt-tip pen, pulling the cap off hastily with his teeth. Using broad strokes, he scrawled **APPROVED** across the unopened letter. He spat out the cap and glared at his son. "Now get out."

Ryan turned and headed for the door.

"William!"

Ryan reached for the door handle and stopped short when he heard his father call out to him in anger, but he didn't look back.

"I hope you know what you're doing, because God knows I'm not going to watch you make a mockery of this company and our family."

Without another word, Ryan left his father's office to the *clang* of his father's polished shoe kicking a copper waste bin, followed by the gentle *click* of the door closing behind him. Ryan let out a heavy sigh. Avoiding the looks of others who worked on the executive floor, he took long strides toward the elevator. He knew that whatever he did, he would never live up to his father's expectations—whether in Chicago, Bayfield, or any other city in the world.

Once the elevator doors closed and he was alone, he pushed the button for the basement level and leaned against the railing of the brightly lit compartment. Then he removed a cell phone from his pocket. Tapping out a brief text to Brad and Pete, he could feel his shoulders begin to relax:

Ryan @ 8:10 a.m.
It's done. If something comes up,
u know where to find me.

Chapter 13

BRUISES

It was the first weekend in October, which meant Bayfield's annual Applefest celebration was in full swing. Everywhere Shelby looked, people crowded together along Main Street eating a gastronomical hodgepodge of smoked turkey legs, kettle corn, and sausage. The crisp air was ripe with a pungent blend of charcoal and fry bread, brown butter, and cinnamon.

And then there were the apples. Thousands of them. Carameled and quartered. Candied and spiced. Pies, sundaes, streusel, and brats. Transient vendors peddled apple bakers, peelers, corers, and dippers. And in the center of it all, the Big Top Chautauqua band played bluegrass from a flatbed truck.

As Shelby unloaded fruit at the Meyers Orchard stand, she considered the apple's resilience. It was once believed that apples should be stacked with their cores in a horizontal position, so that the stalk of one apple would not pierce the one above it. Today, farmers knew that even the slightest amount of pressure would permanently bruise an apple that was left on its side. An upright apple, however, could be bumped and jostled and still come out unscathed.

Excitement over Will Chambers had waned since the Duluth newspaper article came out. Both for the town and for Shelby. She had put aside her pride, stood tall, and resumed her life with as much resilience as the unscathed apple.

"How many people do you think we'll get this year?" Ginny called out to Olen while stirring a kettle of melted caramel.

"Considering how busy it is already, I'd say more than forty, maybe even fifty thousand for the weekend," Olen answered before giving their inventory another check. Their modest booth was painted barn red and shelved with bushels of Honeycrisp, Haralsons, Cortland, and McIntosh. Although no one said it aloud, they were all concerned about turning a profit. The few storms in August hadn't produced enough rain to make up for the dry summer; the weather had taken its toll on the orchards and production throughout the county was low.

"You should have seen this event fifty years ago. Just a handful of farmers and some out-of-town buyers," Ginny marveled, directing her comments to Shelby. "Just imagine what this will look like when you're working this booth with *your* daughter someday, Shel!"

Daughter? Shelby kept her thoughts from Ginny. *I have no intention of getting married, let alone having children—or grandchildren—to carry on the business. Besides, at this rate, there may not be anything left to pass on.*

"Shel—grab the customer down at the end, would'ja?" Olen asked Shelby as she was arranging pie boxes on a table-side display.

"You bet," she replied, seeing the man standing near their cider jugs with his back to her.

"Can I help you?" she asked while readjusting her Badgers cap. She raised her voice to be heard over the Big Top's amplified, nimbly strummed rendition of "Dueling Banjos" just down the street. "We have samples, if you'd like to taste anything. . . ."

Shelby bent down to grab a small stack of disposable sample cups from a lower shelf when the man spoke.

"I'll take a bag of Honeycrisp," the man said above the blaring music. "And a pie."

"Got it!" she called out over her shoulder. Shelby was reaching into the crates behind her to grab a bushel for the man when she heard him speak again. This time she recognized the sunny lilt of his voice.

"Actually, I'll take three," he said.

She spun around with a bag of apples held tightly to her chest. "Ryan?"

"Hey," he replied with a dimpled grin. She had forgotten about those dimples.

"What are you doing here?" she stumbled, rising slightly on her toes to peer around his shoulder. She expected to see his friends, but he appeared to be alone.

"Buying apples, of course." Ryan helped himself to one of the single apples in the basket that sat atop the counter between them and shined it on the front of his cable-knit sweater.

"I don't understand."

"I actually came to ask you out for dinner," he answered matter-of-factly before biting into the apple with a full, mouth-watering crunch, juice dripping down his hand.

"Dinner." Still holding the apples tightly against her body, she shifted her weight to one hip. Shelby shot a glance at her grandparents, who were trying to appear busy and unaware of Ryan's surprise appearance. They were terrible actors.

"Are you free?" He casually sucked the juice from the apple before taking another bite.

"Are you kidding me?"

"I wouldn't have driven here from Chicago if I was kidding."

"Miss? Can you help me?" interrupted a man dressed in a red flannel shirt and jean jacket, flanked by two young boys who were eagerly eyeing the caramel apples.

"Yes, of course. I'll be right with you," Shelby answered. Turning back to Ryan, she said, "It's a bit crazy right now. And, I . . . well, frankly I didn't expect to see you again." She shook her head, trying to make sense of it, set the bag of apples in front of Ryan, and then made her way toward the new customer.

"Is that a no?" He walked opposite her and then stopped to stand behind the customer's boys. "I shouldn't have surprised you like this."

"What? No—I mean . . ." she faltered while grabbing hold of the counter's edge so tightly that a splinter of wood broke off and pierced her skin. "Damn it!" She jerked her hand up to inspect the fragment that was now embedded in the throbbing palm of her hand.

"I didn't think you'd react so harshly," Ryan said curiously.

"It's not that. It's . . . I don't know what to say to you right now."

"Miss? The apples?" the man with the children persisted.

She smiled weakly at the customer and tried to regain control of her voice. "I'm sorry—which variety would you like?"

"Two caramel apples, and my wife asked me to buy baking apples," said the man as he surveyed his options. "I really have no idea which ones would . . ."

"Haralsons. Definitely." She grabbed a bag for the customer, who fumbled with his wallet while simultaneously keeping his boys from poking their fingers into a pie.

"You have to work. This is bad timing," Ryan apologized. "I'd like to talk. What time do you wrap up?"

"Five?"

"Can I meet you somewhere?"

The man paid Shelby for his purchases and looked curiously at Ryan, before ushering his children back into the bustling crowd.

"My truck is parked up by the library." She could feel heat flushing her cheeks, and was uncertain which emotion was causing it—nervous excitement or unresolved anger.

"Then I'll see you at five." Ryan flashed her the same charismatic grin that he displayed in the newspaper photograph. "And Shelby?"

"Hmm?" *Please leave before this village idiot says something she'll regret!*

"It's good to see you." And with that, Ryan stepped into the crowd and disappeared.

Shelby wasn't sure how long she stood there looking after him. The festival's noise seemed to soften to a dull hum. It was replaced by Ryan's voice echoing in her head. *Drove here from Chicago. . . . Are you free . . . Good to see you . . .* Lost in her thoughts, she jumped when someone put an arm affectionately around her shoulders.

"Shelby! How's it going so far?" John asked. He had just arrived to help, wearing a Meyers Orchard apron over his black jacket and a concerned look on his face. After discovering Ryan's identity, she had gone to John to talk about it all. He supported her, as he had done so many times in the past. If she told him that Ryan was back in town and interested in seeing her, she knew exactly what John would say to her. *Run.*

"John. You're sweet to come down to help us."

"No problem. Everything okay?" he asked, looking at the way she was holding her right hand.

"Splinter," she said with a slight shake of her head. She pushed down on her palm until the end of the offending splinter appeared and she could remove it. "I just can't get over these crowds. It's going to be a crazy couple of days."

"That's why I'm here." John sounded pleased while giving her a hug and a warm kiss on the cheek. "Now come on—let's get rid of these apples!"

John was always so good to her. Too good. He didn't have to volunteer his day off to help her family, and yet he gamely pitched in. Later, she felt guilty declining his invitation for an impromptu dinner back at his place. Nevertheless, she said good night and headed toward her truck alone.

Shelby felt more anxious with each passing block. She was angry. And curious. And filthy. She wiped her hands on the sides of her jeans and then stopped to take off her baseball cap and hold it between her knees. After running her fingers through her hair and rebinding a messy ponytail, Shelby positioned the hat back on her head. Realizing there wasn't anything else she could do to make herself more presentable, she turned the corner and continued uphill. One more block to go.

Then Shelby saw Ryan. She couldn't miss him. He was leaning casually against her truck, wearing dark sunglasses and a bright green knit hat that was clearly too big for his head. She wondered if the family of five who were passing him knew that the guy with the ridiculous hat was Will Chambers. Probably not. That would be like expecting to see Prince pull up at a drive-thru and order a Big Mac.

Ryan watched the family make their way down the street before he noticed Shelby approach. A smile warmed his face as he took steps away from the truck to greet her.

Keep cool, she reminded herself. *Let him do the talking. Then walk away.*

"Shelby!" he said, reaching his arms out wide in welcome. She sidestepped his embrace and made her way to her vehicle, then leaned against the tailgate for support.

"Hey, Ryan. Or . . . should I call you William?"

"What?"

"William Chambers Jr., to be exact," she said flatly, folding her arms across her chest.

"Right," he started. "About that."

"Yeah, about that," she replied. "Congratulations. You fooled me."

"I wasn't trying to fool you."

"Mmm." She pressed her lips tightly together. *Hold your ground,* she told herself. "So, what's going on? Why are you here?"

"To see you."

"Come on, you and I both know that's not true." She eyed a round stone by her boot and gave it a swift kick down the street, watching as it skipped and rattled away. "Listen. Nothing lasting is ever built on a lie—so you're off to a lousy start. Why don't you cut to the chase?"

"Shelby, I—" he stumbled.

"Nice hat, by the way," she interrupted, looking up at his bright green knit cap.

"You like it?" He tipped his head down far enough that she could see the embroidered message: **Rotten to the Core.** "I couldn't pass it up."

She smiled in spite of herself. He looked ridiculous. And handsome. *God, he's handsome.* "It suits you."

"Ryan isn't a false name, by the way," he said, returning to their conversation. "If I want to use an alias, I usually go by Charlie."

"Charlie?"

"Long story—the point is, my friends call me Ryan. My parents call me William. And everyone else calls me Will." Ryan leaned his body to rest his hip against the truck so he could face her.

"But you didn't know me. Shouldn't you have introduced yourself as William—or Will?"

"Definitely not."

"Why . . . ?"

"Because you aren't one of my parents, and I know you could never fit into the 'everyone else' category."

"And why is that?" She rapped the toe of her boot against the asphalt in agitation. "Because I'm some hick off the farm? Because I don't run to my mailbox for the weekly tabloid so I can read up on the *exciting* lives of people like you? Or, better yet, search all of those online gossip sites? I'm sure this has all been quite amusing for you and your friends."

"Don't you get it?" Ryan asked. "Because I knew you were special from the start."

"Right." She was exhausted and, considering how hard she had worked that day, probably smelled like an old gym sock. *Oh yeah, I'm real special.*

"I'm sorry about the whole name thing," Ryan continued. "You're right. I should have been straight with you from the beginning. I'd like to talk to you about all of that."

They were interrupted by the sound of a car engine and muffled music with a banging bass beat coming over the hill. A silver Jeep then stopped beside Shelby's truck. When the back passenger door opened, blaring music and two teenaged girls tumbled out.

"Thanks for the ride, JT—see ya 'round," said one of the girls with curls of black hair.

"Later, guys!" echoed the young man's voice from inside

the Jeep before the second girl slammed the car door shut and the Jeep sped off down the hill.

Still questioning Ryan's words and motives, Shelby peered down at her soiled boots with their bright red laces to think.

"Can I ask you something?" asked Ryan. "Be honest. Would you have spent time with me if you had known who I was?"

Still looking down, she considered his question and shook her head. She would never have followed her grandfather's advice and gone to meet him at The Inn on that first night.

Shelby had the feeling that they were being watched. Sure enough, when she glanced at the teenagers, they were now standing in front of their house and looking intently at Ryan. Recognizing him.

Ryan must have noticed, too. "Can we go somewhere private?" he asked quietly. He leaned his shoulder against hers and gave a gentle nudge. She nudged back. When Ryan kissed the top of her head, she pulled away and stepped back onto the sidewalk. *You're not getting off that easily, Chambers.*

With an endearing look on his face that made it difficult for her to refuse, he whispered quietly enough that the gawking teens couldn't hear, "So, how 'bout it? Join me for dinner?"

"You have a lot of explaining to do," she whispered back.

Ryan had asked Shelby to follow his car without saying where they were headed. She was having second thoughts long before they arrived at the South Point Marina just outside of town. She took a moment to sit in her parked truck, wondering why they were there. Why he had returned. And what compelled her to agree to this when she was still wearing work clothes and a lovely layer of festival dirt? *This is such a mistake.*

She watched as he stepped out of his car and grabbed something from the backseat.

I should start the ignition.

Ryan then walked toward her truck.

Shift into Reverse.

He was carrying a small duffel bag that looked vaguely familiar.

Get out of here.

And now he was standing just outside her door, motioning for her to roll down the window.

Run.

"Everything okay?" he asked through the closed driver's side window.

"Never better," she replied, rolling down the window.

"I hope you don't mind, but I brought some things for you—so you could clean up a bit. Only if you want them, that is." Shelby opened her mouth to protest, but he cut her off before she had the chance. "I know what you're thinking, so let me explain," he said. "I arrived yesterday and headed straight to your place. I should have called first, but honestly, I didn't know what you'd say. So I decided to surprise you instead and take my chances. Ginny told me I could find you at the festival today."

"You went to the house? I can't believe that—"

"Can I finish?" he interrupted.

Hearing the insistence in his voice, Shelby leaned back against her headrest to listen.

"When I asked her permission to take you out tonight, she said—"

"What?" Shelby blurted, bolting upright. "You asked for her permission? What about *my* permission?"

"She said you might be a bit irritated with me—something about my reputation."

"Well, that's just great," Shelby muttered under her breath, crossing her arms and leaning back again.

"She said if I could get you to agree to dinner, which she

admitted was a long shot, she was sure you'd want to freshen up. That's why she pulled together this bag for you. It was her idea." He extended the bag through the open window. "There's a ladies' room just inside those front doors," he suggested, pointing toward the marina's clubhouse. It was a modest, one-level building painted white and blue and surrounded by evergreens. It had remained virtually unchanged until three years ago, when the owners added a public dining room and deck that faced the marina and pleased its members.

She took the bag and set it on her lap to collect her thoughts. Shelby had confided in her grandmother. Ginny knew that she felt betrayed and humiliated by Ryan. In packing the bag, was Ginny trying to send Shelby a message to give him a second chance? She rubbed her thumb back and forth against the strap of her bag. Eventually she asked, "Where are we having dinner?"

Ryan's face brightened with relief. He told her that he had chartered a forty-foot sailboat called the *Spindrift* and had packed a dinner to share on board.

"When did you have time to charter a boat?" She recalled her encounter with Claire Dollins at the library and her story about Ryan meeting with someone at this marina.

"A while ago," Ryan said without expounding. He opened the door for her and helped her out of the truck.

"You must not be staying long."

"Why do you say that?" He slammed her car door shut.

"Most boats are already out of the water." She slung the bag over one shoulder. "I'm sure the *Spindrift* will be hauled out within a week or two. That doesn't give you much time."

"It's all the time I need." And then, with a mischievous, dimpled grin, he added, "For now."

CHAPTER 14

FORGIVEN

"Feeling better?" Ryan asked Shelby as she approached the sailboat. He reached out to grab her duffel bag, tossed it into the open cockpit, and then took her hand to help her aboard.

"I have to admit, it felt good to get rid of those clothes." As Shelby took a seat on one of the padded benches, Ryan couldn't help but notice the rosy glow in her cheeks and how good she looked in a turtleneck sweater, hooded jacket, and faded jeans that skimmed her curves to perfection. "Too bad my hair still smells like grilled sausage."

Ryan leaned toward her and took some of her hair gently in his hand, inhaling deeply. "Hmm. Apple brats. Delicious," he teased. "You could always go for a swim."

"Right. Have you felt this water?"

"Do you remember our first date? When I dove in for that boy?"

"Of course, but your heroism aside, I'd hardly call that a date."

"I suppose not. Good thing, too. That water is cold enough

to raise a man's voice by two octaves!" Ryan said while climbing down the short wooden ladder that led into the boat's cabin. He pulled out a cork from the wine bottle in his hand with a satisfying *pop* and called up to her. "I was joking, of course. Then again, aren't you used to the cold, having grown up here?"

"You never really get used to this lake," she called back. "You learn to respect it."

When Ryan climbed out of the cabin a moment later, he was holding the bottle in one hand and two glasses in the other.

"Thirsty?"

"That depends. Are we staying put or sailing?"

"I'll take that as a yes, because I'd rather share a bottle of wine with you than navigate this boat in the dark," he replied. He filled their glasses and offered one to Shelby before returning below deck to prepare their meal.

"Will you sleep here tonight?" she called down.

"That's the plan," he replied from the narrow galley amid the clatter of clinking plates and banging drawers.

"Wouldn't a room in town be more comfortable? And warmer?"

"Are you offering?"

"No."

"Heads-up!" He surprised her by tossing up a plaid wool blanket. When he rejoined her in the cockpit, Ryan was carrying a tray filled with crackers, smoked lake trout, cheese, olives, and, of course, a sliced apple that he had purchased from her earlier in the day. "Help yourself," he encouraged before turning on a camping lantern on the opposite bench and sitting down. As the sun sank lower on the horizon, he could feel the temperature drop.

Shelby wrapped the blanket tightly around her shoulders and tucked her legs beneath her, then she reached for a few apple slices and her wineglass. "This is oddly familiar," she teased. "Isn't this pretty much the same thing you made that other night—when we had a picnic on the beach?"

"I'm not much of a cook, I'm afraid." He chuckled, recalling the night they shared beneath the northern lights. "But I can put this kind of meal together in a snap."

He gave his glass a gentle swirl, lifted it to his nose, and took in the wine's bouquet. Tobacco, vanilla, and berry. It felt right being back on the lake, away from CM, and in the company of someone quirky, unpredictable, and incredibly alluring. Now, if only Shelby could enjoy his company again.

"What do you think?" he asked, gesturing toward her wineglass.

"It's perfect."

"It's a tempranillo."

"It's red."

"You know? That's one of the things I like about you," he said. "You see things exactly for what they are." *Including me.* He raised his glass and clinked it lightly against hers.

She looked around the small, deserted marina, taking another sip of wine, before asking Ryan why he chose to charter a boat in October.

"I've been looking at boats for a while now. I'd like to buy one in the spring. So I decided to test out this Dufour for a few days before it gets too cold." Ryan cut off a wedge of cheese and grabbed a handful of crackers. "Do you sail?"

"I'm more of a passenger. But I used to spend a lot of time on the lake with a close friend of mine. I know just enough to be a pretty good second mate," she said. "Is this the kind of boat you want to buy?"

"I might. I have a Beneteau in Chicago. I take it out on Lake Michigan as often as I can. There's a guy at the marina who has a boat similar to this. I've been out with him a number of times, but I've never sailed one on my own." Ryan leaned forward to cut another slice of white cheddar. "They're designed to handle long distances, but they're also comfortable and easy to handle. And I love their look. I'm excited to take this one out tomorrow."

"Have you ever sailed on Lake Superior?"

He shook his head while cutting into the sausage.

"All I can say is, make sure your radio and instruments are in working order, have a life jacket and a current chart, and keep a keen eye on the skies," she warned.

"Thanks, Gilligan," he teased, noticing how she was pulling the blanket tighter around her legs. "Are you warm enough? Or would you rather go inside?"

"No, no. This is fine," she said, reaching for the discs of sliced sausage. "I'm suddenly famished. Thanks for putting all of this together."

There was a lot of small talk and she still seemed reserved. He wanted to tell her everything—his plans for the photography project, the cottage he would be renting for the next several months, the conversation he'd had with his father, leaving CM. His interest in her. All of it. But he couldn't yet find the words. So instead, he popped olives into his mouth, one by one, and discreetly spit the pits over the boat's railing and into the water.

"Classy," she observed, before doing the same thing herself.

"Just trying to make a good impression."

There were glimmers of the connection they shared in August. The light humor. The teasing. But something was missing. At the festival and now on the boat, her smiles were either forced or quickly withdrawn. There was an uneasy tension between them and she seemed to be using the blanket as a shield—a barrier to keep him a safe distance away. He hadn't come all this way for nothing. It was time to be direct.

"You're angry," he said simply.

She showed more interest in slicing a wedge of cheese than replying.

"There's more to this than withholding my background, isn't there?" He waited until she returned his look. "I should have called."

She held his gaze and casually replied, "I never expected a call." She raised a buttery piece of Brie to her lips and took a bite.

"What is it then?" he asked, trying to read her expression.

"I just don't get it," she said, her voice slow and steady. "I'm just sitting here wondering why you'd want to come back to Bayfield. There must be a million other places that would be more interesting for someone of your . . . status."

"I was trying to explain this to you earlier," he said. "It's simple—I came back because of you."

She raised her wineglass and took not a sip, but a gulp. And then another. After a moment, she set down the glass and simply asked, "Why?"

"Why not?" he asked, puzzled.

"Here's the thing," she began. "We had a good time. A really good time. But we live two completely different lives. All of this—you showing up at Applefest, this beautiful boat, the wine . . . none of this is normal for me. This isn't my life."

"If I could just—" he started, but Shelby was quick to cut him off.

"Don't you see? I know who you are now. That changes everything," she insisted. "You lead an exciting life—a public life. And here I am, schlepping apples out of a run-down booth. Sorry. It just doesn't add up. Look around, Ryan. This town isn't glamorous. And neither am I."

"Actually—" Ryan began to say in his defense.

"And to answer your earlier question—yes. I *am* angry that you deceived me," she said, her voice growing in agitation and stabbing her fork into a chunk of trout. "I was crazy enough to think that after a few short days I could trust you. And then I read about you in the paper and realized you had been lying to me all along!"

Ryan knew there was no stopping her at this point. And from the look of the pulverized trout, he thought it best to let her continue without getting too close to the end of her fork.

"I was probably one of the few people around here who didn't recognize you. Ha! Can you imagine? In fact, I didn't know much about you at all until I looked you up on the Internet," she continued, shaking her head in disbelief—her fork now on to an undeserving piece of cheddar. "Jesus—there are hundreds of photos and pages about you, did you know that? Of course you know that. And do you know how many times my name comes up in a search?"

"I don't think it's important how many—" he began to say, his voice quiet. In August, she had mentioned her general lack of interest in social media and only used the Internet when necessary. He suspected there must be mentions of her on the local news sites, or the Meyers Orchard Web page. It had never been important to her. It wasn't important to him.

She dropped her fork and turned toward the lake. When she spoke again, the tone in her voice was replaced with the quiet that comes from self-doubt. "There's hardly any mention of me at all."

Less than forty-eight hours ago, when Ryan had returned to Bayfield unannounced, he did so without considering her reaction. All of his actions leading up to now had been selfish. He assumed it would all work out. He thought it would be easy. He was wrong not to put her needs ahead of his own. Ryan thought carefully when choosing his words. "I'm sorry," he said humbly, shifting on the seat to move closer to her.

She put her hand out to block him, so he sat still.

"I'm not the guy you read about. If someone happens to

recognize me, whether it's here or anywhere else, nine times out of ten I'll be a disappointment. I'm not bright enough. Tall enough. Interesting enough," Ryan confessed. "So there's a lot of freedom when I'm not recognized. It's the difference between being the guy someone thinks I am, and being just me."

He noticed that her hands, once clenched in her lap, were now beginning to uncurl. And the tense lines between her eyebrows appeared to relax. Encouraged that she was listening, he continued. "You weren't like that. In fact, when we met, not only did you not know who I was . . . you didn't *want* to know."

"That's not true, I . . ." she said, turning toward him.

"Shelby. You turned me down flat."

She started to say something, but tightened her lips together instead and shifted her body so she could pull the blanket up over her shoulders.

"You *still* are," he said, gesturing with his hand at the distance between them on the seat. Ryan took a sip of wine and looked past her to see the breakers and the marina entrance with its red and green nautical lights. The lake was dark except for a dimming sliver of crimson that remained of the sunset. The halyards clanged against the *Spindrift*'s mast as the boat swayed back and forth with each languid wave. "I didn't come here to take a break from my daily living," he said with sincerity. "I was taking a break from my life. I need this."

"What do you need?" she asked.

"A new way of life. I need open spaces." Ryan paused. "New connections." His eyes found hers. "We were just starting to get to know one another, and I didn't want it to end. I knew that before I left this summer. It was a mistake to keep it to myself before now."

A shiver ran up his spine. He shuddered against the chill and tucked his hands beneath his arms. It was getting too cold to stay out much longer and he knew the conversation would soon end. He hoped it would end well, but sensed she might get up and leave at any moment.

"I wasn't completely honest with you, either," she said, breaking his thoughts. "I don't know how to tell you this, but . . . I can't bake."

"What?" he asked as he braced himself against another brush of cold air.

"It's true. I can't bake. Back at the store, the day we met, I told you that I baked those pies, but I lied." She made a poor attempt at keeping a straight face. "Usually, when I'm introduced to new people, they recognize me immediately and are only interested in meeting the person whose pictures hang all over our store. They only see the girl from the orchard, rather than the real me."

Relieved, he said sympathetically, "I can only imagine how difficult that must be for you. How do you retain any sense of normalcy?"

"Fooling around with the tourists usually helps. Particularly the photographers," she answered playfully. "They're easy."

Despite the warmth of her forgiveness, another chill rippled through his body.

"You're shaking."

"I'm fine."

"I can share," she offered, lifting up one end of the blanket that covered her.

"As long as we're being completely honest, I've been freezing for the last half hour and I thought you'd never ask," Ryan said with chattering teeth. He moved closer and pulled the blanket across his body and over his shoulder, settling in next to her. He was keenly aware of her warm body as she leaned against him.

"So, you never told me—how long are you staying?" she asked.

Ryan tilted his head so that his lips were a touch away from her ear. "That depends," he said softly.

"On what?" she asked in a hush.

Beneath the blanket, Ryan reached his hand across until he touched hers. When her fingers entwined with his, the chill between them melted away. "Was it a mistake for me to come back?" he whispered, wanting to kiss her.

"Probably," she said, turning to look into his eyes.

"Are you still angry?"

"You're forgiven."

Ryan smiled and pulled her closer. Forgiveness. Promise. Change. It felt liberating to chart his own course, away from the Chambers family and the public eye. He pressed his lips gently upon the cool softness of Shelby's cheek. He heard her slowly exhale and felt her body sink into his. He gently tucked her hair behind her ear and took his time exploring her neck with light kisses. When she reached her hand up to touch the side of his face, he leaned in to kiss her lips, softly, tasting the sweetness of apple and wine. He forgot about the cold as they kissed away the misunderstandings.

Together, under the blanket of a starry October sky, they embraced the possibilities.

CHAPTER 15

STORM

"Well, whad'ya know," Nic said, settling into a quiet corner table with Shelby at Spill the Beans, Bayfield's one and only coffee shop. "Will Chambers—back in town." The petite young woman with a loud mouth and a love for gossip was wide-eyed and eager for details. "You have to tell me *everything*. Don't leave out a single detail." Nic slid her hand into her canvas bag and Shelby knew her friend was rummaging for the cigarettes she had given up in July. Coming up empty-handed, Nic grabbed her mug with two hands and took several eager slurps of coffee. Black. No sugar. Nic always said that sweeteners were for chumps.

"There's not much to say, really," Shelby explained while unabashedly stirring sugar into the froth of her cappuccino. "He arrived a few days ago. He came down to Applefest to say hello. And now he's staying on a sailboat over at South Point Marina."

Shelby loved Nic, but she wasn't ready to tell her everything. Ryan planned to stay aboard the *Spindrift* through the week. After that, he would return to the cottage he had rented with his friends back in August. While Shelby worked on the farm, Ryan had mainly kept to himself, spending his time sailing the Dufour and experimenting with the aperture settings and lens filters on his camera while photographing the lake. Shelby doubted anyone other than her family, Boots at the grocery store, and the gal at the marina knew he was back. And Nic, of course. But that wasn't a surprise—Nic always seemed to know what was happening in town.

"How long will he be here?"

"I'm not sure," Shelby said, licking her spoon before setting it down on the saucer. "A while."

"A while. What does that mean—a week? A month?" Nic was tapping her fingernails on the tabletop in an agitated rhythm. "This is major."

Shelby smirked behind the brim of her coffee mug before taking a sip, enjoying her friend's impatience.

"He's back because of you, isn't he?" Nic asked with a knowing nod. "Holy crap—Will Chambers!"

"He's here to do some work."

"Jesus. Do you think I just fell off the turnip truck? This is *me* you're talking to," Nic burst out in a voice loud enough to turn the heads of the three other patrons in the coffee shop.

Shelby looked over her shoulder and threw up her hand to quiet Nic.

"Oh. I get it, I get it." Nic became overly theatrical, lowering her voice and leaning forward across the table as if she were in on a conspiracy. "You're keeping this all on the down low, aren't you? A clandestine romance?"

"Hardly," Shelby muttered, now rubbing her thumb along the handle of her ceramic mug.

"Come on, I know you're dying to tell me . . ." Nic said, with an unnaturally sweet smile mounting across her elfish freckled face.

Shelby took a drawn-out sip of her cappuccino.

"Hang on a second." Nic's eyes lit up. "You like this guy!"

"I hardly know him," Shelby said, shaking her head slightly.

"That's it! Oh my God, Shelby—you're really into him, aren't you?"

"Seriously, Nic, can you please keep it down?"

"Have you told John?" Nic whispered.

Shelby cringed. She hadn't returned any of John's calls since she'd left him at the apple stand. Ginny had spoken with him and said he was sounding increasingly concerned. And insistent. "I should probably walk down to the shop to see him."

"He's not going to take it lightly, you know."

"I know. After everything I said to him about Ryan, John will think I'm crazy for giving him a second chance."

"That's not the half of it."

"Why? What do you mean?"

Nic leaned forward again. "He's been waiting for you to move on after Jeff and take notice of him. The guy has been interested in you for, like, forever!"

"That's not true."

"You wanna know why he'll get bent out of shape? Jealousy."

"John?" Shelby put her hand to her forehead and winced. *John?* she repeated inside her head, trying to make sense of it. "How could you possibly know that? You two can hardly stand to be in the same room together, let alone talk about his feelings."

"Shelby, you know I love you. But seriously. You can be clueless." Nic's chair creaked as she leaned back, reaching her clasped hands behind her head. "Ever since Jeff died you've basically been going through the motions. It's time the old Shelby came back, don't you think?"

First being oblivious about Ryan. And now John? Shelby thought. *Am I really that unaware? And if I am, what else am I missing?*

"It's time to take the blinders off, girlfriend," Nic said.

"I never imagined that he . . . really? John?" *We* have *been spending a lot of time together, especially this past year. And I do love him. But not in the way I loved Jeff.*

"You'll sort it out with John. He's a big boy," Nic said. "But back to a more interesting topic—what are we going to do about Will-slash-Ryan?"

"*We* aren't going to do anything."

Nic sighed. "Fine. What are *you* going to do?"

"I'm not sure." She contemplated Nic's question while rubbing her thumb over her warm mug. "The thing is, I don't think he usually associates with people like me."

"What kind of people does he associate with?" Nic raised an eyebrow and pushed her finger to the side of her nose. "Chicago mafia?"

"Of course not." Shelby laughed. "The type of people who are followed by paparazzi, that's who."

"Eh. That's nothin'," Nic said with a dismissive wave of her hand. "When will you see him next?"

"Actually, he has asked me to go sailing with him today—an overnight." Shelby tried to sound casual, but the thought of it made her nervous. The night before, Ryan had said he wanted to spend more time with her, but he wasn't ready to be public. When she questioned him about it—saying that nobody would care—he shook his head and asked her to trust him.

"So, you're going, right? I mean, you *have* to go!"

"How am I supposed to just pick up and go? Leave my family when we're at the height of the harvest?" Shelby shook her head. "It would be irresponsible. I'm not like you. I have responsibilities."

"Excuse me? First of all, I have plenty of responsibilities, thank you very much. I just have different priorities," Nic said. "And second, you'd be a flippin' idiot to pass this up. Fall colors, a cozy little sailboat, a drop-dead gorgeous man . . . it would be as romantic as hell! You have to live a little, Shel. Come on—let me live vicariously through *you* for once!"

"What's that supposed to mean? I don't live vicariously through you."

"Uh-huh. I saw the look on your face when I told you about my road trip to the Sturgis Bike Rally." Nic wagged her finger in Shelby's direction, saying, "You totally wished you had been on the back of Hank's Harley—wind in your hair, rockin' a leather jacket, bugs in your teeth."

"You know me so well," she said with a chuckle.

"It's settled!" Nic announced, suddenly standing up and grabbing her coat. "Here's the plan. I'm going to take over for you on the farm and do my best to drive your grandparents crazy, and you're going sailing with Mr. Wonderful. Let's get your bags packed!"

It was to be an easy trip. Ryan and Shelby set sail by noon and spent a leisurely day on the water. Shelby enjoyed taking the wheel whenever Ryan photographed the islands, which were dressed in autumn foliage that was ablaze in orange and gold with splashes of pomegranate red. At the end of the day, they dropped anchor in Julian Bay at Stockton Island. For dinner, Ryan deviated from picnic fare and prepared steaks on the grill, which he rigged off the stern, and they shared a bottle of wine—"I brought a red," he said with a wink, and without ostentation. It was a tranquil evening—there wasn't another boat anchored in the bay. In the absence of distractions, pressures, or pretense, the couple continued to fall deeper into a relationship.

"Are you up for a sail around Devil's Island tomorrow?" Ryan asked playfully, holding her open hand in his and following the lines in her palm with his finger, like a captain would mark a nautical chart. "We could anchor off Bear Island for the night, and I'd get you back to Bayfield before Sunday dinner."

"And what if we get to Devil's and end up with dead winds?" Shelby asked seriously. "Or worse? The weather on this lake can change on a dime, especially when cold fronts move across the islands. Devil's is the last place we'd want to be."

"I checked the weather broadcast on the marine radio an hour ago. There's nothing but clear skies ahead. Five- to ten-knot winds. It will be perfect," he assured her. "I'd love to get some shots of the caves on Devil's north shore." He wrapped both hands around hers with a tenderness that eased her fears enough to reconsider. "What do you say?"

She hesitated. There was nothing beyond the northern tip of Devil Island's but unforgiving lake water that stretched far beyond the horizon. She had several reasons for saying no—those waters were treacherous, temperatures were dropping, and the weather on Lake Superior was never predictable—even with a favorable weather forecast.

While a voice of reason screamed inside of her head to say no—*Suggest somewhere else. Anywhere else!*—the other voice, the one that sounded oddly like Nic's, told her to take a chance. *Don't be so afraid of life. Be bold!*

"Sure," she conceded, looking down at their clasped hands and then into his eyes that seemed to sparkle with the excitement of a child. "Let's do it."

When Shelby and Ryan headed out to Devil's Island the next morning, the sky was clear and the wind was steady. They traveled at a steady six-knot clip in full sail with a fully bat-tened main. Once they reached Devil's, they dropped the sails and anchored offshore in water that was so clear they could see the lake's rippled, sandy floor beneath the boat. Shelby relaxed onboard and watched as Ryan rowed the dinghy into the caves, disappearing and reappearing, gesturing to her with his arms and hands that the experience was spectacular.

Once the exuberant photographer was satisfied and back onboard, they lifted anchor and traveled along the eastern side of Devil's Island. They had been sailing for less than an hour when Shelby felt a sudden drop in air temperature that sent a shiver through her core. She instinctively looked skyward.

"Ryan? Turn the radio from Sixteen to the weather station," she said gravely, facing west above the island's thick tree line. Shelby sensed that just beyond the island, out of sight, something ominous was coming. And it was building strength over the lake.

A monotone, computer-generated male voice broke through the radio static to broadcast the weather alert. "Doppler radar indicates a line of thunderstorms. Capable of producing water spouts. Mariners can expect sustained winds of nearly thirty knots gusting to fifty, small hail, four- to six-foot waves, lightning, and heavy rain. Boaters should seek safe harbor immediately. Locations in line of the storm include Duluth, Herbster, Port Wing, and Bayfield. Moving east to southeast at thirty-five miles per hour." Just then, as the weather report droned on, Shelby and Ryan saw the base of a massive, greenish-black wall cloud appear over Devil's Island.

"Oh . . . My . . . God," Shelby gasped, staring at the largest storm she had ever seen from the water. Like a Goliath rising up over David, the cloud grew in height and width. Although the weather was almost upon them, everything was eerily quiet except for the frantic call of seagulls flying ahead of the impending storm.

For a moment, she stood frozen in fear as every thought in her head fell silent. . . .

"Shelby, we need to move fast!" Ryan's voice snapped her back to reality with a jolt. "The motor will be useless in this weather. I figure we can furl the jib and use a storm-rigged mainsail," Ryan said urgently. "The storm is going to come up behind us real fast. We don't have a chance of outrunning it. I need you to find a sheltered area!"

"Right!" They had to make a run for it, and Bayfield was a harrowing twenty miles away. Since Devil's didn't have any protected harbors, Shelby knew their choices were limited. *Think!*

"Shit! This thing is going to be a monster," she heard Ryan curse under his breath as he worked swiftly on the lines.

Damn it! Shelby thought, seeing the storm surging angrily behind them. It began to rain hard, as if the entire sky had opened up and was spilling down upon the lake. She had to keep calm. Ryan was an experienced sailor, and she knew the Apostle Islands well. They had a chance. *Think!* screamed her thoughts as she cinched her life jacket tighter around her chest. *We can do this!* She quickly scanned the chart while hearing the whizzing, flapping sound of Ryan furling the sails. Shelby pressed her finger firmly on the chart to mark their course. Taking a quick look around to get her bearings, she began to shout out directions loud enough to be heard over the downpour and howling wind. "Okay! Keep this tack. We need to get to the southeast point of Rocky Island. There's a small bay where we can try to anchor. It's our best shot!"

"Got it!" he called back, working frantically and stumbling in his haste.

"Before this thing hits, put on a safety harness and attach yourself to the jackline." She handed him the harness and put the other one on herself. If he had any objections, the look on her face must have stopped him short.

The wall of clouds rolled in above them like a phantom chasing away whatever residual light was left in the sky. As the water and sky darkened around them, Ryan flipped on the boat's nautical lights. It was reassuring for Shelby to see his focused expression. He looked steadfast and strong. She put her trust in him.

When the storm wall hit the *Spindrift,* the boat heeled sharply to the port side. Shelby was caught off balance and fell headfirst into the storage locker beside her. In the cabin below, she heard a cabinet door slam, books hitting the floor, and the loud clatter of kitchenware shifting in the galley.

"Shelby!" Ryan jumped to her aid, but she motioned him back to the wheel.

"I'm okay!" She regained her balance and managed to stand up on the vessel, which was already getting bounced around in the frigid, choppy water. She felt a hot, stinging pain on the side of her mouth.

"You're bleeding," Ryan shouted over the storm's menacing howl. "Sure you're okay?"

Shelby touched her swelling lip with her fingertips and could taste the iron-like saltiness of her blood, but there wasn't time to worry about it now. "I'm fine!" she yelled back, instinctively crouching down and grabbing hold of the boat as a wave splashed over the starboard gunwale.

Shelby was in a partially protected area of the cockpit and worried about Ryan, who was entirely exposed. She saw him tighten the harness around his waist and brace himself behind the steering pedestal to stand up to the force of the weather. The stern of the boat lifted with every white-capped wave that heaved in from behind and caused the bow to thrust dangerously downward toward the water.

Although they were traveling at a good speed, it seemed as though they were barely making headway against the mounting waves, spray blowing horizontally off their crests. Visibility was so poor that the islands had disappeared behind the sheets of rain and they relied entirely on the gauges for direction. Their hands and faces were now numb in the icy wet. The wind whipped their hair and screamed in their ears.

Just then, a flash of lightning lit up the sky like a strobe as thunder clapped so loudly that Shelby could feel the sound vibration. *Dear God,* she prayed, trying to suppress her mounting fear. She knew lightning strikes could hit the water and jolt back up into the air. And if that happened directly next to their boat and the electricity . . . she couldn't think about it.

As she and Ryan raced the storm, memories collided in her mind like the waves that slammed against the *Spindrift's* hull. *Jeff. All alone on Lake Superior. Sailing on the* Cadence. *Had he been scared? Or had adrenaline taken over? Did he feel any pain? This goddamned lake!*

She heard Ryan's voice and turned to see him standing solidly at the wheel, wet black hair slick against his face, his drenched clothing flapping against his body. He asked her to take the helm.

"We can do this!" he assured her as she made her way to the helm, keeping her body low and holding on to anything she could for fear of slipping on the slanted, wet deck. When she took the wheel, Ryan gave her a quick, reassuring kiss on the cheek. "Just keep us on course for the southern tip of Rocky, adjust the main sheet." He hurried to the port side of the boat to adjust the lines.

Shelby smiled bravely before spitting blood onto the cockpit deck. The hammering rain washed it away in an instant. She could feel the vibrations and pull of the wheel in her hands as she held on tight. She was using all of her strength to keep the rudder steady against the power of several thousand pounds of water pressure. With burning muscles and a racing heart, she looked away from the bow just long enough to check on Ryan. In that instant, the wind changed direction and caught the mainsail.

"Shelby, turn back into the wind—NOW!" Ryan commanded, cranking the winch and leaning against the angle of the boat's heel to stay balanced.

Shelby watched helplessly as the metal boom of the main swung across the cockpit like a baseball bat. "*Jeff!* Look out!" she screamed, reliving the tragedy that had been haunting her for the past three years. Ryan ducked and fell forward just in time for the boom to flash past him and career out over the water. "Oh God! Are you hurt?" She dared not leave the wheel for fear that the boat would turn direction and become vulnerable to capsizing.

"Shit!" he cursed, while pulling himself up from the floor of the deck, his face flushed and his eyes squinting up at her through the pelting rain.

"Ryan?" She continued to grip the wheel with white knuckles while her eyes darted between Ryan and the bow of the boat, which was chopping into the oncoming waves. "Please tell me you're okay!"

"No better than you," he answered, looking at her bruised jaw, swollen lip, and terrified expression. Then he began to laugh. Lightly at first. And then louder, fuller. Despite being consumed with fear—or perhaps because of it—the sound of his laughter was contagious. With tears in her eyes and throbbing pain in her jaw, Shelby started to laugh, too.

If someone had told her a week ago that she'd be caught in the middle of a wildly dangerous storm, struggling to stay afloat somewhere off Devil's Island, with William Chambers Jr., she wouldn't have believed it. And doing it while laughing like kids on a joyride? It would have seemed ludicrous.

"Come on, Meyers," Ryan said, back at the winch and cranking in the boom. "Let's get the hell out of here."

CHAPTER 16

LUCKY

"Who's Jeff?" Ryan asked Shelby as they huddled together inside the teak-paneled cabin of the *Spindrift*, which now floated securely in a protected bay along Rocky Island. The storm had thundered through and left a steady, early evening rain in its wake. Within the cabin, the narrow space felt intimate and safe. Around them, they could hear rain tapping against the boat's decking and showering into the lake. Even though they were anchored close to shore, ribbons of water cascaded over the cabin's portholes and blurred it from view.

"You called me Jeff earlier, when the boom nearly clipped me."

The side of Shelby's lower lip was slightly swollen, the greenish-blue bruising on her jaw was becoming noticeable, and her hair was drying into a tangled mess. And yet, he thought she was still as beautiful as ever.

"I did?" Shelby looked at him, her eyebrows pinched together, folding her legs beneath her as she sat on upholstered seating.

He nodded, not wanting to make an issue out of it, but curious to know whose name she had shouted out in that moment of fear. Ryan slipped the blanket they shared off his legs and went to the galley to flip on some overhead cabin lights and make a pot of coffee.

"I didn't realize . . ." Ryan heard her say softly as he filled a stainless-steel pot with water.

"Friend of yours?" Ryan lit the propane burner on the stovetop and placed the pot down with a heavy *clank*. Disliking the smell of the natural gas that came from the stove, he cracked open a porthole in the galley just enough to help ventilate the cabin and laid a towel beneath its narrow ledge to catch the drops of rain. The flow of crisp air against his face was refreshing.

"He's an old boyfriend," she said, and then corrected herself. "*Was* an old boyfriend."

"Was?" Ryan turned to look at her.

"He died a few years ago, when we were still in college." She spoke softly while sitting alone, wringing a corner of the blanket with her hands.

"Shelby—I don't know what to say." Ryan rejoined her on the seat and when he placed his arm over her shoulders, she closed her eyes and leaned into his chest. "I'm so sorry."

"Me, too," she said, placing her hand over his.

"Can I ask what happened?"

"He, um . . ." she stammered. "He died in a boating accident." She gave him a hopeful smile, but he knew the irony was not lost on either of them.

"So that's why you called me. . . ."

"I really said his name?"

Ryan nodded.

"I don't remember doing that."

He looked down at her and noticed a catch of light in the

corners of her closed eyes as they welled with tears. Not want-ing to push her, he sat quietly beside her and watched the rain through the portholes on the opposite cabin wall. The boat rocked gently from side to side like a hammock swing. He felt peaceful in the stillness, the intimacy of the space, and the warmth of her hand.

A shrill whistle then shattered the moment, screaming from the spout of a boiling teapot. Ryan quickly pulled away from Shelby and nearly stumbled as he rushed to the stove. The pot was now spewing coffee and grounds through its spout like a muddy geyser. Ryan hastily transferred the mess from the stove to the sink without getting burned in the process.

"Did you put the grounds *in* the pot?" Shelby asked with amusement.

"Aren't you supposed to?" Ryan asked as he grabbed the rain-soaked dish towel from the porthole ledge and used it to wipe away the coffee spill.

"Not when you're using a plain coffeepot." Shelby chuck-led, wiping her eyes with the back of her hand. "Did you think it was a French press or something?"

"No," he said, regaining his composure and glad to see that, although it took a bit of a coffee fiasco, he had managed to cheer her up. "This is how I always make coffee."

"Oh, really."

"Okay. Maybe not," he admitted. "Hang on, I think I can salvage it." He opened a drawer and rifled through various kitchen gadgets until he found a handheld sieve. With a ques-tionable amount of finesse, he poured gritty coffee from the leaking pot into two coffee mugs, using the strainer to catch the grounds. He then held up a round Tupperware container of sugar and a pint of milk from the small refrigerator for her approval. She nodded, smiling. After a quick stir, Ryan brought two mugs of coffee back to Shelby.

"Just ignore the little bits floating at the top," he said sheepishly. Shelby lifted an end of the blanket so he could slide in beside her.

She fished out the few black granules that had settled along the edge of her cup and took a hesitant sip. "I'm surprised," she said, looking up from the steam. "This isn't half-bad. You may be on to something."

"If you don't mind picking Folgers out of your teeth," he said before running his tongue along his gum line. He took a few more sips before bringing up the boyfriend again. "Do you want to talk about him?"

"You know what's interesting? I think about Jeff nearly every day, but I rarely talk about him. No one does." She held her cup with both hands. "He and I basically grew up together. We knew all of the same people. Our families were friends. So everyone seemed to grieve his death at the same time, like we were holding on to one another in a collective hug. But now, no one seems to want to talk about him much anymore. I don't understand why that is."

"I can see that you loved him."

"I still do," she admitted without hesitation. "I always will."

"Then he was a lucky guy." Ryan meant it.

"This might sound strange, but I think you would have liked him. He loved the outdoors as much as you do. And he was an excellent sailor. He practically worshiped this lake. We finished up our junior year at Madison in mid-May, and as soon as we were back home he couldn't wait to get out on his boat—the *Cadence*. How big is this boat?"

"Forty feet."

"His was much smaller. And a bit run-down. He and his family took great care of it but between the lake, the weather, and age, it ended up with so many dings and scratches over the years. No matter how hard he worked on it, that boat would never be as nice as this one." Her eyes gazed around the boat's interior, as if seeing it for the first time.

Ryan nodded, encouraging her to continue.

"The *Cadence* had just been put back in its slip for the season and Jeff's parents had barely started the spring routine—cleaning the boat, engine maintenance, making minor repairs and replacements, and so on. Jeff was in such a rush to go out that he didn't bother to check to see that the life jackets had been stowed on the boat. His parents always stored them in their basement over the winter and they hadn't been returned yet. It was so unlike Jeff not to check. . . ." Her voice trailed off. She stared into her mug. "He took off on his own that day. Ordinarily, that would have been fine. But when a storm came up, they say Jeff faced two problems. An old boat and not a single PFD on board."

"What happened?" Ryan asked carefully, already knowing how the story ended, but also sensing her need to recount it to the end.

"The storm that hit him was similar to the one today—it came out of nowhere," she continued. "He was always so careful, you know? He followed weather reports, he knew how to navigate in poor conditions . . ." When Shelby set down her coffee and pressed her hand over her eyes, he reached out to hold her.

"That's why it was so hard for all of us to believe he was gone." Shelby spoke with a quavering voice and a brave smile. "Jeff was the last person anyone thought would get into trouble out here."

"Was he over by Devil's . . . like us?" Ryan asked carefully.

She took a deep breath. "No. He was just on a day sail, going around Madeline. The Coast Guard said he was in the channel between Michigan Island and Madeline, making his way toward Big Bay. Based on some evidence recovered from his boat, they believe the boom swung across and struck Jeff in the head. He fell overboard."

"So when the boom almost hit me . . . ?"

"Is that when I said his name?"

"Yeah," Ryan said softly. "Where did they find him?"

She shook her head and began to cry. Jeff's body was never recovered. Ryan had always heard that about Lake Superior. As the coldest and deepest of all of the Great Lakes, legend said that Superior didn't give up her dead. If you went down, chances were your body would never be found. He was angry with himself for putting Shelby in danger and triggering such tragic images to run through her head.

"I am so sorry. I know you didn't want to go out to Devil's today, but you did it anyway. And I know you did it for me. I should have listened to you last night, when you were telling me about the weather at this time of year—and about Devil's being so exposed. I should have listened to you. You know this lake far better than I do, and I didn't take it seriously." He pressed his lips against the crown of her head. "It won't happen again." He rubbed her shoulder and smoothed out her hair to help soothe away the tears.

An image came to Ryan's mind of when he met her in the orchard on that first day. She was wearing a red baseball hat. In fact, he was fairly certain she was wearing it again when he saw her at Applefest. "That cap you wear . . . the UW Badgers?"

She lifted her face to his and looked at him with mournful brown eyes. He knew without her answering that it had been Jeff's. Ryan imagined it was a way for her to feel connected to him, so he didn't ask anything more. He understood.

"Do you still see his family?"

Shelby dried her eyes and took a calming breath. "Of course, but not very often," she said, the strength in her voice returning.

"Is it difficult for you to have those reminders of him?"

He felt her body relax in his arms. "It's just the opposite, actually. I love seeing them. I never want to lose the memory of him," she answered. "In fact, Jeff's older brother and his wife had a baby boy just a few months after Jeff's accident. His name is Benjamin and he has these amazing blue eyes, just like his uncle Jeff's. Seeing him—hugging him . . . it helps."

Another image came to Ryan's mind. It was the moment after he had run into Shelby at West Bay Outfitters. *I hardly noticed her,* he thought to himself. *Until I saw her holding that little boy.* While Shelby was basking in Jeff's memory and expressing her love through the child—lifting him off of his sandaled feet and twirling him around in giggles—she was also taking Ryan's breath away.

Chapter 17

ORCHARD

It was early November and the wind was racing across the lake in shifting shades of gray. Frigid air blew off the water and up into town. Pedestrians wrapped their coats tightly around their bodies, pulling their arms across their chests and leaning into the wind. Dry leaves were swept up and scattered along the edges of porch steps, boulevard gardens, and brick-laid streets. Jack-o'-lanterns sat on doorsteps in post-Halloween stupors with tired eyes and drooping, toothy grins. And neighborhood scarecrows, once well dressed and standing straight, now appeared haggard—their hats askew, jackets slipping off their shoulders, and straw stuffing falling out of the seams and blowing away with the leaves.

But in the fields and orchards above town, where farmers were coming to the end of a marginal harvest, the wind blew softer. The Meyers family had been working feverishly with a temporary crew of hired hands to bring in the remaining crop before the first frost. Most of the work was now complete. And it was Sunday. They would spend the day indoors with a fire burning in the hearth and a pot of wild rice soup simmering on the stove.

Ryan and Shelby stepped out of the house, bundled up for a brisk walk on the property. The orchard, once colorful in fruit and foliage, was now an empty grove of gnarled branches and leaf-covered paths. Shelby tightened the Badgers cap upon her head and zipped her coat up higher around her neck. A breeze lifted the leaves at her feet and whipped up the scent of her family's land. The woodsy aroma of the autumn harvest was now replaced by the smell of crisp leaves, damp soil, and rotting vegetation. It was the natural end to another season.

While the orchard was going dormant, Shelby and Ryan's relationship was in full bloom. By this time, Ryan was settled in his new routine and engrossed in his work, and the couple was spending most of their free time together. Despite the closeness Shelby felt for Ryan, some topics had been avoided. The thought of Ryan's certain departure back to Chicago often lurked in the back of her mind. Her belief that his time in Bayfield was provisional, and that their lives were only temporarily aligned, made it all seem as fleeting as the spring blossoms on an apple tree. As hard as it would be to say good-bye, there was a certain sense of comfort in knowing it would eventually end as planned. Having a finite relationship was far better than having one end in tragedy.

But on this cool November day, he was with her and, as far as Shelby knew, not leaving anytime soon. So she decided to ask the questions she had been keeping to herself. His background. Ryan's answers wouldn't change their situation, but they could help her to better understand why he was taking refuge in her small lake town.

"I know I've said this before, but Olen and Ginny really make me feel at home," Ryan said as they walked hand in hand. "It's more than welcoming me into your house. It's the way you feel when you're *in* the house—they treat people like family."

"I know what you mean," Shelby agreed. "They haven't had the easiest life, but they've had a loving life. There is this unbreakable bond between them. It always made me feel safe. I think it also affects the way they treat you and others."

He nodded, looking ahead as they plodded across exposed stones and tire ruts in the path.

"How about your parents?" She threw out the question lightly, hoping this time he would be open to sharing. "Do they have a good marriage?"

He glanced at her with furled brows. "My parents?" he asked, then turned his focus back on the path that lay ahead. "I suppose. It depends on your definition of a good marriage."

She paused a moment before asking more. "How long have they been together?"

"Thirty-some years."

It went against her nature to pry, but enough was enough and her curiosity could no longer be contained. She asked again and, this time, Shelby noticed the muscles in his face tighten as he clenched his teeth. They walked and she waited, until his expression softened and he was finally ready to talk.

"They met when my mom was a college senior," Ryan began. "Dad is five years older than her—he was working his first job as a journalist in Boston. They met through mutual family friends." He kicked a stone out of the path before admitting, "Their introduction was arranged."

"Really?" She came upon a stone of her own and gave it a swift kick in solidarity.

"My grandparents on both sides of the family traveled in the same social circles, but they were more business contacts than friends. Dad's parents invited my mother's family to a Christmas party at their club. My grandparents encouraged

Dad to take my mother out on the dance floor, and I guess they ended up hitting it off right away. They married the following December. Mom likes to say their wedding was one of the social highlights of the year."

"It must have been beautiful." The few weddings Shelby had attended were small affairs held in backyards, church basements, or the Bayfield Community Center. When her friends Abby and Luke Gordon married, they exchanged vows at a secluded beach on Madeline Island. Shelby had never been to a country club or a formal wedding, let alone a reception that made it into the social pages.

She hesitated before asking more questions because the picture he was painting made it clear just how different his life was from hers. But the pause was brief. She wanted to know everything about him. "Did your father start his company soon after?"

"No. At first, everyone expected him to work with his father or father-in-law, just as two of my uncles had done. My father refused. He wanted to start something of his own and wasn't afraid of the risk." They had come upon a downed tree limb, so he took hold of its branches and dragged it to the side of the dirt road. "My parents were young and from wealthy families. They had a financial safety net and a network of possible benefactors," he continued.

She collected the smaller branches that had broken off of the limb and cast them aside. "So he was about your age when—" she started, but cut herself short.

Ryan nodded. "Dad set his sights on communications—broadcasting, actually. He knew he needed firsthand knowledge of the industry before leading his own business. That's what he was doing when he met my mother. He was working his way up the ladder, so to speak, gaining experience in print media before moving into broadcast news. Our family moved to Chicago when my sister and I were very young. Chambers Media was a success before Dad turned forty." Ryan stopped talking and turned to Shelby. "Sorry. I'm rambling."

"Not at all," she said, taking his hand in hers.

"CM started out small, broadcasting strictly in the Chicago area," he said as they resumed their walk. "It didn't take long before he proved his knack for journalism, as well as entrepreneurism, and the company grew quickly."

"Let me get this straight," she interrupted. "Your father didn't follow in his parents' footsteps, but now he's insisting that you follow in his?"

"Bingo," he replied with a forced smile. "He always said it would be my choice. I don't think it ever occurred to him that my choice wouldn't involve CM. He's been grooming me to eventually take over for him when he retires."

"*Grooming* you?" It occurred to Shelby that her grandparents had been teaching her their business for as long as she could remember, but somehow it didn't seem the same. Or was it?

"I've been getting business instruction from him for as long as I can remember. Lately, he's been putting on a lot more pressure. I'll just leave it at that."

"For argument's sake, is there a way to stay involved in your family's business and still pursue your photography?" The idea of compromise had been on her mind lately as she considered the future of Meyers Orchard and the aspirations she had as a university student but never acted upon. Hell, she never even went back to finish her degree.

Ryan stopped abruptly, dropped her hand, and looked at her with an expression that proved just how much she didn't understand. "No! How could I? Photography keeps me outside. It helps me feel connected to *life,*" he said, raising his voice and gesturing to the trees that surrounded him. "Working at CM means I miss out on all of this! I can't be that guy who sacrifices his dreams just to make a living, trapped in an office and barking orders from behind a desk!"

She was taken aback by his reaction and raised her open hands to calm him down. "What about the guy behind the desk who employs good people? The guy who uses his influence to make dreams come true that would otherwise be impossible? Not only for himself—but for others," she challenged. "As far as I can tell, you keep running away from opportunity. You were born into a privileged life." She set her hand on his forearm before saying, "You don't have a problem, Ryan, you have a blessing—but I think you have too much resentment to see it. Instead of running from CM, why not use it for something that's important to you?"

"Art isn't important enough for you?"

Shelby shook her head and took a step back, not recognizing the bitter tone in his voice. "Of course not. That's not what I meant."

"What would you know about business, Shelby? Or life beyond the comforts of this farm? You cling to this land as if it's a security blanket!" Ryan said with anger that caught Shelby further off guard.

She had obviously hit a nerve and he was now swinging back. Then it occurred to her that the loss she was bound to face when Ryan left Bayfield would be nothing compared to the loss he'd ultimately feel from missing opportunities if he stayed. This reaffirmed her earlier thoughts. His stay in Bayfield had to be temporary.

"Your family has built a successful company that has the ability to shape people's perceptions, affect cultural change, reflect the times," Shelby said, with more sensitivity this time, carefully watching his reaction.

"Jesus, Shelby, it's not that simple," he grumbled while rubbing the back of his neck.

"It's just that I'd hate to see you mistake obligation for opportunity. Joining your father's business doesn't necessarily mean that you have to continue what he started. Think of it like this—at your father's company, you would have a platform to speak to people. You'd be behind the lens—a place you love—and you could share the stories you're passionate about."

"Shelby, you don't understand how—"

She ignored his resistance and pressed on. "Despite your earlier dig about me and this farm—which I'll forgive—I don't need to be a hotshot from the city to know what's right. If you find meaning in your work, your business will prosper. And if you stay true to yourself, you won't become your father in the process."

"All right. Now that we're talking, let's shine the spotlight in your direction for a minute," he said with an unsettling edge to his voice. Shelby realized too late that her search for the truth was about to backfire. "Are you fulfilling *your* dream, Shelby?"

"This isn't about me." She thrust her hands into the pockets of her coat.

"You're so good at analyzing my situation, I can't help but wonder if you're living with the same inner conflict?" He folded his arms across his chest and shuddered against the wind that suddenly rose up over the bluff. "Me and CM. You and this farm. I think we're more alike than you realize."

"Believe me, Mr. William Ryan Chambers the *Second,* we don't have a thing in common," she said flatly. "It's getting cold—I'm ready to head back." As she turned toward the direction of the house, Ryan unfolded his arms and reached for her.

"Hey—wait," he said, sounding more like the Ryan she knew and liked than the ass who had lashed out at her. She pulled away. "I'm sorry," he continued. "I didn't mean to raise my voice at you. You just said something I didn't want to hear."

Shelby stood there, in the middle of the orchard, searching his face and seeing a vulnerability that hadn't been there before.

"The truth is, I wish I had your optimism," he added.

Without thinking, she touched the brim of her red cap and pulled it down lower over her eyes. She didn't know where their relationship was headed, but she resolved not to run away from it. Cowards ran. Her mother ran. And she was nothing like her mother. She'd see this thing through to its inevitable end.

"Come on. Let's keep walking," Ryan said, offering his gloved hand like a gentleman. "Please?"

She accepted it and walked alongside him in silence. She knew they were both considering the gauntlets that had been thrown down before them.

A honking flock of migrating geese flew over the orchard so low that Ryan and Shelby could hear the rustling *whoosh* of their flapping wings as they passed overhead. It helped to break the silence.

"What do you love most about this place?" Ryan asked.

"I could tell you what you'd expect to hear—that I've grown up on this land, farming is in my blood, I love seeing things grow, yada-yada. That's all true. But it's only part of it." Shelby reached her hand up to touch the remaining yellowed leaves that dangled like loose teeth from an overhead branch. "When I'm out here, I connect with something greater."

"Spiritually?"

"God, yes, but I was actually referring to the orchard. It reminds me of family."

"Family?" Ryan cocked his head and looked at her curiously.

"You asked . . ."

"How so? Tell me."

"Imagine that every tree you see here represents a family. Some are newly planted, while others have spent years on this land and their roots are deep." Shelby pointed toward a row of saplings just beyond where they stood. "See those over there? The ones we planted last spring? They're transplants. New arrivals to the community."

"Okay . . ."

"Remember, I've spent years in this place, so I've had a lot of time to think about this," she said, smiling for the first time since their heated exchange about dreams and obligations. "I'm reminded of how families pass traits along to the next generation. Each generation is a new harvest."

"I never pegged you as the poetic type," he said while using his free hand to pull his collar up to keep out the chill. "What else?"

"Are you really interested, or just humoring me?" she asked as they resumed their walk.

He reached over and gave a playful tug on the brim of her hat. "Interested."

"Okay, so take this tree." Shelby stopped at the next tree and slipped her hand out of Ryan's grasp so she could reach up to pick a few of its last remaining apples, cold and overripe. "One tree, and yet none of the apples are exactly the same." She gave an apple to Ryan and he gently tossed it back and forth in his hands. "Some apples aren't as strong as others. When a storm blows in, they can't withstand the pressure and drop to the ground. Others fight to hang on so they can reach their full potential—like these two," she said, holding up the pair in her hands. "Others are full of color, texture, and beauty."

"I remember Olen saying something similar—I think he said his apples might not look great on the outside, but they're perfect on the inside." Ryan sank his teeth into the apple with a wet crunch.

"He stole that line from me."

Ryan laughed and wiped the sweet drops of juice from his chin. "What else can you tell me about this crop of yours?"

"Now you *are* making fun of me," Shelby said, joining him in laughter while threatening to hurl an imperfect apple in his direction.

"Hey! Hold up!" Ryan dodged and held his hands up to protect his face.

She lowered her arm and, instead of throwing it, took a hearty bite. "What can I say, I love my family trees," she said with a mouthful.

"What about the guy who comes from a deeply rooted family, is strong enough to handle both the hardships and the good days, but who wants desperately to drop off of his tree?"

"None of us can choose where we came from, but all of us can choose where we go," she said simply, sounding like she had it all figured out, when in truth she was trying to convince herself as much as Ryan.

"Life's not that easy."

"Why do you say that?" Shelby took another bite and licked the juice from her lips.

"Nothing," he said with a shrug. "Forget it."

"Can I be honest with you?"

He tossed his half-eaten apple beneath the tree, where it rolled against the others that lay rotting in a bed of leaves.

"You're looking at it in the wrong way," she said.

"Really."

"You were born into a family that offered you financial security, a stable home, and an excellent education and opportunities."

"Don't leave out the best part," he said with more than a hint of sarcasm. "Prestige."

"Give me a break. You say that like you're a victim. Instead of running away from the reputation and exposure, why not make it work for you? Why not use your visibility to do something good—something you can be proud of?"

"I never said I was a victim."

"You implied it," she said, tossing her apple alongside Ryan's. "Most people will work their entire lives and never come close to achieving what you have. I don't understand how someone as strong as you—as good as you—doesn't seize it as an opportunity."

"I hear what you're saying, but consider this—as I tried to say before, you're not much different. We're both tied to our family's business. But I'm not interested in continuing *their* life's dream. I want to live each day pursuing something that is important to me. Making a difference my way, rather than simply stepping into their shoes. Are *you?*"

"What—you're turning this on me again?"

"You're asking me to take a look at myself. I'm just asking if you're doing the same. Do you see yourself living here indefinitely? Or do you think you'll branch out on your own?"

There was a time when she wanted to explore a life outside of her hometown. But those dreams, along with her mementos of Jeff, had been carefully boxed up after his death. This was her home. Meyers Orchard would be her past, present, and future. That's what she had been telling herself for the past few years.

But now, looking up at Ryan, she felt a pang of doubt. Was the orchard truly where she belonged? Or had it become her safe haven?

"What do you want out of your life?" he asked again, stepping toward her with an extended hand. Talking about Ryan's future was easy. But this? She took several steps out of his reach and found herself beneath an awning of branches. He continued to move toward her—asking the questions she wouldn't ask herself. *What am I doing with my life? Why am I still in my childhood home? Why am I always making safe choices?*

Shelby kept taking small steps backward until she couldn't go any farther. Her back pressed against the tree trunk, the roughness of the bark and pruned branch stubs pressing into the insulation of her jacket.

Ryan ducked his head under low-hanging branches and entered the sheltered space beneath the tree. They stood close together. He removed a glove and reached up with his bare hand to tuck a fallen curl of hair behind her ear, and then rested his palm against her cheek. The chill on her skin warmed beneath his touch.

"If your dream is to continue the life your family started for you here, then embrace it," he said gently. "But if you want to do something more, then don't be afraid to pull up your roots and follow your own dreams. That's all I'm trying to do, Shelby. That's why I'm here."

She stared up at the branches, realizing something about herself that she was ashamed to admit. After a moment of thought, she looked into Ryan's eyes. "I'm twenty-four years old," she said, her voice cracking and barely above a whisper. He leaned closer to hear her. "I stopped dreaming years ago and now, the only future I can imagine is tied to this land."

Ryan reached around her waist and pulled her closer. Ducking under the frayed brim of her hat, Ryan's nose brushed past hers as lightly as a butterfly's wing. He was warmth, strength, and tenderness. He was everything she needed.

Shelby welcomed the affection from this man who had appeared in August and found her in the orchard. She closed her eyes, and felt him slowly lift the cap off of her head. As her hair fell down heavy around her shoulders, sadness welled up in her throat. Shelby looked up and gulped to hold back a cry, her eyes brimming with emotion. Ryan held her gaze while holding Jeff's hat in one hand. It probably meant nothing to Ryan, but to her, it meant everything.

His lips, warm and full, fell on her cheek rather than her expectant lips. She held her breath in anticipation, and he reached behind her, set his hand on the small of her back, and held her close. Shelby cradled his face in her hands and kissed him in a flood of emotion.

Later that evening, after Ryan returned to his cottage, Ginny was in the kitchen leafing through recipe books to find holiday dishes while Shelby and Olen sat down together in the living room. If the weather had been warmer, they would have retreated to the barn. Without Olen saying a word, Shelby knew he wanted to "have a chat."

When he eased into his favorite armchair, Olen and the seat cushion both let out a sigh. And as he leaned back into the chair, its springs groaned with age. Shelby curled up on the couch, which, over time, had faded from vibrant red into an uneven shade of pink. She leaned her head back and closed her eyes, exhausted from the day. Before she had met Ryan, every-thing was simple. She enjoyed her predictable routine. She could count on it as much as her grandparents could count on her.

"So . . . you wanna tell me about it?" Olen asked as he raised his feet onto the fringed ottoman in front of his chair, exposing his blaze orange thermal socks that were thinning at the heel.

She kept her eyes shut. "About what?" She and Ryan had already told her grandparents about their close call on the lake, with Ryan assuming full responsibility and the brunt of Olen's worry-fueled safety lecture.

"The effect that young man is having on you," he said sim-ply. Her grandfather seemed to have the uncanny ability to read her mind.

"I like him," she said simply.

"I'd say the feeling's mutual," Olen said. "It's fairly obvious that you two make each other happy. And for what it's worth, your grandmother and I like him, too."

"That's good." She heard rain beginning to tap against the roof and turned to look out the living room window. It was dark outside, aside from occasional strobes of lightning in the distance. *It will probably turn over to snow tonight,* she thought. Her mind went back to the *Spindrift,* when she was sheltered from the rain in the warmth of Ryan's embrace.

"But that's not what's on your mind now, is it?"

"Not really," she said, returning her attention to him while grabbing an embroidered pillow off the couch to hold in her lap.

"So what is it?" Olen readjusted his feet on the ottoman, crossing them at the ankles and wiggling the kinks out of his toes.

"The problem is . . . it's getting complicated. At some point, he'll have to go back to Chicago. He has an incredible life there."

"And?"

"And my life is here," she said, running her fingers along the pillow's white fringe. "So I can't help but wonder—what's the point? One day soon we're going to go our separate ways."

"I see." He paused before speaking again and she could feel the intensity of his stare. "Let's put that thought on hold for a moment and get back to a conversation you and I have had many times over the past few years."

Great. Here it comes, she thought. "I don't want to talk about that right now."

He disregarded her objection and asked anyway. "Have you given any more thought to going back to college? One more year and you'll have your degree."

"I thought we were done talking about college, Grandpa."

"I know, but your grandmother and I were thinking—"

"Stop. We've been over this. You're stuck with me."

He shifted in his chair and his voice took on a fatherly tone. "You never know. Someday, you may decide that you want to explore something different. See new places. Share a life with someone?" He raised his eyebrows, inviting her to open up.

"Subtle."

"You know we love you. But here's the kicker . . . we don't *need* you."

"But I—"

"Listen to me, honey. This farm has been our life. It's part of who we are. The land, the town, and even the lake—we chose this for ourselves," he said warmly. "If this is your life choice, too, then we'll be overjoyed. It has given us a great deal of happiness and I know it would be no different for you. But if your heart isn't in it, then I need you to promise me that you'll take another path. And if you ever decide to leave this farm, do so with your head held high, knowing that you have our absolute love and support."

Before Shelby could utter an answer, Ginny walked into the room with a cooking magazine in her hand. "I need your opinions," she said, placing the magazine on the coffee table and opening it to a spot that was bookmarked with a white envelope. "Thanksgiving dinner this year—should we try this Southern corn bread stuffing with chestnuts? Or this Italian bread stuffing with sausage and shallots?" Ginny was a traditional Midwestern cook eleven months out of the year. During the holidays, however, her inner chef came out and she enjoyed trying something a bit more adventurous.

Olen said "corn bread" at the same time Shelby voted for "Italian."

"You two are no help at all," Ginny said, shaking her head. She grabbed the letter from within the magazine and handed it to Shelby. "Sorry, Shel, this arrived for you yesterday and I completely forgot to give it to you."

Shelby's heart sank when she saw the crooked stamp and her name and address scrawled across the front of the envelope in purple ink.

Dear Shelby,

Word is you have a new gentleman friend. Good for you. Don't take this the wrong way, but I'll admit that I was a bit surprised. After Jeff's accident I thought you'd thrown in the towel for good. You were such a mess. Not eating, crying all the time, dropping out of school. I didn't say anything at the time because, let's face it, you have a fragile personality. You're much more suited for staying at home with your grandparents than getting your degree. You're like a sweet, well-trained puppy dog, never wandering far from home.

So imagine my surprise when I found out this young man comes from such a distinguished family! My, my. Like mother, like daughter! Maybe you do like the finer things in life. I'll just have to meet him one of these days. I think Thanksgiving would be perfect. Wouldn't that be nice? A little family reunion.

Love, Mom

CHAPTER 18

IMAGES

From: wchambers
To: wrc_charlie
Re: Personal

William—

It has come to my attention that you are involved with a new young woman. What you do during this sabbatical of yours is your own business. However, when it comes to our family's reputation and the future of CM, it becomes my business.

You would be wise not to become entangled with someone who does not fit into our long-term goals and, of course, your return to CM. Though it pains me to say this, your actions are becoming increasingly disappointing to your mother and me. It is time you pack up your camera bag and return to Chicago and your responsibilities here.

As you are aware, the annual meeting is set for January 15. I'll expect you to be here so we can properly announce your new position and you can address the shareholders. Do not disappoint me and I'll forgive our differences.

William R. Chambers
Chief Executive Officer
Chambers Media

Pete @ 9:12 a.m.
Ran into your dad at Sutton's last night.
He asked re: you and S. Look out. He's pissed.

William Chambers
P.O. Box
Bayfield, WI

From the Desk of Charlotte Chambers

    Dear William,
    Thank you for your recent call. I'm delighted to hear that you are well. But I am anxious for you to wrap up your project and return home. Will you be joining us for Thanksgiving? We'll be hosting a lovely dinner party for some guests from New York. Your sister and her family will not be making the trip this year. You'd make us immensely happy if you came home for the holiday.
    Love, Mother

"Any news from home?" Shelby asked while kneeling on a plush rug that lay before a crackling fire in Ryan's cottage. She was rosy-cheeked and unaware of how beautiful she was in nubby wool socks, faded jeans, and a white sweater that looked irresistibly soft. A baby blue scarf was draped loosely around her neck. As always, Ryan felt at peace in her company.

"Nothing interesting," Ryan replied, speaking easily to her from the compact kitchen space that opened into the intimate living room. He sat at the pinewood table he had been using as a makeshift desk—filing proofs, editing photographic images, and staying connected to life beyond the walls of his rented home. Ryan had been working all day on final edits to a series of photographs he had taken in October. An hour earlier, Shelby had burst into the cottage bringing a flurry of snow, groceries, and excitement with her. In exchange for Shelby cooking dinner, he was finally going to show her some of his work.

Ryan looked away from the computer screen to glance out the kitchen window, which was delicately framed with a brushstroke of frost. Snow floated lazily past the pane. The intimacy of the snowfall, which was blanketing everything around them, made it difficult for him to focus on his work rather than the woman by the fire.

"Can I see them now?" she asked, bubbling with eager anticipation.

"Sorry, but I'm not that easy. You'll have to wine and dine me before we take that next step," Ryan teased.

"You have the wrong idea, Mr. Chambers," she teased back. "Just finish up whatever you're doing over there. The wait is killing me!" Shelby stood up to attend to the fire, which had petered down to a weak flame over ashen logs and glowing embers. Shelby grabbed hold of the metal poker and gave the wood a few nudges, then added another log to reenergize the fire. Ryan looked up again from his computer upon hearing the *clank* of the tool and a *pop* of sparks jumping out of the flames. He breathed in the scent of wood fire that filled the cottage. He was ready.

"Okay, Shel, come take a look," he said casually, although his stomach was twisted in nerves. Were the photographs good enough? Would she think he had talent? He was anxious for her approval.

She smiled broadly, set down the fire poker, and closed the mesh fireplace screen. "This is so exciting . . . the big reveal . . ." Shelby said as she bounded eagerly to join him at the computer. She stood behind Ryan, reached her arms around his shoulders, and leaned in to see the first photograph on the screen. It was taken from within a sea cave on Devil's Island, the morning before they were caught in the storm. Ryan had captured a ray of sun that reached into the shadow of the cave and pierced through the water, casting light on an arch of rust-colored stone that curved just beneath the surface.

She sighed. "Beautiful."

Melting into the warmth of her cheek upon his, he clicked to the next image. It was the storm cloud rising above Devil's Island. A flash of light highlighted its northern rim in a way that was both ominous and striking. It was taken just before they took off ahead of the impending weather. Shelby gave his shoulders a reassuring squeeze.

Another tap of the mouse changed the screen once more. This time it was a black-and-white photo—a close-up image of Ginny's hands gripping an aged rolling pin, its handles smooth from use and its core darkened from the oil of countless pastries. Ryan had captured the contrast between her aging hands and the supple disc of flour-dusted dough. It was simple. It told a story.

"Ryan. These are . . . *good* . . . really, really good." Shelby kissed him behind his ear, sending a current of heat through his body.

The combination of her praise and allure made it nearly impossible to focus on his work. He took a deep breath and advanced to the next photograph, which was cropped to show another pair of hands. This time, the woman's hands held a round mug in front of her full, pregnant belly. Natural light from a window illuminated the steam as it gracefully swirled up from the mug and around her protruding middle, like an angelic spirit protecting the unborn child. Shelby said she immediately recognized her as Rachelle Yaeger, the owner of Spill the Beans coffee shop in town.

"Lovely," she whispered into his ear before brushing her lips down the nape of his neck with tantalizing kisses.

He continued advancing through the photographs, barely looking at the screen himself. He closed his eyes, distracted by the desire she was stirring in him. Each word of praise felt like a caress. Each compliment, a kiss.

Ryan stood from his chair to face her, reached his hands around her waist, and pulled her to him in one fluid movement. He leaned his face close enough to hers that their lips nearly touched. "Thank you," he said, the words catching in his throat. Overcome with emotion, he blinked back welling tears of gratitude.

"You have a gift, Ryan," she said, taking his face in her hands and looking intently into his eyes. "You have a gift."

The word "thanks" didn't come close to expressing what a profound impact she was having on his life, his well-being, and his self-esteem. But "love" was nothing he was prepared to declare, although he felt it deeply. Love would complicate everything. Love would pull her away from all she held dear. Love would cast her into the Chambers family spotlight and strip Shelby of her privacy. Yes, he loved her. More than she could imagine. However, Ryan's underlying instinct to protect her from that life kept him from saying it out loud.

Instead, he showed her. Ryan ran his fingertips up her back

and down her arms. Then, taking her hands in his, Ryan led Shelby back to the living room. In the firelight, he unwrapped the blue scarf from her neck and let it fall to the floor. His hands found their way beneath her sweater and traveled up her smooth body. He lifted the white sweater carefully over her head and let it, too, fall to the ground. She raised her arms gracefully and allowed him to remove a lace bra from her gently curved breasts.

Ryan pulled his sweater and undershirt over his head and cast them aside. He became lost in the sight of her silken, pale skin as it reflected the fire's glow. Shelby then unbuttoned her jeans and easily stepped out of her remaining clothes. She was exposed, radiant, and lovelier than he had imagined. His entire body longed for her. Then it was Shelby who ran her hands down his chest until her fingers took hold of his belt and she eased him toward her. When he moved his hands across the warmth of her back and kissed her fully on the lips, she sighed beneath his touch.

As the snow continued to fall upon the quiet cottage in the woods, Ryan realized that with Shelby, he was home.

CHAPTER 19

THANKFUL

"I'll apologize now for anything my mother might do or say to make you uncomfortable, angry, annoyed, or flat-out shocked," Shelby told Ryan on Thanksgiving Day as she paced back and forth across the Meyerses' kitchen floor. She already regretted her decision to wear black wool slacks and a cable-knit sweater. "Are you hot? God, it's hot in here!" She hastily opened the kitchen junk drawer and rummaged around for a hair binder. *Why'd I even bother with my hair this morning?* she grumbled to herself, tying her hair up in a floppy knot. There wasn't time to change her clothes again and she was desperate to cool off.

"Shelby, relax. It's going to be okay," Ryan tried to assure her, putting his hand on her shoulder and closing the kitchen drawer. "Maybe you should go outside for a minute—let the snow cool you off."

"It's just nerves," Ginny said while rolling out pastry dough between two pieces of wax paper. Over her shoulder, she asked Ryan to grab a citrus zester out of the utensil drawer.

Ginny was teaching Ryan how to make pies, and while Shelby thought the sight of them baking together was endearing, she was too nervous to enjoy it.

"Relax, dear," Ginny continued with Shelby. "Your mother will behave herself. It's a holiday and we have a special guest." She nudged Ryan, who had returned to her side with a mandoline instead of the zester.

"I'm not so sure," Shelby said, pushing up her sleeves.

"Shel, I've met a lot of characters in my life. I'm sure I can handle your mom." Ryan used his forearm to wipe flour from his cheek. He had mentioned to Shelby how much he enjoyed being in the kitchen with Ginny because he never had the opportunity with his own mother. According to Ryan, what Charlotte Chambers lacked in culinary skills she excelled in managing cooks and caterers and orchestrating perfection.

"Uh-huh," Shelby replied to Ryan absentmindedly as she stood at the kitchen window, keeping watch for the family's white truck. The snow was light enough to be easily cleared by the county's plows. Her mother's flight was expected to arrive in Duluth at 9:50 that morning, so they were bound to drive up County J that very minute. She wondered what they were talking about during that two-hour car ride. *How is Grandpa holding up?* Shelby would know the instant he walked into the house whether there was a glimmer of hope that Jackie was going to behave—or if she was already throwing punches.

Behind her, Shelby could hear lively chatter between her grandmother and Ryan, but she was too preoccupied to focus on their words. The clock ticked on. The anticipation was agonizing. *Why was I crazy enough to agree to this? To subject Ryan to this? Whose idea was this, anyway?*

She turned away from the window to look at Ryan. Here he was, spending the holiday with her family. Shelby was truly thankful for him. But no matter how handsome he looked wearing Ginny's paisley yellow apron around his waist, this day was sure to be a disaster. It was much too soon for him to meet Jackie. After all, Jackie could make "pass the cranberries" sound like an offensive remark. Shelby wouldn't be surprised if Ryan left her family's holiday table and hightailed it all the way back to Chicago. She wouldn't blame him at all.

"Step away from the window, Shelby. Now you're making *me* nervous," Ginny said as she retrieved a jar of cinnamon from her spice drawer. "Come over here, sweetheart. See what a great pastry chef your boyfriend is turning out to be."

"Boyfriend?" Ryan mouthed to Shelby with a wink. Why did he have to be so damned charming? *The poor guy has no idea what's coming. But at least this will be a Thanksgiving he'll remember.*

"Maybe we should have a signal, Ryan," Shelby said, drumming her bluntly cut fingernails against the edge of the kitchen sink. "You know, when things become intolerable, you can give me a hand signal or something that says you've had enough. We'll just get up and leave."

"How 'bout a peace sign?" he suggested, raising two fingers in the peace gesture. Then he repositioned his hand with his thumb down. "Or would this be better?"

"Maybe just give us the bird, dear. That should be a clear enough sign," Ginny said with a twinkle in her eye and a cinnamon-dusted middle finger held high. "It certainly would liven things up around here, now, wouldn't it?"

While Ginny and Ryan continued making jokes and finishing the pies, Shelby returned to staring out the window at the vacant, icy driveway. Chewing nervously on her lower lip, she remembered a time when she was seven. Like today, Jackie had decided to grace them with her presence over the Thanksgiving weekend, just in time to see Shelby perform in a 4H dance recital at church. "You're such a creative dancer, Shelby," Jackie had said mockingly to young Shelby. "Not every girl is as brave as you are, to disregard the choreography and do your own steps while the others stay so beautifully synchronized. You're a unique bird."

Or the time Jackie ended a disappointing letter when Shelby was thirteen by writing, "Don't worry your pretty little head about your math grade. Problem solving simply isn't in your nature."

Or the phone call, years later, when Jackie asked her teen-aged daughter, "Why on earth would you break up with that nice boy, Brett?" At the time, Shelby was still shaken over being pinned in the backseat of that "nice boy's" grungy Gran Torino with her hand forced down Brett's unzipped pants while his friend drove the car down a dark forested road. "I hear he's one of the most popular boys in school. Just think of what he could have done for your social life."

The sight of Olen's truck turning onto their property and crunching across the icy driveway interrupted her thoughts. Shelby ducked away from the window and was tempted to rush into the living room and peek from behind the curtains, just as she had done as a child. Instead, she followed Ginny's lead and walked calmly to the front door to greet them.

Jackie entered the home with ostentatious flair, like a flamboyant showgirl greeting her backstage admirers. There she was, dressed in leggings tucked into knee-high patent leather boots, sequin tunic, and a faux-fur bolero jacket. The acrid scent of jasmine perfume permeated from her cleavage. Her hair was the same color and texture as Shelby's, but unlike Shelby's, it fell in curls that were tightly coiled and sprayed stiff.

Shelby clenched her fists and felt her mouth go dry.

"Mother!" Jackie shrieked, rushing to Ginny with outstretched arms and air kisses, all the while tracking snowy footprints into the house. Olen walked in behind Jackie, lugging an oversized, hot pink suitcase behind him, its tiny wheels caked in snow. The forced smile on his face told Shelby everything she needed to know. *Man your battle stations,* she thought, taking a deep breath.

Ryan appeared at Shelby's side while removing the apron from his waist. "She looks harmless," he leaned in to whisper in her ear before wrapping his arm protectively around her shoulders.

The mouthwatering aromas of thyme, lemon, roast turkey, and nutmeg filled the house. The table was set beautifully. Everyone had chipped in to help Ginny prepare their favorite dishes. In appearances, it was a picture-perfect holiday scene. That is, until Jackie turned her attention to Ryan. She rushed toward him with audacious flirtation and then caught him off guard with a full kiss on the lips.

Ryan pulled away, Ginny's jaw dropped, Olen stumbled and knocked over the pink suitcase, and Shelby lost her appetite.

"How did you meet our Shelby, Ryan?" Jackie asked with a winsome smile as she forced a hard pat of butter across the warm dinner roll in her hand. "May I call you Ryan? Or do you prefer William?"

"Ryan is fine," he replied, shooting a quick glance in Shelby's direction.

"Jackie, I already told you how they met," Olen said while raising a forkful of mashed potatoes to his lips.

Jackie ripped off a piece of the buttery roll. "Oh Dad, you know how us girls are—we all adore a good *love* story," she purred.

Shelby thought she actually saw her mother bat her eyes in Ryan's direction.

"Let's let them enjoy their meal in peace," Olen said, offering Shelby a supportive nod.

"No, no—it's fine," Ryan said, to everyone's surprise. He

took hold of Shelby's hand beneath the table. "I don't mind one bit."

"You see, Dad?" Jackie said to Olen, who chose to dip a piece of turkey into the pool of gravy on his plate rather than look at his daughter.

Ryan spoke easily about their chance meeting, the pies, surprising Shelby at the orchard, and his return to Bayfield for a photography sabbatical. The more he spoke, the more Shelby was able to relax. And every time Jackie threw out a sugar-coated insult, Ryan acted as a buffer, shielding Shelby with his charismatic replies.

"So, tell me, Ryan, what are your intentions with our Shelby?" Jackie reached toward him and ran her finger up his arm suggestively. Ryan leaned away from her as Olen dropped his fork against his plate.

"For God's sake!" Olen added.

"Jackie!" Ginny scolded.

"Relax, Mother," Jackie said, pulling her heavily glossed lips into a sneer. "We're just having a friendly little chat, aren't we, Ryan? I'm not prying, am I?"

Olen pushed back his chair and picked up the bottle of wine at his end of the table. He walked over to Ryan and re-filled his glass without having to ask. "What Jackie is trying to say, *I'm sure,* is that we're all happy that you and Shelby are enjoying each other's company and that we're celebrating Thanksgiving together." Olen continued to walk around the table with the wine and, when he reached Jackie, took a firm hold of her shoulder and whispered, "Enough!" loud enough for everyone to hear.

"Actually, Dad, that's *not* what I meant. A mother has the right to know if there are any long-term plans," Jackie cooed, brushing off Olen's hand and dismissing his stern command. "Since I hardly *ever* hear from my daughter, I thought I'd catch up on all the news while I have the chance." She turned back to Ryan and waited for a response while Olen returned to his chair. When he refilled his own wineglass, he did so generously.

Shelby exchanged looks with Ginny, who then raised an eyebrow and discreetly lifted her middle finger above the edge of the table. *The signal,* she thought. Shelby shook her head and covered her mouth to hide a smile. They were on her side. It was enough to make her see things differently and she almost felt sorry for her mother. Perhaps Jackie behaved badly because, like a feral cat trapped in a corner, the only thing she could do was lash out at the people who tried to bring her home. Maybe she felt caged in. Disconnected. Unaware that she could have a life with them if only she would retract her claws.

Shelby surprised everyone at the table, even herself, when she looked directly at Jackie and raised her glass. "A toast, to my mother," Shelby began. They all rose their glasses with slight trepidation. "Although we live apart, we have certain . . . connections . . . that hold us together. I am thankful for you, because the decisions you made in your life have profoundly influenced mine. I am grateful to live with Gran and Grandpa in this ordinary town where I have met extraordinary people, like Ryan. For that, I will be forever thankful."

Everyone looked between Shelby and Jackie, whose veneer of a smile had disappeared.

"Cheers!" Ginny burst out, clinking her granddaughter's glass.

"Cheers," the others around the table joined in reluctantly, clinking glasses and sipping their wine, no one knowing what would happen next.

Jackie pulled her lips back against her teeth in a forced grin and took several gulps of wine while eyeing her daughter intently. "What a lovely sentiment, Shelby," she said finally, pushing back her chair and standing with her glass raised. "And now, let me add a toast of my own."

"Jackie, *please,*" Ginny insisted. "Sit down."

"Relax, Mother," Jackie said, before addressing everyone around the table. "It's just a harmless little toast. After all, it isn't every day that Shelby invites a man over to meet her mother, let alone someone with Ryan's impressive pedigree. So let's raise our glasses again. This time, to the happy couple—may Ryan continue to find sanctuary by hiding away in our little town, and may Shelby continue to hold his interest by hiding her precious insecurities."

CHAPTER 20

TREASURES

Later that evening, after the table was cleared and the dishwasher was humming, Ryan and Ginny drank coffee in the kitchen while Olen cornered Jackie in the living room for a serious talk. With a moment to herself, Shelby slipped down the hallway and entered her bedroom. She walked past her antique bed with its matching dresser, her tidy desk, and the chest painted in rustic rosemaling.

She paused when she reached her bookshelf. It was once filled with fairy tales and chapter books and now held a collection of novels, along with college textbooks and journals that had sat untouched for far too long.

Tucked in among the books was a small diary with a red leather cover and a delicate gold script that spelled out *My Diary* along its aged spine. It wasn't what she had planned to retrieve from her room, but there it was, begging to be noticed after so many years. She knelt down in front of the bookshelf and pulled out the diary. The lock was broken. The key long since lost. But the pages were still tinged with a golden luster.

She carefully opened to the first page. There, she read the

thoughts of her six-year-old self, as written with a tender hand on Christmas Day.

> i Met mi MoMMy. she is nOt like gran. Or johns MoMMy.
> mine is sad. she Makes me sAd to. I thOt she was r frend.
> i have a new frend. my dOl. I luv her n gran n grapa.
> but not mi new MoMMy. i think she cAn go hoMe.
> then we wOnt be sad.
> luv shelby

Shelby's eyes began to well with tears as she continued to thumb through the pages of her diary. There were large gaps of time, over which her handwriting and vocabulary improved, and other memories were recorded. Birthday parties. Spelling bees. Games in the orchard played with John. Her first time meeting a spitfire named Nic. But the recurring theme—the words that couldn't be missed—was the constant reminder from Jackie that Shelby was an unwanted child.

With the diary in hand, Shelby stood up and walked to her closet. She pulled a stepstool from the back and used it to retrieve a shoe box from an upper shelf, tucked beneath her sweaters. Shelby then stepped down and made her way back to the bed, where she sat cross-legged, opened the box, and carefully spread its contents out across her blue duvet.

There was a pair of Badgers football tickets. Several Valentine's cards. Jeff's caricature of their twelfth-grade science teacher conducting a botched lab experiment, which still brought a smile to her face. Frayed friendship bracelets. Letters, neatly folded and bound with a thin orange ribbon. And a photograph of them sailing on the *Cadence,* laughing uncontrollably about something she could no longer remember.

Jeff had been Shelby's childhood, her best friend, her love, and, at one time, her future. With tears pooling in her eyes, she held each object with bittersweet remembrance before tucking it back into the box. She then slid off of her bed and took hold of one last item, something that had been sitting on her nightstand every night since the accident. Jeff's Badgers hat. She closed her eyes, let the tears fall, and hugged it tightly against her chest. The memories of him were as strong as ever, but the pain was easier to bear. She raised the cap to her nose and inhaled deeply. His scent was long gone. Shelby ran her finger over the threadbare brim of the hat before bringing it to her lips and then carefully laying it back down into the box. *I'll never forget you,* Shelby thought.

Before closing the lid, she picked up the diary once more and ran her hand over its cover. It was time to put those memories behind her, as well. While her experiences with her mother would always be a part of her, they wouldn't haunt her. Even with Jackie in the room next door, Shelby would be strong. She owed it to that little girl who cried beneath a Christmas tree to find true happiness.

After what seemed like a lifetime since Jeff's accident, she felt that a part of her former self was coming back. She was beginning to see the possibilities of a future beyond Bayfield's city limits, and beyond her fears, doubts, and deeply rooted feelings of obligation.

She returned the box to its place on the closet shelf, feeling thankful for the person who inspired her to dream again. It was the man sitting in the kitchen with her grandmother. It was the man with whom she had fallen in love.

CHAPTER 21

CROSSROADS

"What are you going to do?" Brad asked Ryan over the phone as they neared the end of their call. Ryan was in the cottage, seated at the computer and scrolling through his gallery of work. He was proud of the photographs he had compiled over the past several months. In fact, the final collection exceeded what he imagined he was capable of doing. There were edits to complete, and some winter photographs still to take, but essentially, his work in Bayfield was nearly finished. He should have been ecstatic but instead, he felt himself at a crossroads.

"I should probably head back," Ryan told Brad, continuing to scroll through the images. He stopped when he came upon a photograph of Shelby and Ginny in the Meyerses' kitchen. He had taken it from the doorway without their knowledge, hours before Jackie had arrived at the house on Thanksgiving Day. The light that shone on their faces from the window above the kitchen sink illuminated their faces as they laughed together. It was one of his favorite shots from the weekend.

"And leave Shelby?" Brad's words came through Ryan's phone and hung in the air.

"I've already stayed longer than planned, and there's not much left for me to do here. I really want to get these photos printed and framed. See if I can get them shown somewhere in the city," he confided to his friend. "I don't know, Brad. What would you do?"

"Come back to Chicago. Bring Shelby with you," Brad said with encouragement. "Don't worry about your family. They'll love her."

"It's not my family that worries me." Ryan stood up from the table and walked to the kitchen window. Looking out, he marveled at the expansive frozen lake and the massive shards of translucent ice that were piled up haphazardly along its shore. "Even if I thought she'd ever leave this town, it's the lifestyle, Brad. I can't subject her to that. You know how it is."

"From what you've said, she seems tough enough to take on all of the attention and craziness that comes with your family," Brad said on the other end of the line.

"I don't know."

"Do you love her?"

Silence filled the distance between them while Ryan contemplated his answer. "Yeah," he finally said, running a hand through his hair and then rubbing the back of his neck. "I do." Thinking it was one thing—saying it out loud felt like a commitment.

"Well, I'll be damned," Brad said with so much pleasure that it made Ryan wince. "I wasn't sure it was ever going to happen to you! Ryan Chambers. In love."

"Easy," Ryan warned.

"So what's the problem?"

Ryan placed his palm upon the cold windowpane and watched the frost melt beneath his touch. "The problem is, I can't tell her."

"Why the hell not? Doesn't she feel the same way about you?"

"I think she does. Maybe. I'm not sure."

"I don't know, Ryan, I guess I'd just be honest with her. Take a risk."

"But she loves her family—and this place—so much. The last thing I want is to force her to choose. I can't ask her to change her life. And I definitely don't want to drag her into the circus."

"And you don't see yourself settling in Bayfield."

Ryan took a pause before answering. "No," he said. "I don't."

As Brad talked him though his options, Ryan absentmindedly scratched frost off of the window edges with his fingernail, watching the delicate shavings collect under his nail and pepper the windowsill. Rather than spend Christmas with the family he was avoiding in Chicago, Ryan decided to stay with the family he had come to love in Bayfield. He'd figure out the rest in time.

"I don't take Shelby as the type of woman who's going to wait around for you," Brad concluded.

Ryan could hear Brad's infant son crying in the background. "Sorry, man—I have to go," Brad said in a rush.

"Give Holly and that baby boy a kiss for me, will you? Tell her I'll come down soon."

"I'll hold you to it." And then, before hanging up, Brad added, "Don't underestimate Shelby. If you really love her, you'll know what to do when the time is right."

CHAPTER 22

PESTS

Like much of the wildlife in northern Wisconsin, the Meyers family slowed down during the winter months. Although work on the farm was less rigorous in early December, there were chores to do. Namely, keeping watch over the acres of frozen soil for pests that fed on the bark of dormant trees. As organic farmers, their most successful method for ridding the orchard of pests was by supporting natural predators.

On a quiet Friday evening, while most of Bayfield's residents were tucked away in the warmth of their homes, a stranger slinked into a dimly lit town bar on Main Street. Like a field rat, Avery Martin had crept into town with a wet nose and a keen eye, nibbling on bits of information she could pick up on William Chambers Jr.

Fortunately for Ryan, Nic was sniffing out the reporter before she had a chance to sink into anything juicy.

Snow was falling steadily in downy clusters the following day when Shelby arrived in town at Spill the Beans, at Nic's urgent request. The coffee shop's windows glowed golden from the light within and were decorated with garlands of holiday evergreen adorned with silver bulbs. Even before opening the shop's blue door, Shelby could smell the nutty scent of coffee percolating inside.

The *ding* of a delicate bell rang above the door as Shelby entered. She brushed snow off her coat and looked around the space. Seeing Nic seated at the far window with her nose in the Duluth paper, Shelby decided to go straight to the counter to place her order before joining her friend.

"Hey, Shelby, how's it going?" asked Rachelle Yaeger, the shop's owner and the subject of one of Ryan's portraits. She rubbed the small of her back and arched slightly, trying to ease the strain she felt in her pregnant, perfectly bulbous belly. A petite woman with an unruly mess of hair, she looked like a character from an illustrated book on gnomes that sat on the Meyerses' coffee table. And like a gnome, Rachelle was most content in the comfort of her small home, which usually smelled of baked mushrooms and a wood-burning fire. She looked particularly wholesome this morning, with her round, rose-colored cheeks, green eyes, and swollen fingers.

"Hey, Rachelle," Shelby said in a singsong voice.

"Cappuccino?" Rachelle asked as she finished wiping the counter with a damp towel.

"Absolutely," Shelby answered, peering into the bakery case, a mischievous smile coming over her face. "And a blueberry muffin. It'll be my lunch."

"You bet."

Shelby glanced at Nic again. It was unusual for her not to jump up when Shelby arrived and start chatting and throwing her arms about to dramatically regale her with one story after another. Considering Nic's boundless energy and general dis-interest in current events, the sight of her quietly reading the paper was out of character.

"Has she been here long," Shelby asked.

"Um, about an hour maybe?" Rachelle said. "She grabbed a black coffee and the paper and then plunked down in that spot and hasn't budged. Huh . . . it's not like her, is it?"

"Not at all."

After paying and thanking Rachelle, Shelby walked across the room to join Nic, who still hadn't bothered to look up from behind the newspaper.

"Anything interesting?" Shelby pulled out a chair across from Nic with a scrape against the wood floor and took a seat.

"Not today, but something's brewing," Nic said with a sour tone while setting down the paper.

"What do you mean?" Shelby inched her chair in closer to the table.

Nic gave a quick look around and then placed her forearms on the table and leaned forward. "Hank and I were at Captain's last night, sitting at the bar, when a woman walked up next to us. She orders a beer and finds a spot in the corner. Then she sets up shop."

"Sets up shop?"

"You know—laptop, phone . . . Anyway, she's drinking her beer, typing, and watching people. It's like she's looking for someone," Nic said. "She gave off this weird vibe. Hank noticed it, too."

"Okay, so?" Shelby said, unsure of where this was going. She began to peel away the paper wrapper from her muffin.

"So when Boots and his wife walked in, this woman looked interested."

Shelby broke off a piece of the muffin top and popped it into her mouth. "Please don't tell me you spent the entire night watching this poor woman," she said, brushing away a crumb from her lip.

"Just hear me out. As soon as they settled into a booth, this woman saunters over to him acting all casual-like. Ya know?"

"Did you call me down here to tell me that Boots was talking to some stranger? I don't understand why I would—"

"I overheard her question, Shel."

"And?" Shelby lifted her mug to take a sip.

Nic pointed her finger at Shelby. "She asked him about *you.*"

"What?" She splashed coffee onto her napkin as she fumbled to set down her mug.

"She wanted to know about you and Ryan."

"Ryan? Who was she?" Shelby nervously pulled off another piece of her muffin. "Why would she care about us?"

"I think she's a reporter, hon." Nic tapped her finger on the folded newspaper that lay on the table between them. "She's doing a story, but not for this paper. I scanned the entire thing and there's no mention of you or Ryan."

"But why?" Shelby rubbed a piece of the muffin between her fingers, oblivious to the small pile of crumbs that was piling up on her plate. "What for?"

In a rare act of tenderness, Nic reached across the table and took Shelby's fidgeting hand in hers. "Maybe you should ask Ryan."

"Why? I doubt he'd know anything about this," Shelby said.

Nic shrugged her shoulders. "I'd bet money that he does."

Shelby slipped her hand out of Nic's and pushed away from the table. She knew people wrote about Ryan; he had told her numerous stories about the media preying upon his personal life, but she had naïvely believed it wouldn't happen up north. Feeling anxious, a variety of possible explanations running through her head, Shelby stood up and pulled her coat off the back of her chair. "Did you happen to see this person talk to anyone else?" she asked while shoving her arms into her coat sleeves. She glanced out the window and was surprised by how much snow was coming down. The heavier bands weren't forecast to arrive until mid-afternoon.

"No. She didn't stay long. But there is one more thing you should know," Nic said carefully.

"There's more?"

"Yes, but first—are you going to eat this?" Nic pointed at the remaining muffin on Shelby's plate.

"Come on!"

"Okay—sorry! Sorry. On her way out of Captain's, she was walking past Hank and me when her cell phone rang. She stopped to answer the call when she was right behind me, and . . ." Nic pursed her lips together and stalled by reaching for Shelby's plate and pulling it across the table.

Shelby zipped her coat and slipped on her gloves in haste, eager to speak with Ryan. "And . . . ?" she said, trying to hurry Nic along.

"Maybe you should sit back down."

"Nic!"

Nic looked up at Shelby and said simply, "I heard her thank John Karlsson for returning her call. Maybe it's time you checked in with your so-called *friend*."

CHAPTER 23

SIGNATURES

It was Sunday, which meant a football game would be on in the Meyerses' home and Olen would be seated in front of the television. Although Ryan had been raised a Bears fan, as long as he was under Olen's roof and in Packers country, he'd root for the green and gold. The two had formed an unexpected bond over the past several months. For Ryan, being welcome in a stable home was a blessing. As for Olen, it was no secret that after years of living with women, he appreciated having a little extra testosterone in the house for a change.

When Ryan had arrived at the farmhouse for the noon game, Olen told him Shelby was in town and would be returning shortly. As if on cue, Shelby walked through the front door just after kickoff.

"Shelby! You're back early," Olen called out to her from his recliner without bothering to look at the front door. "The snow's really coming down out there! It's a good thing you came back when you did—we're going to get walloped today."

"The plows are out, so it's not too bad yet." She shook out

her coat and brushed the snow from her hair before hanging up her things and entering the room.

"At least it's a great day for football," Olen said as he reached into the bowl of potato chips in his lap.

Ryan stood up to greet Shelby with a light kiss. "Have a seat—the game's just getting started."

"Actually, can I talk to you for a minute?" she asked.

"Sure," Ryan replied at the same time Olen let out a cheer. Ryan's attention shot back to the television screen. "Come on—come on—come on!" He leaned his body to the right as if he could help maneuver the quarterback past his opponents during a sprint down the sideline. "Almost there . . ."

"Doh! Fumble." Olen smacked his hands on his knees and leaned back into his chair.

"Sorry about that," Ryan said with a boyish grin as he turned back to Shelby, who was now standing behind the couch with her hands dug deep into her jean pockets. "You wanted to talk."

Shelby nodded and motioned for him to follow her into the kitchen. "We'll be right back, Grandpa," she said over her shoulder. Olen murmured something inaudible with a mouthful of chips, his attention focused on the instant replay.

Once they were alone, she leaned against the kitchen counter and turned to Ryan.

"Something wrong?" he asked, standing beside her with his arms crossed loosely over his chest.

"I was with Nic down at the coffee shop," Shelby began. "She thinks there's a reporter in town."

"A reporter." He had known that it would only be a matter of time. In fact, he was surprised it had taken this long.

"She overheard a woman asking Boots some questions."

Ryan's fists, hidden from view beneath his crossed arms, clenched tightly. "What kind of questions?"

"Nic's pretty sure she was asking about me—and you."

Ryan glanced out the window above the sink. The snow was coming down so fast and heavy now that it looked like heaven itself was breaking apart and falling to the ground. "Did Nic get her name?"

"No." Shelby shifted her weight to the other foot and watched Ryan carefully.

"Any idea which publication she works for?"

"She didn't say."

"Shouldn't be too hard to find out." Looking out on the expanse of land that surrounded the farmhouse, he was grateful to have been sheltered in privacy for this long. "Did Nic say if this reporter spoke with anyone else?"

Shelby dropped her eyes and said, "Only Boots and his wife."

"Boots doesn't strike me as the type of guy who'd say much." Ryan reached into an overhead cupboard for a glass and filled it with cold well water from the tap. "He's pretty protective of you." He took several long gulps.

"There's something else you should know," Shelby said, waiting until their eyes met before she continued. "Nic's pretty sure that John called the woman on her cell phone, just as she was heading out."

"Perfect." Ryan took one last drink and wiped his lips with the back of his hand before setting the glass down beside the sink.

"I can't figure out why he would be talking to a reporter," Shelby said. "Why would she care about us? We're hardly making news up here. No one around here cares."

"Maybe she's doing an exposé on the apple industry, or a winter travel piece on Lake Superior," he offered with a slight smile.

"Seems unlikely, doesn't it?" She returned his smile. "But

maybe it's nothing. Nic could have misunderstood this whole thing. I mean, there isn't anything newsworthy about you working here, is there?"

"Absolutely not." *But nothing they've covered about me in the past was ever based on legitimate news.*

"And it's not like John or anyone else would say anything to make me look bad. I mean, to make *us* look bad."

Ryan leaned over to give her a kiss. "I'll find out who she is. Hopefully she's not here to stir the pot. Some reporters tend to blow things out of proportion." He put his hands on his hips and looked out at the snow blowing into drifts behind the Meyers' house. He knew he didn't have much time before the roads would become impassable. "I'm sorry you have to be involved in this." He turned back to Shelby, wrapped her in his arms, and kissed her forehead for reassurance.

"So what do we do now?" Shelby hugged him back and buried her head in his chest.

"I'll track down the reporter." Reluctantly he added, "And you'll need to call John."

A heavy snowfall wasn't enough to cover the tracks of a city reporter in a small town. Finding Avery Martin at the only motel that stayed open during the winter had been easy. Convincing her to cancel the story for the national weekly magazine, however, was not.

"Listen, I'm just doing my job," Avery said when Ryan met with her in the vacant, poorly lit motel lobby. "When my editor sends me all the way up here to the boondocks to check up on some rumors, I sure as hell am not going back to the office empty-handed."

As it turned out, Ryan learned that she was an aspiring reporter who wasn't about to drop a story that could lead to something bigger in her as-yet-uneventful career. Despite

Ryan's attempt to downplay his involvements in Bayfield, Avery was undeterred.

"I get it," he said calmly, careful not to be overheard by the curious, bespectacled woman peering at them from behind the reception desk. "But what you don't understand is that no one in this town needs attention from your magazine. *I* don't need this attention."

"Can I quote you on that?" she asked with a wry smile, fumbling for a pad of paper in her oversized leather purse.

He shook his head. "There's a chance I'll be back in Chicago after the new year. Why don't you give me your card. We can talk then."

"That won't be necessary. We can either talk now, or I'll just have to rely solely on my sources. Either way, we're running this story over the Christmas weekend. You may even make the cover."

There was nothing left to say. Getting angry would only make it worse. Without another word, Ryan zipped up his jacket and turned to leave. Before he reached the door, the reporter called out to him. "Listen, there's no need to worry—I mean, it's just a love story, right? Nothing beats a good holiday love story."

Two weeks later, Ryan sat on the edge of the bed in his dimly lit bedroom, waiting for Shelby to wake. Upon opening her eyes, she looked baffled to find him already dressed and wearing his winter coat and knit wool cap. She reached for the alarm clock, cleared her throat, and asked him what time it was.

He leaned in to the bed and kissed her good morning. "Merry Christmas."

"Merry Christmas," she replied groggily, sitting up and rubbing her eyes. "You're up early. Are you going somewhere?"

"Actually, I just came back." He reached to turn on the bedside lamp and handed her a glossy magazine.

She took the publication from him and squinted to adjust her eyes to the light. "What's this?"

"It came in early this morning. Boots met me outside the store to give me an advance copy. It goes on sale tomorrow," he said of the issue, which contained a brief article along with a photographic exposé of the two of them.

"On Christmas? They're running this over the holidays?"

"What can I say, it's a slow news day," he offered, trying to make light of it.

"You're a terrible liar."

"Really, it will be okay," he said. "There's not much here."

"It's national—"

"It's not credible."

"Please tell me John was honest with me—that he refused to speak with that woman," she said with rising concern, reaching for the magazine.

"He wasn't quoted, but—" he said, and then caught himself. "I'm just going to let you read it. When you're finished, come on out to the living room. I'll make a fire. And make some coffee. Then I think we should talk." He brushed aside a tangle of her uncombed hair and kissed her again, then left her alone with her first bitter taste of tabloid news.

Apple of His Eye

Farmer's Daughter Snags William Chambers Jr.

by Avery Martin, Staff Writer

When one of America's notable bachelors headed north for vacation in August, Lake

Superior's breathtaking landscape wasn't the only draw. While traveling under the radar, William Chambers Jr. has been discreetly seeing Shelby Meyers, a Bayfield, Wis., apple farmer.

Although Chambers and Meyers are both closed lipped about their relationship, there have been confirmations that this romance is definitely in full bloom, with Chambers taking up temporary residence in the picturesque town.

"They come in once in a while and pretty much keep to themselves," said Morrie O'Neil, proprietor of the Bayfield Chocolate & Bread Shoppe. "It's obvious that they're keen on each other."

While the townspeople were reserved on the subject—unusually protective of the couple's privacy—Meyers's mother was happy to confirm that her daughter is indeed in "a very serious relationship" with Chambers.

"She is head-over-heels in love with him, and the feeling is definitely mutual," Jackie Meyers offered during a phone interview from her home in Alhambra, Calif. "I had the pleasure of meeting him over Thanksgiving and he is as gorgeous and successful as I imagined he'd be. It truly makes a mother proud to see her only daughter land such a great catch."

Will Shelby Meyers be the one to finally take the prominent Chicagoan off the market? Her mother would put money on it.

"I'm sure she'll be calling me up soon so we can start hunting for that perfect wedding dress!"

While *Signature* magazine did confirm that Chambers has been living in Bayfield since early October, he declined to comment on the record about his relationship with Meyers, claiming that the intrusion would not be welcomed by the couple or the residents of his new home away from home.

According to Chambers Media, William Chambers Jr. is expected to accept a senior management position at the company's annual shareholder's meeting in January.

Is there a crack in the Chambers empire? Is a small-town farmer charming her way into Chambers' heart—and his fortune? Only time will tell.

CHAPTER 24

EXPOSED

Considering the cold never stopped Shelby and her grandfather from venturing outdoors, it wasn't surprising to find the pair walking through the town park on a morning when the wind chill hovered just above zero.

As she and Olen trekked through the snow, dressed warmly in thermals, parkas, and wool, Shelby reflected on all that had transpired over the past several weeks since the *Signature* article ran. It had caused a collective gasp throughout town—not only in response to the magazine's intrusion into Shelby and Ryan's private life, but also because photographs of their beloved town had been featured prominently in a national magazine. In their eyes, that was far more newsworthy than Shelby's love life.

Since Ryan hadn't been able to dissuade Avery Martin from running her story, Shelby knew he felt responsible for the media storm that followed. Everything that had once been personal was now exposed. Every place that had been private seemed to be on display. After Avery Martin's visit, a few journalists and photographers braved the trek north in January while others barraged Shelby's family with intrusive long-distance phone calls.

As someone who rarely used the Internet, Shelby was saved from reading the online reports. But the stories reached her nonetheless. Many well-intended friends and neighbors mailed news clippings along with handwritten notes of "Did you see this," "Can they say these things," and even, "Is this true?" The more the story spread, the more Ryan seemed to withdraw.

"This is a good spot," Olen declared once they arrived at a snow-covered bench, the same spot where Ryan and Shelby had shared their first date back in August.

They brushed the snow away with their gloved hands before taking a seat. Olen leaned against the back of the bench with a heavy sigh and removed a black thermos from the canvas bag Ginny had packed for them earlier that morning.

Suddenly, her grandfather's eyes darted toward a cluster of white pines that edged the park grounds. "Hey, Shel—don't look now, but—"

"What?" Shelby looked in the direction he was facing.

"I think there's someone hiding behind those trees over there," he whispered.

"Seriously?" she groaned, leaning forward to scan the trees with their snow-laden branches.

"Shh!" He flung out his arm and pushed her back. "Don't look!"

"What's gotten into you?"

"Over there. Three o'clock," he said with a surreptitious tone.

"What . . ."

"Paparazzi!" Amused by his own antics, he broke out into a wide grin and a chuckle. "You're a bit of a celebrity these days. You can never be too careful. Better keep an eye out."

"I'm glad someone thinks this is funny," she said, sharing a smile with the gray-haired comedian seated beside her.

"I do, indeed." With the thermos squeezed between his legs, he unscrewed the lid and watched steam swirl up and dissipate into the cold air. Olen inhaled the deep aroma of coffee while carefully pouring a mug for Shelby and handing it to her. She always appreciated the way he presweetened it with cream and sugar before leaving the house. "Nothing compares to sitting lakeside with a perfect cup of coffee in your hand, Shel. This is where I belong," he said, looking out onto the snow-covered ice and bright sky.

Holding her cup with both hands, Shelby could feel the warmth of the coffee through the thick lining of her gloves. "I feel the same way."

He screwed the lid back onto the thermos and returned it to the bag at his feet. "So tell me, how are you holdin' up?"

"Good question," she said, pondering her answer while taking a sip. "Let's see . . . I feel that Ryan is pulling away. After he finished his project, he started to get agitated. You know how it is up here in the winter. Everything shuts down. I think he's bored and anxious to go home," she said. "If that wasn't enough, I know the phone calls to the house were especially hard on Gran. And—oh yeah—my own mother sold yet another story about us to the media. Other than that, I'm terrific."

"Hmm," Olen considered while raising his cup to his lips and blowing away the steam. "Could be worse."

She pulled her nubby wool cap down lower over her ears. "How? How could it possibly get worse?"

"Your mother could move back here and sign us all up for one of those god-awful reality shows."

"You know what, Grandpa? At this point, as ludicrous as that sounds, I actually wouldn't put it past her!"

It felt good to laugh with her grandfather. Sitting in the deserted park brought back all the times spent together, just the two of them. Talking. Joking. Sometimes saying nothing at all. But always feeling a connection that ran deeper than the lake.

"I know this has been hard on both of you, but at least the coverage has been positive," Olen said.

Shelby raised her eyebrows.

"Okay, mostly positive." Olen reached back into the bag at his feet and pulled out a sandwich bag that contained several Oreo cookies. "It's not like you two are a modern-day Bonnie and Clyde. You're not in the press because you've done anything wrong. You're just two kids falling in love." He opened the bag and held it out to her.

"Tell that to Ryan. One more intrusion and he's going to snap." She removed her glove long enough to grab an Oreo and pop the entire cookie into her mouth.

"How much press has there been since that first article in *Signature*?" Olen didn't bother removing his gloves while dipping into the bag of treats.

"I honestly couldn't say," she mumbled with her hand over her mouth while she finished chewing. Olen joined her, opening his mouth wide and shoving in a whole Oreo. "You know me—I'm not much of a tabloid news expert." Shelby felt a shiver run up her spine and, in an effort to restore feeling to her extremely cold backside, she fidgeted on the bench and shook out her legs. "Grandpa, are you getting cold?"

"Freezing," he said, finishing off the last of his coffee.

"Let's head back."

"Can't," Olen said. "My ass is frozen to this bench."

Shaking out the last drops of her coffee into the snow and rising to stand, her legs felt stiff and numb. "You and me both!" She took Olen's hand to help him up, then reached down to grab the canvas bag.

Olen rubbed his hands together and asked, "Are you still

upset with John? I've seen him around town a few times. We miss seeing him up at the house."

"Of course not. Nic thought he was a source for the *Signature* story, but after it came out and I saw that he wasn't quoted, I went to his house to talk. You know I love him. I mean, we've been friends forever. I should have known he'd never betray me, unlike my . . ." Her voice trailed off.

"Like your mother did?" Olen removed the bag from her shoulder and insisted on carrying the load.

Shelby nodded as they followed their snow tracks back out of the park.

"I can't imagine what goes through her head," Olen said. "All kidding aside, I don't understand how she manages to disappoint, time after time. I'm sorry, honey."

"You have no reason to be." Shelby took his arm, as she had done countless times in the past.

"I know it's been hard on you. And Ryan. He's keeping up a good face, but I think he feels responsible for all of this."

She thought back to how troubled Ryan had been since that first article came out on Christmas morning, and how he had virtually said those exact words. And what made the situation even more difficult were the headlines that proclaimed Ryan had fallen in love, when in fact, neither of them had yet to say "I love you."

"Is there anything I can do?" Olen asked.

"Just keep being you." Shelby gave his arm an affectionate squeeze.

Just as they were about to step out of the park and onto the plowed street, they heard the roar of a high-powered engine blaring off of the frozen lake. The two turned to look, just as a red-and-white-striped wind sled zipped past the marina. They continued to watch the enclosed boat-hulled craft, propelled by two enormous fans in the stern, speed off toward Madeline Island.

"That's odd," Shelby said. "I thought the ice road to Madeline was open. Is there still unstable ice out on the lake?"

"I don't think so. Maybe the sled was just in town for repairs. But it gives me an idea," Olen said as he led Shelby to the truck. "Come on—I think I know just the thing to get Ryan's mind off this whole publicity mess."

CHAPTER 25

ICE

"Say, Ryan—Shel and I were down at the park this morning and it occurred to me that you've been holed up here for months, but you haven't been out on the ice yet," Olen said, holding a bottle of cold beer in one hand while the other fished through a bowl of unshelled peanuts that sat on the knotty pine end table beside his recliner.

"Well, I took my camera out on the ice a few times already, if that's what you mean," Ryan said from the couch, turning away from the television to face Olen during a commercial break from the NFL playoff game they'd been watching.

"Nah, I mean ice fishing." Olen cracked a shell and popped the nut into his mouth. "So, whad'ya say—you game?"

"I'm in!"

"Good. It's just what you need. Get you away from all the hoopla." Olen extended his snack bowl in Ryan's direction. "Peanut?"

Ryan shook his head, and Olen shrugged.

"We'll head out first thing tomorrow morning," Olen said. "John lets me keep my old snowmobile parked down behind

West Bay Outfitters. We can strap our gear on the sled and head out to a great spot I know. I checked the weather an hour ago and they say there's a storm heading our way, but it won't be here until late tomorrow night. So, if we're going to get some fishing in, tomorrow morning's our best shot. Quick and easy." He leaned back in his chair, turning his head toward the kitchen, and called out, "Ladies? How would you two like a nice lake trout dinner tomorrow night?"

"Boots isn't selling trout this week," came Ginny's reply.

"Who needs Boots? Ryan and I are going fishing!"

Ginny poked her head out of the kitchen doorway. "But there's a storm coming."

"Not until late tomorrow night. We'll be back here enjoying our fish well before the first snow falls."

"You better be right about that," Ginny said before rejoining Shelby in the kitchen. Ryan could hear the hushed objections between the women, but couldn't make out the words.

"And, dear?" Olen called out sweetly. "When you get a chance, my lovely wife, could you please help me find my old coveralls for Ryan?"

An audible groan came from behind the doorway. Olen then gestured to Ryan.

"No offense, Ryan, but that fancy parka of yours won't cut it out on the ice," Olen said. "You're going to need to wear some of my old duds—and I gotta warn ya, they're not pretty. We'll need to pick up a license for you, too."

"You're the boss." Ryan laughed.

A short while later, during half-time, Olen snatched another fistful of peanuts before the two took their beer and their boyish enthusiasm out to the barn. They gathered the gear they needed for their outing, including Olen's well-used ice auger, skimmer, reels, spoon lures, and bucktail jigs.

"Just one more thing." Olen opened the freezer chest, reached in, and grabbed a plastic Cool Whip container that held frozen bait. "Between you and me, I don't know what's more fun. The prospect of fishing or seeing Ginny's face in the morning when she finds these dead smelt on her pristine kitchen counter. They can give off quite a stink."

"I imagine she'll raise a bit of a stink herself," Ryan said.

The ice gave Olen and Ryan a frigid welcome as they set out among twenty or so fisherman the following morning. A silver-white sundog, a reflection of light that shone off of the ice crystals in the atmosphere, made a luminous halo around the morning sun as it rose over the islands. As forecast, it was to be a bitterly cold, perfect day.

Ryan worked quickly and efficiently, helping Olen load the snowmobile trailer with all of their gear. His face radiated with exuberance, as he was eager to try a new outdoor sport with someone who knew the lake well. A group of ice-fishing enthusiasts had gathered on the shoreline, but no one seemed to have recognized Ryan, dressed in Olen's coveralls, thermal fishing gear, wool hat, and face mask. Or else they just didn't care. While Ryan knew he would stay warm, the stench of stale sweat and pungent fish oil that clung to the clothes would take some getting used to.

Climbing aboard their heavily loaded snowmobiles, pick-ups, and cars, some towing portable icehouses, the ragtag group of men and women took off in a roar of diesel engines. Ryan sat behind Olen as their sled joined the others in darting across the ice like a gypsy caravan.

They turned onto the ice road, a plowed path that ran across the bay from Bayfield to Madeline Island and was lined with small evergreen trees. Ryan noticed the signs that warned "At Your Own Risk," written in vibrant red paint and placed strategically at the road's entrance, but it was too late to turn back. Olen's sled raced along with the others.

At various points along the ice road, snowmobiles veered

off to find their fishing holes. "Not much longer now," Olen shouted back to Ryan. And then he, too, turned off the road and headed left toward Basswood Island. The crisp outer layer of the frozen surface crackled under the sled's skis.

A thin haze of lake fog shrouded the surface, enhancing the thrill and enticing the men to venture out farther. Racing ahead, wisps of fog swirled upward and curled around them before falling back to place like a bedsheet that had been shaken out and then laid smoothly over a mattress.

As the sun continued to rise, the suspended ice crystals in the air lifted and added moisture to the clouds forming overhead. It was a beautiful setting that offered no indication that storm clouds were gathering strength and velocity only a few miles away. But Ryan wouldn't know that until it was too late.

Olen brought his snowmobile to a stop near the southern point of Basswood. As they walked on the ice, Ryan heard it moan and crack somewhere deep down, reminding him of the sound a large ship makes as it lists and heels in ocean swells. This particular spot was windblown and void of snow. Although it was immensely thick, the ice was also extraordinarily clear, a phenomenon unique to Lake Superior. Looking through the ice reminded Ryan of an aquarium exhibition in Chicago where a single pane of glass stood between him and a massive polar bear swimming on the other side. The sun was high enough at this time that the light shining down through the ice was able to illuminate what lay below. As a result, Ryan had the sensation of walking on water as he moved across the ice. Underfoot he observed a floating leaf, bubbles, ripples, and even a slow-moving fish that taunted them before they drilled their first fishing hole. He shuddered to think that nothing but this twenty-inch shell of ice separated him from one hundred and fifty-foot depths of arctic temperatures and certain death.

★ ★ ★

"Not too shabby," Olen said several hours later, grinning as he surveyed their catch. "Some lake trout and a couple of herring. Not to mention the throwbacks. You earned your supper, Rookie." He gave Ryan a hefty whack on the back for good measure.

The skies had been a tranquil gray all morning, but now, without warning, their color turned sinister. In the time it took the two men to pull in the lines and pack their gear, the intensity of the wind had grown and snow began to fall heavy and wet. They had no way of knowing that just around the point, a swath of ice was breaking apart and open water was churning. The waves were building quickly and surely, creating powerful movement beneath the ice. Section by section, the underwater force was shattering the serene, glass-like surface that Ryan had admired all morning.

Olen was about to start the snowmobile engine, with Ryan sitting behind him, when he pointed to some equipment lying on the ice some fifteen feet away. If there hadn't been a slight break in the snowfall just then, they wouldn't have seen it at all. They would have hopped on the sled and taken off ahead of the storm. Instead, Olen left Ryan by the snowmobile and went back to retrieve the rest of his gear.

Ryan took that opportunity to secure the cooler onto the back of the sled when he heard a tremendous crash—like the sound of shattering glass. He whipped around just in time to see the ice heave and surge, as if the lake were taking a deep breath before breaking free of its frozen restraints. He turned back to Olen and shouted, "Run—RUN!" He was breathing rapidly and could feel the pain of frigid air filling his lungs.

The icy floor, which they had trusted to be solid and safe, broke apart before Ryan's eyes. The lake opened up and waves splashed over a rapidly expanding area of fractured ice.

Ryan started up the snowmobile's engine and took off in Olen's direction, but it was too late. Everything was happening too fast. A crack tore through the ice and separated the men. Ryan stopped the sled abruptly and, without thinking, jumped off of it and leapt over the gap in the ice. Instead of reaching Olen, Ryan slipped away from him. Another break shattered the surface and caused a shift—the two men and the snow-mobile, with all of their provisions, were now floating sepa-rately on ice floes that were no bigger than eight feet across.

Cracks like shotgun fire exploded in Ryan's ears as more sections of ice crumbled under the water's pressure. The ice moved and swayed, grinded and gnashed, creating more dis-tance between the men, who bobbed helplessly on the floes.

The cold was now working its way through the layers of Ryan's clothing, numbing his extremities, and turning the wisps of hair from beneath his wool hat stiff and white with hoary frost. He knew Olen must be feeling just as cold. "Are you okay?" he called out.

"That was the stupidest move of my life!" Olen called back. "Whatever you do, don't tell Ginny. Once we get out of this mess, she'll have my hide."

"I can't reach you—" Ryan stopped mid-sentence when he heard a scrape and splash to his right. He turned just in time to witness the lake claim her first victim. "Shit! We just lost the snowmobile." His heart sank.

Realizing their situation was dire and he couldn't get to Olen, Ryan searched for an escape. There was simply too much water between his ice slab and the larger surface. Swimming across the gap wasn't an option. And then, to make matters worse, the waves picked up and knocked him down. The slab was wet and slippery. It was a merciless life raft.

Then, although consumed in an adrenaline rush to survive, his inner thoughts drifted and became reflective. Ryan took an inventory of his life. He didn't think about what he had achieved—but what he had yet to do. His mind filled with images that, until this moment, had seemed loose and disconnected. Clinging to a slab of ice, his ideas came together with absolute clarity. He thought of his parents. He considered the family business and what Shelby had said about using his opportunities to make a difference in the lives of others. He embraced his dream of becoming a father someday and could imagine the faces of his unborn children. And he thought of Shelby. Beautiful. Resilient. Warmhearted.

The vision in his mind of a future beyond that day's storm gave Ryan a rush that was entirely new. It was what he had been searching for all along. It's what had brought him to Bayfield. It was the very thing he'd explored through photography. It was why he'd fallen in love with Shelby. He now had a purpose. Ryan realized he wanted to put someone else's life above his—and now, he knew with absolute clarity, whose life it should be. Shelby's. The hope of sharing a life with her gave Ryan the strength to cling to the ice.

"Ryan? I'm having trouble seeing you!" came Olen's voice through the blanket of snow.

"I'm still here! Everything's going to be okay—I can still see you." His stomach twisted in fear for Olen, whom Shelby loved as a father. Although he was a distance away and visibility was poor, Ryan could make out enough to see that Olen was lying facedown across his slab of ice. He appeared to have a strong hold, but looked terrified. The men continued to call out to each other for what seemed like an eternity, trying to remain calm. Trying to stay alive.

"It doesn't look good," Olen shouted over the howling winds. "I don't know how much longer I can hang on!"

"We can do this!" Ryan shouted back. Looking out at the vast mass of churning ice, he refused to acknowledge how difficult it would be for anyone to reach them. "Someone will come for us!"

"Damn it!" Olen cursed in distress. "The ice is splitting again!"

"Can you move to your left? Is it stable?" Ryan tried to push up on his arms to get a better look at Olen.

"I'm fighting here, Ryan. I'll be damned if I'm going to let this lake take me after all these years," Olen yelled back. "Oh God!"

Worried that Olen was starting to give up, Ryan shouted out words of encouragement.

"Watch over my family." Olen's voice was still loud, but less angry and afraid. "They'll need you." He called out hurried instructions for Ryan about insurance, accounts, money put aside for emergencies. Olen wasn't afraid for himself. He was concerned for his family.

"You have to hold on! Of course I'll help them, but they won't need me—you'll be back on the farm tonight," Ryan insisted, restraining the sound of panic in his voice. They were now roughly thirty feet apart and the ability to hear one another's words was lessening.

Ryan had already lost feeling in his fingers and now the biting pain in his feet was fading into numbing warmth. He could see the shape of Olen's limp body on the ice and knew that he, too, was losing strength. Turning toward the Bayfield shoreline, he looked for any sign of help.

"Can you see those lights?" From Ryan's vantage point, he couldn't determine if the lights were coming from an approaching boat, or if the sweeping winds were blurring the town's distant skyline and creating the illusion of a rescue. He wouldn't share his doubt with Olen.

"Olen?!" Ryan willed Olen's body to move. It didn't. "Can you hear me?"

Nothing.

"Please say something. . . ."

There was no answer but for the ghostly moans beneath

the unforgiving ice. "Help is on the way!" He said it for Olen as much as he did for himself. "Help is on the way," he repeated quietly.

He tried to sit up, squinting against the snow to find the lights again, when a powerful wave filled with the debris of broken ice shards hit his slab with such force that he was knocked off balance. His ice slab was now listing slightly to the left, causing Ryan to slide toward the black water.

Although it happened in an instant, time seemed to slow down and Ryan moved his feet and hands quickly across the slick surface, trying to feel for any crack or impression to hold on to and stop his slide. His fingers desperately clawed at the ice. Slipping. Grasping. Then, feeling a deep crevice to his right, Ryan jammed as much of his hand into the narrow crack as he could, just as he felt water seeping into his left boot, which was now dangling off the edge of the ice and taking in water. With a rush of adrenaline, Ryan yelled into the storm and used all of his remaining strength to pull himself back to the center of the ice floe and away from the water. With his energy spent, he clung to the ice like a child holding on to his mother.

"Olen?" Ryan called out again, weaker this time. He didn't lift his head or look in Olen's direction. He simply listened for a reply. Hearing nothing, Ryan continued on, hoping that Olen was able to hear him. Praying that Olen was still alive.

"I'm in love with Shelby." He had been stubborn—a fool to have kept those feelings to himself. But in that moment, captive by the storm, Ryan was inspired to confess his love to the one man who knew her best. Although he was covered in frost and snow and his boot was beginning to ice over, Ryan was beginning to feel warm again. The pain was leaving his body.

"I love her!" he cried out weakly, one last time, declaring his love to the wind, to the ghosts of French explorers, Ojibwa spirits, and lost sailors whose ships had been consumed by these superior waters.

"Make her happy," came Olen's feeble but determined voice. Ryan wasn't sure if it was real or an imagined whisper carried on a whirl of snow.

"It's going to be okay!" Ryan's voice cracked. *He's alive. Thank God he's alive.*

And then, once again, Ryan was left alone in silence.

Before long, two lights appeared in a blur of snow that swirled around a vehicle that skimmed over churning water and unstable ice.

"They're coming—they're coming . . ." he whispered hoarsely, knowing that Olen couldn't hear him.

Just a short while longer. Hold on.

The lights flashed more clearly now—red-orange, red-orange—luminating the snow like a warm fire. A spotlight then shone directly on Ryan. He heard the muffled shouts of several men over the roar of whirling fans. It took all of his strength to raise his head. He tried to make out the vehicles. A boat. No, a wind sled. His vision blurred. But he was alive. He would hold her again. He would make it right. *I'm here,* he thought. *I'm here.*

Save Olen.

CHAPTER 26

SNOW

While Shelby and Ginny waited anxiously for Olen and Ryan's return, the storm raged on. Snow continued to build up around the Meyerses' farmhouse. It clung heavily from the limbs of apple trees, causing branches to snap and fall to the ground. The snow drifted over their driveway in deep, wave-like formations that were whipped and sculpted by the howling winds.

Aside from the creaks, rattles, and bangs of an old house standing up to the weather, everything was quiet. Shelby paced the kitchen floor, often stopping to look out the frosted window. Ginny sat silently at the kitchen table with her hands clasped beside a lukewarm cup of tea. The men were late.

An hour earlier, they had been nervously making excuses for Ryan and Olen's delay.

"They're probably warming up down at Captain's before driving home," Ginny had said.

"I'm sure they're conjuring up some excuse about why they didn't catch a single fish," Shelby had teased.

By now, however, too much time had passed and they were genuinely worried.

They had confidence in Olen, of course. His knowledge of the lake and storms was unsurpassed. Nonetheless, here they were, with their hopes deteriorating as quickly as the weather. As a precaution, Ginny had called the Coast Guard's office and spoken with Marty Hudson, who was manning the phones. "I understand. Thank you for checking," Ginny said into the receiver. Shelby watched her grandmother closely, hoping to see a glimmer of good news expressed in her eyes. "Thank you again, Marty. Yes, please call if you hear anything. Good-bye."

Ginny set the phone receiver back into its cradle, before turning to face Shelby. "They'll be fine, dear. You know your grandfather," she said with forced optimism that reminded Shelby of all the times in the past when Ginny had made excuses for Jackie's failures. "He always gets himself in the middle of things. I'm sure they'll have quite a story to tell."

"And retell." Shelby tried to smile.

"And then retell again," Ginny said with assurance. Ginny extended her arms to Shelby and pulled her in close, giving her a kiss on the cheek just as she had when Shelby was a child.

Shelby stopped pacing the kitchen floor and took a seat across from her grandmother. And, since there was nothing left to do, she placed her elbows on the table, rested her chin upon her clasped hands, and closed her eyes. *Dear God, please let them be okay.*

The telephone rang.

Ginny rushed to pick up the phone before the second ring. "Marty," she said calmly, clenching the receiver tightly in her hand. As she listened to the man on the other end of the line, Ginny kept her eyes locked on Shelby's. "I understand . . . No, we can make it out—a neighbor plowed out our driveway a short while ago. . . . We're on our way." With a quick nod to Shelby, they rushed to the front hall closet, leaving the wall phone receiver hanging from its tangled cord.

"What did he say?" Shelby asked as the women threw on mismatched mittens, hats, and scarves—whatever they could grab quickly.

"I'll tell you in the car—let's go!" Ginny insisted as they shoved their feet into boots. "That damn truck better start," was the last thing Ginny said as she slammed the front door shut.

Thankfully, the driveway had been cleared. But the truck was still half-buried in snow. "Damn it!" Shelby cursed the storm. "Hang on, Gran—I have to grab a shovel," she called out as she lurched through the deep snow toward the barn.

"Right behind you!" her grandmother called back while trudging into the storm.

Arriving at the marina, Shelby slammed on her brakes and fishtailed to a stop.

"Go ahead—I'll catch up," Ginny said, with urgency, holding tightly on to the handrail.

Shelby set the emergency brakes, jumped out of the cab, and raced toward a nearby ambulance with its bright lights flashing color into the torrent of snow. Realizing it was a mistake to leave her grandmother, Shelby turned back to rejoin her. But, to Shelby's surprise, Ginny had been right on her heels and now passed her.

"Come on!" Ginny called out, breathing hard and rushing ahead.

The women surveyed the scene. The Coast Guard boat, emergency workers, blinking lights, fishermen, trucks with their headlines turned on to spotlight the rescue area, and no sign of their men except for Ryan's car, left abandoned and snow-covered in the parking lot. Shelby hadn't taken the time to zip her coat or lace her boots, and now her coat flapped like an unfurled sail, the cold air whipping through her.

They held on to each other as they made their way toward the commotion, trying not to slip on the icy road. A fireman appeared to help Ginny with her footing. "Come with me," he said, escorting them to the ambulance just as several EMTs arrived with a man wrapped in blankets and lying flat on a stretcher.

"Ryan!" Shelby gasped.

"Go to him," Ginny insisted, giving Shelby's hand an encouraging squeeze before letting go.

Shelby rushed to the stretcher and peered down at Ryan. His eyes were closed and his warm complexion was unnaturally pale. Tufts of hair stuck out from beneath his hat, stiff with frost. And the lips she had kissed so many times, always soft and inviting, were now blue and trembling.

"Hey," he whispered hoarsely. She noticed his hand move slightly beneath the blanket.

"Shh." She rested her hand carefully over his.

"You with him?" came the abrupt voice of the paramedic inside the ambulance. Shelby nodded and stepped out of their way so they could move Ryan into the vehicle.

Ginny joined Shelby and watched as the EMTs secured Ryan's stretcher in place. "Oh, thank God he's safe." Ginny put her arm around Shelby's waist. "Now go. He needs you, honey."

"But what about you? And Grandpa?" Shelby spun around, squinting her eyes against the blowing snow to spot another stretcher. Another rescue. There was nothing.

"Now, don't you go worrying about us," Ginny said, giving Shelby a nudge. "I'll find him, and then I'll find you."

"Miss, if you're coming, we need to go *now*," one of the paramedics insisted.

Driving away with Ryan meant abandoning her family,

and she found it impossible to make that split-second decision. Until another man raced up to them, out of breath, and made the decision for her.

"Shelby, go ahead," John insisted. "I just heard they're bringing in Olen. I'll take care of Ginny."

"I know you will," she sighed, raising her gloved hand in thanks and feeling undeserving of such a good friend. She had paid little attention to him since Ryan moved to Bayfield, and yet, here he was, coming to her rescue again.

"I hope he'll be okay," John replied solemnly, looking into the ambulance at Ryan. And then, like a gentleman, he turned to accompany Ginny down toward the marina entrance where more emergency lights could be seen flashing through the falling snow.

An EMT took Shelby's hand and led her into the back of the ambulance. As she slid into the seat at Ryan's side, Shelby heard him quietly sobbing. She instinctively held his listless hands in hers, willing his body temperature to rise. "Everything is going to be fine," she assured him as the paramedics worked to stabilize Ryan's vitals and administer a sedative.

"Olen . . ." Ryan's voice cracked.

"Gran and John are with him." She stroked his hand and peered out the window, wishing she could see what was happening down at the marina. "He's so cold," she said with concern to the paramedic who was adjusting Ryan's hypothermia blanket.

"Don't worry, he's going to come out of this just fine," the man said with such composure amid chaos that Shelby believed him. "He's very lucky."

"I'm so sorry, Shel," came Ryan's anguished voice.

"Shh . . . you have nothing to be sorry about," Shelby said soothingly, leaning in as close as she could. "Just rest."

"I couldn't . . . There wasn't enough time . . ." He winced and closed his eyes.

"Time for what?" she asked gently.

The other paramedic, a broad-shouldered man with a ruddy, chapped complexion and heavy brows, told Ryan to do his best to stay calm. He held Ryan's wrist to check his pulse and watched the monitor. "Try to breathe deeply for me," he said. "That's it . . . Nice deep breaths."

It was clear to Shelby that Ryan wouldn't relax until he told her something about the accident. She delicately wiped the melted snow from the corners of his eyes.

"I couldn't reach him," he choked with a cry that came from somewhere deep in his chest. She looked at him wide-eyed as the sedative began to take effect. "I'm so, so sorry." His cries softened, and then, mercifully, his anguished expression became peaceful and Ryan fell asleep.

A female EMT in the driver's seat called out an "all clear." Her ponytail whipped from side to side as she checked the road before shifting the ambulance into gear.

"Buckle up, we're heading out," said the paramedic, who remained admirably calm. Shelby heard the tires spin on the ice and then, taking hold, propel the ambulance forward with a jolt. She fell back into her seat as they bounced hard over a snowdrift and sped out of town, sirens screaming.

In the days that followed, time wasn't measured by the hands that turned around a clock or the dates on a calendar. Time was a series of moments, some remembered and some forgotten, all blurred by grief. For Shelby, the only part of the day that had clarity was at dawn, when the sun forced its way through the narrow slit between her drawn bedroom curtains. Like a long finger, the light reached through the dimly lit room and touched her face. She would get out of bed, nudged by the light. It wasn't a dream. It happened. He was gone. Carry on.

Her beloved grandfather had died.

In some ways, the time spent with Ryan in the hospital just after the accident was easier than being home. In the stark environment of the hospital, Shelby could take her mind off of her own life by focusing on Ryan's. She kept busy—she would speak with his medical team about hypothermia and minor frostbite, manage his pain, make him comfortable, keep him from seeing the news headlines that linked his name to the words "ice," "tragic," and "fatality." And, despite Ryan's protest, she'd call his parents periodically to update them on his recovery.

After Ryan was released from the hospital, everything seemed more difficult at the farmhouse. It was her new reality. Every time she passed by the barn or glanced at her grandfather's empty chair in the living room, she imagined his final moments on the lake. Like a bone-chilling film clip, her imagining of the scene kept playing in her head.

Olen had slipped into the water just as rescuers reached him that day, but it was too late. They found his lifeless body pinned beneath the ice. If there was any mercy, it was that the lake—known for keeping the dead—took her grandfather's life, but gave up his body.

Shelby and her grandmother planned Olen's cremation and memorial service and even her mother flew up from California to help. For once, Jackie placed others' needs before her own. Ryan stayed at the house, too, sleeping on the couch and doing what he could to take care of the Meyers women. No one wanted to be alone, so they needed to put aside their differences so they could grieve. There was a blessed truce during their time of sorrow.

As they carried out the tasks that families do—accepting meals and visits by friends, reviewing wills and legal documents, preparing a service, and offering each other comfort—Ryan and others praised the women for their strength. Particularly Shelby's.

But at the end of each day, lying alone at night, she was exhausted. Grief came over her again and again, like rolling waves hitting the shore. Strong, forceful, and unyielding, they continued to knock her down. She clung to her pillow, wet with tears, curled up, gasping for breath, trying to survive the waves that battered her with each bittersweet memory. And with every regret that there would be no more tomorrows.

It was on one of those nights, long after she thought the others had gone to sleep, that she heard a gentle rapping at her door. Left unanswered, the door creaked open. Shelby didn't have the strength to lift her head. She heard the floorboards squeak beneath Ryan's weight as he quietly made his way to her bedside. Without a word, he carefully lifted up an end of her blanket and lay down beside her. She welcomed Ryan's warmth as he spooned his body around hers and wrapped his arm across her waist. "I love you, Shelby," he whispered, lightly kissing her behind the ear. She knew he was hurting, too. Shelby took his hand and gave it a kiss, before pulling it to her chest and curling into his embrace. "I love you so much. I'm sorry it took so long for me to say it."

"I love you, too, Ryan," she whispered. For the first time since her grandfather's death, Shelby fell into a restful sleep.

CHAPTER 27

HOMECOMING

Ryan was as quiet as the twilight shadows that crept in through the wall of windows before him. He was deep in thought, sitting on the edge of the bed in his Chicago apartment beside a partially unpacked suitcase. Although this was home, he no longer felt he belonged in the finely decorated space. His solemn homecoming had been spent alone, doing nothing more than what needed to be done to bring the apartment back to life. Open the curtains. Turn up the heat. Restart the mail. He was back and he had to carry on.

A short time earlier, while unpacking the last bag, Ryan came across the program from Olen's memorial service. He didn't remember packing it in Bayfield and thought it strange to come across it now. When he withdrew the stiff, folded piece of paper out of his suitcase, he felt the sting of grief all over again. His head dropped. He closed his eyes and sank down onto the bed.

His mind traveled back to the afternoon of the service. He

had intended to say good-bye to the friend he lost to the lake. Instead, he reluctantly said good-bye to everything he had come to know and love.

In the days leading up to the service, Ryan had done everything he could think of to comfort Shelby and help the Meyers women with the arrangements, but nothing seemed enough. Shelby was distancing herself from him and seemed increasingly uncomfortable in his arms. One of the things he had always admired about her was now creating a rift between them—her strength. Shelby was so determined to take care of everything herself that she wouldn't allow him to take care of her.

After the service, friends had respectfully shuffled in and out of the farmhouse bringing every sort of hotdish imaginable, from tuna to Tater Tot, as well as flowers, Olen stories, and sincere condolences. It was late by the time the last guest left the Meyerses' home. Ginny and Jackie had gone to bed and Ryan was alone with Shelby for the first time all day.

When Shelby said they needed to talk, he knew he wasn't ready to hear what she had to say. "I've been thinking about you, and me, for some time now. I mean, really thinking about us—even before the accident," she had said, sitting beside him on the faded living room couch with its fringed pillows. "I think you have an incredible gift. Your photographs are lovely. They tell stories and evoke emotion. I want you to share them with people. I know you're still in edits, but you've basically completed the project. You knew weeks ago that eventually you'd need to go back to the city and show them to others."

"Shelby, wait . . ." he said, shaking his head.

"Ryan, you know I'm right," she continued. "Staying here would hold you back from some incredible opportunities. You couldn't accomplish what you were *meant* to do."

"You aren't holding me back from anything," Ryan insisted. He felt like he was back on the ice, slipping into that dark, unforgiving water. "Come with me—come to Chicago." His words stumbled out, surprising himself more than they did her.

"I can't."

"Then I'll stay here." He tried desperately to keep their love intact. "I'm sure there are things I could do to help you and Ginny with the farm. I could hire more seasonal workers so Ginny could continue living here without needing to worry about the—"

She shook her head slowly and placed her hand upon his chest. "I can't let you do that."

"Why? I don't understand." How quickly things changed. He never thought he'd be in this situation, and yet, here he was—in a relationship where he was the only one who could foresee a future together. Despite the media, Olen's passing, and his family's lack of interest, he could see a future with her. He believed in it.

"I appreciate the offer, but we're going to be all right. We can manage alone," she said. "The thing about Chicago is . . . I'm not like you. I don't take chances. I've tried living away from this town and it makes me feel . . ." She turned her face away, now lightly grasping on to his sweater as she struggled to find the right words. "I belong here, where I'm needed," she finally said, looking back into his eyes with an expression that broke his heart. "Loving you isn't enough. My future in Chicago is as improbable as yours in Bayfield."

"Shel, we said good-bye to your grandfather today. You're dealing with so much right now—his death, your mom's visit, and the orchard. This isn't the right time." He put his hand over hers and clung to it, hoping to change her mind. "I know you don't mean this."

"I do. It's very clear to me right now. I also know that, because of me, your life is on hold. And I love you too much to let that happen," she said with a quiet strength. "Ryan, it's time for you to go home."

Home. Where was home? It wasn't Chicago. It wasn't the residence where he spent his childhood. Or his high-rise apartment on North Lake Shore Drive. Home was the lovely, determined, quirky woman sitting beside him. "You're wrong. Nothing in the city is more important to me than what's happening right here. Right now." With that, he moved off the couch and knelt before her, placing his hands on either side of her face, flushed with emotion. "Home means nothing to me if I'm not with you," he whispered. He pressed his lips against her cheek, tasting the salt of her tears and realizing there was little he could do to change her mind. Everything he had come to love was slipping away. He lightly touched his forehead to hers, closed his eyes, and hoped for a better solution. "Please, Shel, I love you." His lips traveled down her cheek in small kisses that led to her trembling lips.

His heart broke, hearing her choke back a cry as she wrapped her arms around his neck and pulled his body closer to hers. He kissed her again, with as much love as he could express—but also with the desperation that can only be felt when something wonderful is coming to an end.

Now, as he sat in his empty apartment thumbing the sharp edges of the memorial program, he wondered whether he had fought enough for their relationship. Could he have said or done anything differently? If only she believed, as Olen had, that Ryan's love was enough. He looked around his expansive bedroom, perched high on a piece of premium real estate, and he knew he would give it all up just to be with Shelby in that shabby cottage in the woods again.

Ryan flipped the program over in his hands and looked at

the portrait printed on the back. It was a photograph he had taken in early November—a simple portrait of Olen, standing in front of the barn, basked in sunlight. He stared at the photograph and remembered their fleeting time together on the ice. *Watch over my family,* Olen had pleaded as they struggled to stay afloat. *Make her happy,* he said of Shelby. Ryan loved Shelby enough to walk away. But in doing so, did he abandon Olen's wishes?

He stood up from the bed and walked to the window, with the program still in his hand. He looked out onto the frozen Lake Michigan, cast violet in the evening twilight and stretching out for miles. Ryan wondered if he'd ever be able to look at that view again without remembering the accident. He laid his hand flat against the window. It was smooth and cold as ice. He had made a promise. Something had to be done, but what?

His move to Bayfield had more to do with breaking away from his family than pursuing his photography. That he knew. What he had never expected was that leaving Bayfield would ultimately bring him heartbreak over losing the people whom he had grown to love like family—the kind of family that served as the wind in his sail, rather than his anchor in the sand. *You have the ability to shape people's perceptions,* Shelby had challenged him months earlier during a walk in the orchard. *Don't run from your obligations. Use your gifts to tell the stories that are important to you.* Passions. Opportunity. Family. Promises to a dying man. Even here in Chicago, he had to find a way to make it right.

Ryan peered out once more toward the lake. It was in that moment that a spark of inspiration, as strong as the one he felt when he saw Shelby sitting on the rocks so many months ago, came to him. He could make it right again.

The idea suddenly *clicked*.

CHAPTER 28

PASSAGES

With each passing year, some people die. Others are born. Friendships are celebrated. Disputes forgiven. People fall in and out of love. And yet the seasons continue on, blissfully oblivious to the passage of time.

And so it was that the ice melted into lake water, the grass was reborn, and flowers colored the landscape. On the Meyerses' farm, Shelby marched through each day without much regard for the next until spring eventually gave way to summer, as it always did, and the orchard was in bloom and full of life again. Shelby was taking care of her grandmother and the farm and that was enough.

"Come on—get in!" Nic called to Shelby from the driver's seat of her run-down, green Jeep Wrangler convertible, which sat idling in the Meyerses' driveway. She rapped her hands anxiously on the steering wheel. "Time's a-wastin'!"

Shelby pulled on the handle and gave the passenger door a swift kick, which released the latch with a *clunk*. "When are you going to get this door fixed?" Shelby grumbled as she opened the creaking car door and pulled herself up into the vehicle.

"Not a priority." Nic grabbed her canvas beach bag from the front seat and threw it in the back.

"I know, I know, just like fixing the soft top isn't a priority, replacing the blinker and wiper lever that broke off last summer isn't a priority, and . . ." Shelby continued, looking around. "Oh yeah, how could I forget the tire carrier that 'fell off' two months ago? Seriously, you need a new car."

"Not. A. Priority."

Shelby pulled the seat belt across her chest and clicked it into place. "So what is your priority?"

"Getting out of Dodge." Nic grabbed hold of the stick shift and forced it into Drive. The friends had a day to themselves and Shelby didn't care where they went. She simply needed some fresh air.

She looked over at her friend, the outspoken gal with a no-nonsense approach to life. If something worked, go with it. If it was broken, fix it or move on. Her Jeep was a good example. Nic considered the task of putting the soft top and windows on and off according to the weather to be "a complete pain in the ass." Shelby recalled driving home with Nic one evening during a rainstorm. The top was down. A pragmatic driver would pull to the side of the road and replace the top. Nic's solution was to accelerate to seventy-five miles an hour so the rain would aerodynamically skip over the top of the vehicle. Shelby returned home that night soaking wet and cold. Rather than being upset, however, she was utterly exhilarated.

"Little Sand Bay?" Nic asked without really asking. At this time of day, they would likely be the only ones walking on the three-mile stretch of sand that was so fine and light it squeaked beneath each footstep.

Shelby nodded and they drove in silence—not from a lack

of conversation, but because the wind and the raucous blare of
an old muffler made it nearly impossible to hear one another.
In the absence of words, Shelby leaned her head back on the
seat rest, closed her eyes, and enjoyed the sun on her face.

"Have you heard from Ryan?" Nic shouted suddenly,
glancing sidelong at Shelby before returning her eyes to the
road.

"What?" Shelby shouted back, eyes still closed.

"I said, what's up with Ryan? Have you talked to him yet?"

"No," Shelby said loudly. She put on a pair of sunglasses to
shield her eyes from her hair that whipped about her head.

"Why the hell not?" Nic threw another quick look at
Shelby.

Shelby shrugged and put her hand to her ear, feigning an
inability to hear Nic's question. But the roar of the engine
couldn't drown out her inner voice that whispered, *You gave
him up because you were afraid.*

Nic surprised Shelby by abruptly pulling off the road and
onto a tractor path that was overgrown with willowy field
grass and purple-tufted thistles. Shelby thrust her arms forward
to brace herself when the Jeep jerked to a stop.

"Are you crazy?" Shelby yelled. "What do you think
you're doing?"

Nic jammed the vehicle into Park and twisted her body to
face Shelby. "The better question is, what are *you* doing?"

"Me? I'm not the one trying to get us killed!"

"Listen to me for a second!" Nic lashed out. The friends
glared at each other without really knowing why they were
upset, until Nic spoke again, softer this time. "I wanted to wait
until we were at the beach to tell you this."

"Tell me what?" Shelby dropped her hands into her lap.
She didn't like the look in her friend's eyes. Was it pity?

"You're making a huge mistake with Ryan, and you
know it."

"We've gone over this before. You know I—"

Without saying another word, Nic raised her left hand. And there it was. A gold diamond ring as petite and original as Nic herself.

"Oh, Nic. It's beautiful," Shelby gushed.

"You think so?" Nic asked, looking down at her hand. And then, with uncommon tenderness, Nic left Shelby speechless by asking, "Here's the thing—if I get married and leave town, who's going to make sure you start living again?"

Over the past several months since Ryan was last in Bayfield, the town had become a beguiling hostess who welcomed a new set of tourists eager to see the place where William Chambers Jr. had fallen in and out of love. The Lupine Huss Inn prided itself on being the famous Chicagoan's "inn of choice." The rooftop bar where she and Ryan had met that first night in August now offered the Chambers, the house twist on a Manhattan. *Odd,* Shelby thought upon seeing it on the menu. *He doesn't even like bourbon.* Even the pizza place up the street was in on the excitement, baking Chicago-themed pizza pies in Ryan's honor.

The increase in tourism was good for the town's economy. Shopkeepers could afford fresh coats of paint and more elaborate window displays. Lush baskets of cascading greens and colorful flowers hung from the streetlights down Main. And the town's inns all displayed "No Vacancy" signs at their entrances. Even Meyers Orchard was having a prosperous summer. Visitors came flocking to the farm, presumably to see "where it all happened." Leave it to Ginny to make sure they didn't leave without a bag of her homemade preserves and sugared doughnuts.

Funny how things turned out sometimes, Shelby thought while walking out of Sonny's Candy Shoppe with a black cherry double scoop in hand. Licking the pink drops that trickled down the side of her cone, she made her way down to the lakeside park and took a seat on a bench. It felt good to sit after a long day at the farm. This would be dinner, she resolved, taking another lick.

Shelby was able to rest unnoticed. She didn't do anything to conceal her appearance. It wasn't necessary. It was quickly apparent that the media interest was more about Ryan than it ever was about her. To Shelby's relief—and her mother's disappointment—Shelby had no more notoriety now than she had before dating Ryan. When someone did happen to recognize her, they either asked her to sign some magazine that had a photograph of her and Ryan together, or they would look upon her with a sorrowful expression that seemed to convey, "poor girl—what will become of her now?" The first encounter she would politely decline. The second she chose to ignore. Inwardly, she wasn't sure which encounter made her more uncomfortable.

As she sat in the park, the taste of ice cream on her lips, looking out on the lake that had been such a big part of her life, her thoughts drifted back to her childhood and an early memory of her grandfather.

"They named this body of water Lake Superior because it is the biggest, grandest body of freshwater in the entire world. And you, my sweet child, get to play in it whenever you want," her grandfather had said as the two enjoyed ice cream while sitting upon a blanket on a patch of grass not far from where she sat now. She remembered that they were waiting, along with countless others, for the Fourth of July fireworks display to light up the sky over Chequamegon Bay.

"These waters captured the heart of the Chippewa. They called it Kitchi-Gummi, which means 'great-water,'" he said.

"Itchy-gummy?"

"Close enough." He had laughed, placing his hand tenderly atop her head and stroking her hair. "A long time ago, French fur traders traveled the Ottawa River and Lake Huron by canoe until they came to a beautiful inland sea. No one knew this place existed! They celebrated their discovery and announced that they had found *Le Lac Supérieur,* which means 'Upper Lake.' And today, we call it . . ."

"Lake Superior!"

"That's right, honey. She is *your* lake. You can count on her being cold. And beautiful. And great. But most of all, you can count on her to always be here for you." He leaned in and kissed the tip of her nose. "Just like your Gran and me."

"Is this seat taken?"

Shelby turned toward the familiar voice and raised her hand to block out the sun. "John." She smiled and scooted over on the bench to make room.

"Hey," he said simply, dropping his backpack on the grass and taking a seat by her side.

She never felt rushed with John or obligated to speak when all she wanted was to enjoy the quiet. He always knew that of her. Today was no different. "Ice cream?" Shelby asked, handing her cone to John. He put his hand over hers and took a lick of the melting treat.

"Thanks," he said, letting go of her hand. "You okay? I saw you over here and you looked so serious."

"Just thinking."

"Wanna talk about it?"

"They're out there somewhere—Jeff and Grandpa. I can feel it."

He nodded and followed her gaze to the water, which was alive with waves and boats and swooping gulls.

"Crazy?" she asked.

"Not crazy," he assured her, putting his arm around her shoulders and pulling her closer.

She welcomed it and leaned into his body. "They both loved this place, you know?"

"They did."

They sat that way for a while, quietly passing the ice cream back and forth until they reached the cone itself.

"Why are you here?" Shelby asked, considering how he had just appeared in the park.

"Wow, that was abrupt," he said, straightening his posture. "Do you want me to leave?"

"Sorry, no—no," she apologized. "I mean, how did you find me?" She hadn't told anyone she was coming to the park and hadn't noticed his car at the shop when she walked past. But then again, she wasn't really paying attention to her surroundings.

"I just came off the ferry and saw you sitting here. Thought you might need some company," he answered matter-of-factly.

"I do."

"This isn't just about Olen and Jeff, is it?" He faced her and leaned forward, setting his clasped hands across his knees.

She shrugged her shoulders and turned the cone around between her fingers.

"I know what's bothering you and I know it will all work out," John said.

"You do?" She knew John hadn't wanted to discuss Ryan after he returned to Chicago for good, so she was surprised he'd be willing to bring him up now. *Is it really that obvious?* she wondered. She had been trying so hard to move on.

"Sure. Nic and Hank will be back here all the time. Just wait," John said. "I never thought I'd be the one to say this, but she's a good friend for you. Just because she's getting married doesn't mean your friendship will change."

Shelby sighed. *This has nothing to do with Nic,* Shelby

wanted to say, but couldn't. She stood and walked to a nearby garbage can. Tossing the cone into the bin, she noticed black flies hovering clumsily over the sticky edges of its rim. The filthy insects reminded her of why she was really downtown, taking refuge in the park. She was avoiding the putrid mess that was awaiting her back at the farm.

"Am I right?" John's voice called out from where he sat on the bench.

She shook her head and turned away from the bin to face him. "My mother came back today. We haven't seen or heard from her since the memorial service." She rubbed the back of her neck. "Guess I've been hiding out, trying to avoid the unavoidable."

Shelby didn't need to elaborate. John knew her well enough to understand the heaviness of her words. He stood up, slung his backpack over his shoulder, and walked over to her. "Why is she here?"

"Now that the ice is out, we'll be dispersing Grandpa's ashes this week." Shelby dug her hands into the pockets of her denim shorts and looked down at her feet, kicking at the grass. "Gran and I didn't expect to see her again, but she called out of the blue yesterday and said she wanted to be a part of it. It made Gran happy, of course."

"And you?"

"I don't know—she's never been the sentimental one, so I'm not sure I trust her motives. But he was her father. So there's that."

John set his hand upon her lower back and looked at her with understanding. "Need some company?" he asked with a look of understanding. Then he raised his fists in a comical boxing pose and added, "If she gives you any trouble, I can take her."

Shelby watched as John danced around her, throwing out jabs and punches into the air, laughing. "Yeah, I'd appreciate that," she said, giving him a slow-motion punch to his chin. His head whipped to the side and he grabbed his chin before falling to her feet in feigned agony.

Perhaps it was the stress of her mother's return. Or the surprise that Nic was moving on. Or the comfort of John's company. For whatever reason, as Shelby walked through the park with John, Ryan was not the foremost thing in her mind. That alone was enough to lighten much of the emotional weight she had been carrying.

As they passed under the broad branches of a maple tree, John stopped.

"What is it?" Shelby asked.

"I'm not kidding, you know." John turned his body away from hers, crossing his arms and looking out toward the lake.

"Kidding about what?" she asked, confused by his sudden change in behavior.

"About you," he said with a pause. "I'll always be there for you, whether it's helping you deal with your family or work or—anything."

"I know that."

"I don't think you do, Shel."

"John, look at me," she said, reaching out to touch his arm. He shifted his body away.

"The truth is, Shelby, I've *always* been there for you."

"Please look at me." She touched his arm again, lighter this time, and his shoulders slumped. "I don't understand. What's wrong?" She stepped into his line of view, forcing him to face her. When he finally did look at her, Shelby saw both pain and adoration in his eyes that she had never noticed before.

"I know you've always been there for me. We've known each other forever. You're one of my dearest friends, John. I can always count on you," she said, her hand still on his arm, comforting him.

John uncrossed his arms and reached for her hand. He held it tenderly and took a step closer. They had held hands on countless occasions in the past. This time, it wasn't platonic. His skin felt charged against hers. Her cheeks flushed and she was suddenly unsure of what to say or do next.

She and John had reconnected soon after Ryan moved back to Chicago. When John told her how much he wanted to take care of her and help her forget the past year, she believed him. When he promised to do everything he could to make her happy, she was grateful. But now, standing close together beneath the tree, his words took on new meaning. He was about to change everything.

"This is about more than friendship, Shelby." John's hand brushed along the side of her cheek and settled behind her ear. Her breath caught in her chest, surprised by how warm and tender his touch felt on her skin. "I can't tell you how many times I've wanted to tell you how I really feel about you." He reached his other hand around her waist, and when she didn't pull away, settled it firmly on her lower back and eased her closer until their bodies were pressed together. She surprised herself with a sudden longing to kiss him. To know if the best man for her had been John all along. Her breath quickened as she raised her arms and wrapped them around his neck.

John embodied everything that gave her contentment— her town, the happier days of her childhood, a love for the lake and its islands. With John at her side, she could care for her grandmother in her later years and carry on the family business. She could give back to those who had given her so much. John was exactly what Shelby always thought she needed. Comfort. Familiarity. Loyalty.

John was home to her.

His lips were soft, luscious. When he kissed her, he didn't rush. It was a savored experience, worth its wait. Generous and full of adoration. After all of the experiences they had shared over the years, she thought it was one of the most expressive and honest moments in their lives.

Being kissed by John was like taking that first deep breath after drowning in a storm. It filled her heart and brought her back to life.

Before leaving the park together, John held her in his arms while she rested her head on his chest. He ran his fingers lovingly through her hair and confessed his love for her. While it was sweet, and beautiful, and a blessing to receive, she couldn't help but wonder: *Is the safest choice always the best choice? By living my entire life in one place, even if it's a good life, would I be cheating myself out of the chance to experience something greater?*

CHAPTER 29

LUGGAGE

After John's confession in the park, true to his word, he escorted Shelby back to the farmhouse to confront Jackie.

"Shelby! So good to see you again," her mother cooed with such artificial sweetness it made Shelby's teeth hurt. Jackie approached her daughter with open arms. Her head tilted to the side and her tight smile gleamed behind a pair of lips that were slathered in pink gloss. Shelby allowed her mother to hug her, though her arms stayed limp at her sides and her head turned away from those wet, glazed lips.

"Hey," Shelby greeted her mother flatly. Looking over Jackie's shoulder, she spotted several moving boxes beside two pink suitcases with gilded handles and stepped out of her mother's grasp.

"Shelby, honey, have you heard the latest about Ryan?" Jackie asked with excitement.

"No."

"On my way here, I grabbed some magazines in the airport and there he was—looking so handsome on the front cover." Jackie swung her hip out to one side, which nearly stretched the synthetic fabric of her dress to its breaking point. "He was photographed at some restaurant, but they said he's still single. That must mean something, don't you think?"

"That's the news that put him on the cover?" Shelby asked without hiding her irritation. "That he eats at restaurants? Wow. Stop the presses." ·

"You don't have to be rude about it," Jackie replied.

"Mother, you remember my friend, John Karlsson."

John stepped forward to shake Jackie's hand. "Hello, Ms. Meyers. We've met a few times."

"Were you that scrawny kid with all the acne? The one who practically lived here all through high school?" Jackie asked with no more than a superficial interest, just before closing her eyes and covering an exaggerated yawn.

"That's me," John said with admirable confidence.

"Well, you certainly have filled out well. I'll give you that," Jackie added, giving her lips a smack. "Still pining away for this one?" She gestured her thumb in Shelby's direction, and John continued to handle the jabs with ease.

"Something like that," he said, sharing a knowing smile with Shelby. He then gave her a nod, which was their signal that he would cover if she wanted to break away. And so she did.

Shelby mouthed "thank you" to John and then brushed past Jackie and her luggage, and walked straight into the kitchen. She marched up to her grandmother, who was standing at the counter stirring a pitcher of lemonade.

"What's with all of the boxes?" Shelby asked in a forced whisper.

"Hello to you, too." Ginny kept stirring without looking up. "I trust you had a nice time in town."

"Seems like a lot of stuff." Shelby leaned into the counter so her grandmother would be forced to look her in the eye. "She's only staying for a few days, right?"

"Would you care to sit down?" Ginny removed the wooden

spoon from the glass pitcher and placed it in the sink before turning to Shelby. "Have some lemonade?"

"No, I don't want to sit. Come on, Gran—what's going on?"

Ginny glanced at the doorway and said, "I think you should sit."

Shelby straightened her back and crossed her arms.

"Suit yourself," Ginny said. "I'm going to sit." She retrieved a clean glass from the dishwasher, poured herself a glass of lemonade, and then took a seat at the table. As Shelby continued to watch, impatiently shifting her weight from her right foot to her left, Ginny took several long sips of her beverage. Ice clinked against the sides of her glass. Jackie's cackle could be heard from the other room. Ginny let out a sigh. "She's decided to move back home."

"What?! Moving? What does that mean?" Shelby strained to keep her voice down. "She's supposed to be here long enough for us to take care of Grandpa's ashes. That's it, right?"

"Actually," Ginny said with a pause. "She just told me that she wants to stay." She took another gulp. "Indefinitely."

"Please tell me you said no." Shelby pulled her arms tighter against her chest and clenched her hands into fists. "You did say no, didn't you?"

Ginny set down her glass and ran her palms over the smooth surface of the wooden table. "I told her she would need to speak with you."

"Fine. She can speak to me all she wants." She began to pace back and forth in the small kitchen, suddenly feeling trapped in her own home, the one place where she had always felt safe. "The answer is no. Four or five days tops and then she has to leave. We've gone through too much already this year."

"Shelby, you should know that she wants to help run the farm," Ginny said, pushing her chair away from the table. "And let's face it. With Olen gone, we could use all the help we can get."

"I'll bet she does." Shelby gulped hard, forcing herself not to cry. *How dare she? After all this time? She's more than twenty years too late.* "We don't need her, Gran—we don't!"

Before Shelby could offer more objections, Ginny gave her that tender, nurturing expression that had always been a comfort. "I know it's a lot to ask, but what else can you say when a loved one asks to come home?"

"No offense, but I'd hardly call her a loved one," Shelby replied.

Just as Shelby turned to leave, her grandmother said, "Don't leave just yet. Come, sit down. It's time we had a little talk."

CHAPTER 30

FAVORS

Ryan found himself back in his father's expansive office with its mahogany and leather furniture, magnificent Lake Michigan view, and Chihuly glass. Although he had returned to the city months earlier, he hadn't discussed business with his father until this afternoon. Partly because of the fallout that ensued after Ryan declined the CM promotion, and partly because Ryan was busy preparing for his first art show and formulating a new business proposal. There was too much he had to sort out. Too many plans to solidify. Ryan wouldn't return to CM until he was fully prepared for a meeting with his father that, until recently, he doubted would ever happen.

At the start of their discussion, Ryan knew he had a lot to lose. While there was a good chance that his father would turn him down, Ryan hoped he would at least respect his loyalty.

"I see you've given this a lot of thought," William Sr. said after listening to Ryan's proposition. He slid his tortoiseshell bifocals off the tip of his nose and set them down on his desk, then leaned his head against his high-backed leather chair and folded his arms neatly across his chest. "I'll admit, I didn't expect this from you."

"Thanks for hearing me out. These last few months haven't been easy." Ryan's posture relaxed slightly while sitting across from his father, feeling the relief of finally having said his peace. "For any of us."

"Sadly, I couldn't agree more." The pinch of distinguished wrinkles across William Sr.'s forehead softened. He rubbed his chin in contemplation. "If there is consolation in any of this, I'd say you've changed in ways I never would have predicted, Ryan. I'm impressed," he said.

After everything that had transpired between the two Chambers men over the years, hearing his father's praise was an unexpected gift.

"I'm glad we had this chance to talk. I wouldn't have come here if it wasn't important," Ryan said while his father nodded in agreement. "Listen, I'm sure you have a lot on your schedule today—I should get going." When Ryan stood up, his father pushed his chair away from the desk and walked him to the door.

"I forgot to mention this earlier," Ryan said as they crossed the room. "I see you named Maria Colton senior VP of operations at the shareholders' meeting back in January. Good choice."

"It's an interim position. What she really wants is a move to the New York office," his father replied. "I think you're well aware that I still have someone else in mind to lead operations. Assuming, of course, that he considers it more than just a 'figurehead' position." The CEO and founder of CM gave his son a sideways glance and then, with the corners of his mouth pulling back into an actual smile, he added, "I'm sure Maria would be very appreciative."

"I guess that remains to be seen." Ryan smiled back, reaching for the door. He thanked his father again before leaving his office and then proceeded to the elevator bay. Once he was in the privacy of the elevator, Ryan leaned against the railing of the brightly lit compartment, let out a heavy sigh, and smiled to himself. He removed his cell phone from his jacket pocket and tapped out a brief text to Brad and Pete:

It's a go!

CHAPTER 31

DIARY

With John keeping Jackie mildly distracted in the front room, Shelby sat at the kitchen table waiting to hear whatever her grandmother needed to say. She watched as Ginny pulled out a step stool and stood on tiptoe to reach an upper cupboard that was rarely used, the one with chipped flower vases, random jars, and coffee cups that people collected as gifts but never end up using for coffee. Pushing aside a tin canister, Ginny reached in and pulled out a small cardboard box.

"What's that?" Shelby asked.

"Something I've been saving for you. It came in the mail last week, but I wanted to give it to you at just the right time."

"For me?"

Ginny stepped off the stool and joined Shelby at the table. She stood beside her and presented Shelby with the box. "For you."

Shelby didn't need to look at the return address to know who sent it. The purple handwriting gave it away.

"I don't understand," Shelby said, rubbing her thumb over

the box's sharp edges, hesitant to open it. "Why would she send me a package when she had plans to come back today? Why not just give it to me in person?"

"You'll notice that it's already been opened. She called me soon after she mailed it and asked me to keep it from you. She was having second thoughts. Once I saw what was inside, I had a long talk with your mother. A *good* talk," Ginny explained, reaching down to set her hand upon Shelby's to steady her fidgeting.

"I don't think this is the best time, Gran. John is here and—"

"It's all right, honey. I'll go out and join them. Give you a little privacy, so you can read what your mother has written." Before leaving, she placed a kiss atop Shelby's head. "Take your time."

Shelby opened the box with a gasp. Inside, tucked in white tissue, was a small red book with gold script and a broken, keyless lock. *How* dare *she take my diary!*

With careful hands, Shelby reached in to take out the diary. As she slid it out of the box, a note slipped out with it.

> *Shelby—*
> *You probably think I was digging through your things. I wasn't. I was simply looking for an old sweater of mine over the Thanksgiving weekend and Dad thought it might have been in your closet. He said you wear some of my old things once in a while, which I think is sweet. Anyway, you were off with Ryan, so I looked for it myself. That's when I found your box of treasures, along with this journal.*
> *Never did find that sweater. But in the end, maybe I was supposed to find this all along.*
> *Love, Mom*

Anger welled inside. Betrayed, again, by her own mother. Shelby was sure she had delighted in pilfering through her innermost thoughts, the innocent expressions of a child, without a hint of regret.

Shelby opened her diary, hoping that she wouldn't find any signs of her mother's trespassing. Instead, she found notes. Dozens of notes, each carefully folded and tucked into selected pages throughout the diary. Her first response was to pluck them all out and tear them into pieces. But there was something about the notes that caused her to pause. They were neat. Carefully placed. Not at all like the letters her mother had sent in the past.

Against her better judgment, she opened the first note, the one that bookmarked Shelby's first diary entry from Christmas Day.

> *Dear Shelby,*
> *I have always regretted my actions on that Christmas morning, so long ago.*
> *It was me who gave you that doll that year, the one you named Polly. I had hoped we could use the doll to begin talking about our relationship, about being mother and daughter. Your grandparents were going to help.*
> *But seeing you there, so beautiful with Polly in your arms, I snapped. I hated myself for not knowing how to hold you in the same way. Instead of taking the blame for my own insecurities, I directed my anger toward you.*
> *I hope, in time, you can forgive me.*
> *Love, Mom*

Shelby wiped her eyes with the back of her hand before folding the note and placing it back in the diary. And so it continued. One by one, she read each note. She found them nestled in among the pages where Shelby recorded the disappointments, fears, and insecurities she felt about her mother. Birthdays. A dance recital. Spelling grades.

Her mother apologized for every misgiving.

When she was finished reading every note, Shelby dropped her head into her hands and cried. The letters contained all of the words she wished her mother had written in the past. Displaced anger. Regret. Responsibility. Pride. Love from afar. It was all there, tucked between pages of her childhood reflections.

What does she expect me to do with these now? It's too late. And it's not enough, she thought, drying her eyes and standing up from the table. *Gran may be ready to welcome her back home, but I'll be damned if I'm going to forgive her so easily.*

CHAPTER 32

CHURCH

Olen had rarely attended services at the Lutheran church on the corner of Pine and Myrtle, but he had been a spiritual man. On most Sunday mornings, while Ginny and Shelby reflected on sermons and sang from their hymnals, Olen had joined Lou Olson and Bernie Cromwell on Bernie's Mainship trawler, the *Nimbus*. It was there where the old friends would go out in search of anything they could nab at the end of a fishing line. During those outings they prayed for fish, worshiped the godliness of the lake, and broke bread together. And yes, they were even known to share a communal bottle of wine—or two. Or perhaps it was simply an ice-packed cooler of Old Milwaukee beer. Regardless, Olen had always said he never felt closer to God than when he was on the lake.

So when it came to Olen's ashes, the Meyers women knew exactly what to do. They would wait for the ice to melt. They would gather on a sunny morning. And then they would take Olen to his church.

"Mornin', ladies," Bernie said as the women climbed aboard

the *Nimbus,* which was idling in its South Point Marina slip. With Shelby and Jackie barely speaking to each other, Ginny was the most animated of the women, dressed in a lavender sundress and carrying a plastic bait bucket that contained her husband's ashes.

Jackie walked unsteadily across the boat deck in her ridiculously high-heeled pink wedges to find a seat, while Shelby rolled up the sleeves of her chambray shirtdress and helped Bernie untie the lines and toss them onto the deck.

Ginny looked around the boat and asked, "Wait, Bernie, where's Lou?"

"Sorry, Ginny, he couldn't make it," Bernie said, coiling the stern line neatly in the corner of the cockpit. "Stomach bug," he added with a sour face. Despite Shelby's somber mood, she couldn't help but appreciate Bernie. On any given summer day, he would have been shoeless and dressed in khakis with frayed hems, faded T-shirts, and a black knit cap that covered his bald head. But on this day, he was dressed in a pair of newly pressed khakis, a navy blue blazer with brass buttons, and a proper shirt and tie. If it weren't for his bare feet, you would have thought he belonged on the *Queen Mary II.*

"Poor man." Ginny shook her head and drummed her fingers against the rim of the orange bait bucket. "I heard it's going around."

At the sound of Ginny's tapping, Jackie shifted in her seat to face her mother. "I still can't believe you put Dad in that disgusting thing," she said with a scrunched-up nose. "It's disrespectful."

"Excuse me, *who's* disrespectful?" Shelby muttered under her breath as she took a seat across from her mother.

"What's that?" Jackie asked, raising an eyebrow in Shelby's direction.

Shelby looked away and Ginny continued with her tapping. "Actually, he would have thought it was funny," Ginny said of the bucket. "When I say good-bye, I want to remember him laughing." Looking down at the pail and running her hands over its surface, she added, "Besides, it's not like there was ever any bait in here. I cared enough to buy him a new bucket. It's even his favorite color!"

"You're right, Mother," Jackie said with a look of mockery on her heavily made-up face. "I'm sure Dad would have *loved* to know that, in the end, his life was reduced to being no greater than a bucket of minnows."

Shelby was about to stick up for her grandmother when Bernie interrupted with perfect timing to say it was time to cast off. He shifted into Reverse and used the bow thrusters to alternate power from the starboard and port side jets to skillfully ease the boat out of its slip. Then, as the boat slowly powered forward, they passed the *Spindrift,* Ryan's former charter. Looking at the sailboat as the *Nimbus* continued to motor out of the marina, Shelby felt as empty as it appeared. *That boat shouldn't be bound to its slip, so lifeless and alone,* she thought. *It should be out on the lake in full sail, crashing over the waves and racing in the wind. It should be alive!*

Once the *Nimbus* passed the end of the dock and the breakwater pilings, it picked up speed and headed out to open water. With the swift breeze whipping her hair back, the sun warming her face, and the beauty of the Apostle Islands surrounding her, Shelby realized she hadn't been on the water since sailing with Ryan. She had missed the lake.

"So, ladies, where are we headed?" Bernie called over his shoulder, loud enough to be heard over the engine. Jackie turned away from the group and stared off toward the mainland as Shelby glanced at Ginny for direction. She was relieved when her grandmother stood and made her way to the captain's chair.

"I trust you, Bernie," Ginny said, clutching the bucket of

her husband's remains against her chest. "You know where he'd want us to go."

Bernie reached down beside his chair and pulled out his black knit cap, stretched it over his bald, sun-freckled head, and grinned. "I do indeed."

She patted his shoulder in gratitude. They would make the hour-long trek to Stockton Island, a favorite with the Meyers family and most area boaters. The island boasted scenic walking trails, and a stretch of sandy beach that was as stunning as any you would find in the tropics. Although one would typically find several boats anchored around Stockton during the weekends and holidays, this was a Tuesday and they knew the island would be virtually deserted.

"Do you remember what Olen used to say about Devil's Island, Ginny?" Bernie asked.

Ginny nodded with a grin, saying, "What's the Devil doing smack in the middle of this heaven on earth?"

"That's right. This heaven on earth," Bernie recalled fondly as the boat skipped across the sun-sparkled waves that led to Stockton.

The women spoke very little during their boat trip through the archipelago. Shelby knew their silence had less to do with the ashes than the upheaval Jackie had caused by returning home. When Shelby first learned of her mother's intention to move back to the farm, her answer had been a firm no. But now, after some thought, she wasn't sure. Watching her grandmother chat openly with Bernie, Shelby knew Ginny didn't deserve to live in a tension-filled home. She deserved a mended relationship with her daughter. As for Shelby, her hope for a true relationship with her mother had been extinguished long ago. Although her grandmother talked about people's inherent ability to change, and of how losing her father had been a profound eye-opener for Jackie, Shelby was more wary of her mother's motives now than ever before.

If only her grandfather were there, Shelby wished. He would know what to do. Sadly, the hub of their family wheel was gone, and without him, Shelby didn't see how they could hold together and move forward.

Once they reached the island, Shelby knelt down at the bow of the boat and signaled Bernie as soon as the anchor caught on the lake floor and held. When Bernie cut the engine, the boat floated in silent isolation off of Stockton's Julian Bay. Shelby stood and leaned over the guardrail. Due to the excellent visibility of the lake's clear water, she could easily see the triangular blades at the end of the anchor hooked securely into the ripples of light sand nearly twelve feet below the boat. She listened to gentle waves lapping against the helm and the hollow *glug* of water resonating underneath the hull. Two gulls passed overhead, calling out in their search for food. Spying nothing on the *Nimbus,* they continued on toward the beach.

"Okay," Ginny said, standing up and straightening the front of her skirt. "I suppose we should get started."

Bernie had climbed down into the cabin and now reappeared with a bouquet of field daisies, zinnia, and white hydrangea. "Before you do, Ginny, I have these for you," he said, standing before her with as much respect as a uniformed soldier presenting a folded American flag to the widow of a fallen comrade. "They're from our garden. Marilyn wanted you to have them."

"They're perfect. Thank you," Ginny said, graciously accepting the flowers.

Bernie turned toward the water, pulled off his cap and held it to his heart, and then tossed a single daisy into the lake. "See ya 'round, pal," he said solemnly before descending back into the cabin to give the family privacy.

★　★　★

Standing at the stern of the boat, the women circled around the open bait bucket and peered down at the contents within. Ginny held the lid to the bucket in one hand and Bernie's flowers in the other. Shelby shifted her eyes from her grandmother and her mother, waiting for someone to say something.

"All right, let's get on with it," Ginny said finally. "We have a ceremony to perform."

"I'm not touching that," Jackie said firmly, taking a step back. "There are pieces of bone in there! I thought it would all be dust. Why are there chunks of bone?"

"It's perfectly normal," Ginny replied.

"It's gruesome."

"It's your father, Jackie," Ginny scolded in a forced whisper, as if Olen could overhear them. "Show some respect."

"What can I do, Gran?" Shelby asked. She wanted this to be over, so she could return home, get back to her routine, and put the past behind her.

"Shelby, I'd like you to take these flowers. Jackie, hold the pail up on the ledge here," Ginny said, passing the flowers to Shelby. Jackie looked visibly repulsed as she stepped forward and held the bucket gingerly by her fingertips, raising her pinkies in the air. Ginny set down the lid and removed a folded piece of paper from her dress pocket, explaining how she had selected a favorite poem for the occasion.

The breeze picked up a bit and the boat began to rock along with the waves, so instead of standing, they knelt on the starboard cockpit bench as parishioners would on a church pew. Shelby felt anxious. She wanted to talk about how much better this day would have been without her mother present. How Shelby resented her mother for being disrespectful. Or how she wished everything over the past year could have turned out differently. She wanted to shout it out loud! Make her mother take notice!

But she didn't. Out of consideration for her grandmother, Shelby remained as quiet as a hushed child at worship.

"Thanks for being here with me today, girls. I know that Olen would be happy to see us all together," Ginny began. "Instead of a Bible verse, I thought this would be more fitting for him. It's by Robert Frost. Your grandfather admired Frost for many reasons, but he always talked about having a sort of kinship with the writer because both men lived on apple orchards and loved the entire growing season, from bloom to harvest."

Shelby gave her grandmother an encouraging nod, while Jackie smacked her glossy lips together with a blatant lack of interest and moved to sit across from them. Shelby disregarded her and looked out at the lake as a gust of wind raced across the water's surface in a shifting orb of ripples and shadow. Like a dark phantom, it spun and darted past their boat and disappeared. It was time to say farewell.

"It's titled, 'After Apple-Picking.' Okay. Here we go." Ginny took a deep breath, composed herself, and began to read:

> " *'My long two-pointed ladder's sticking through a tree*
> *Toward heaven still,*
> *And there's a barrel that I didn't fill*
> *Beside it, and there may be two or three*
> *Apples I didn't pick upon some bough.'* "

Hearing a sniffle, Shelby looked over at her mother. Jackie had one hand clasped over her mouth, trying to hold back a sound, but her eyes were laughing.

> " *'But I am done with apple-picking now.*
> *Essence of winter sleep is on the night,*
> *The scent of apples: I am drowsing off.'* "

Ginny decided that it would be easier to sit on the cush-
ioned benches than kneel, so she and Shelby shifted in their
seats while Jackie dabbed at her eyes and nodded toward the
paper in Ginny's hand. "How long is this poem, anyway?"

"Hmm? Too long?" Ginny asked, a bit flustered by her
emotions and the interruption. "Let's see, maybe I'll just jump
ahead . . ."

"Gran, it's beautiful. Don't rush it," Shelby insisted. "Take
your time."

"It's all right, Shelby. Let's see . . ." Ginny replied, looking
down at her notes. "Okay, I'll just pick it up here."

For reasons that Shelby couldn't begin to understand,
Jackie shook her head and smirked.

"You know what, Gran? It's not all right," Shelby blurted
out and stood to face her mother. "Mom, for once—for one
single day—could you try not to belittle everything we do
or say?"

Jackie grasped her chest in feigned dismay. "Excuse me?"

"Today, of all days, you need to be on our side."

"Be on your side?" Jackie laughed. "Shelby, darling, I'm *always* on your side."

"That's bullshit!" Shelby burst out, surprising everyone,
herself most of all.

"Girls!" Ginny snapped. "Remind yourselves why we're
here."

"I'm sorry, Gran, but I can't take it anymore!"

Ginny's voice softened quickly, saying, "Don't forget the
diary, dear—"

"Please don't bring that up now, Gran. She snooped through
my things and read my personal thoughts—yes, the notes were
nice," she admitted, glancing at her mother to gauge her reaction before continuing. "But let's be real. She comes home and
you and I end up walking on pins and needles. Just like we al-

ways do. 'Let's not upset Jackie.' 'You know how Jackie gets when she's angry.' 'She's only in town for a short while, so we need to make the most of our time with her.' It's crazy. She doesn't deserve it!"

"Really?" Ginny closed her eyes. "Do we have to do this now?"

"Go on, Shelby," Jackie challenged with narrowed eyes. "I'm interested. Tell me what a terrible mother I am. Let's hear *again* how difficult it is to have me around. This is enlightening."

"Why do you care what I think? You left me!" Shelby lashed out in an angry voice that she barely recognized as her own. "Let's get real, shall we, *Mother?* I know why you want to move back. You failed in California. You failed in your relationships. And you failed with me!" Shelby heard her words, but felt disconnected from them, as if she were watching everything unravel from a distance. "You wanna know what I think? You think you can get all cozy with Gran again so you can convince her to sell the farm and make a quick profit for yourself. Selling our home and tearing apart what's left of our family? That would be icing on the cake for you!"

"You're something else, you know that, Shelby?" Jackie said, turning to Ginny. "This is how you raised her, Mother? To be so accusatory?"

Ginny shook her head, clutching the poem tightly in her hands. "No . . ." she murmured.

"Gran taught me to be strong," Shelby declared.

"Strong?! Then why do you follow your grandparents around like a puppy dog? Why are you so afraid to live your life? You're not fooling me, little girl—I grew up in the same house you did. The only difference? I had the strength to leave. Do you hear me? You're locked in and you don't even know it. I'm doing you a favor!"

"Enough!" Ginny cried out, reaching for the flower bouquet that lay beside her and then shaking it high in the air like a white flag, white petals falling to her feet. "We are here to honor my husband and you *will* be respectful, do you hear me?"

"Be real, Mother," said Jackie, folding her arms across her chest.

"You want me to be real? How's this for real, Jackie," Ginny scolded. "Leaving Bayfield the way you did was not an act of strength. I love you, but you were a coward. I never thought I could be more disappointed in you than the day you left Shelby."

"Gran, please." Shelby's guilt for having started this argument was sinking in. If only she had remained quiet.

"But you proved me wrong, didn't you," Ginny continued. "Years of neglect—disappointment after disappointment—abandoning your child over and over again? That kind of heartache has been absolutely devastating to Shelby. And to our entire family."

The clamor of angry voices muffled in Shelby's ears. She couldn't listen to it any longer. She turned away from Ginny and Jackie and cast her eyes on the glistening water around them and imagined how wonderful it would feel to disappear . . . to dive into the lake and wash it all away. . . .

"You want to see devastation?" Jackie jumped and swung her arm squarely into the bait bucket with a whack, *sending it careening into the air. The gray, ashen contents dispersed into the air in a cloud and sprinkled down over the lake water, while the orange bucket hit the surface with a splash. It bobbed for a moment before taking in water. The container, like the roots that held their family together, was barely hanging on.*

Without thinking, Shelby leapt off the stern of the boat and dove headfirst through the ashy film that floated on the lake's surface like algae. She hit the water and descended into its depths. The cold numbed her body and stole her breath. Her clothes wrapped tightly around her body and weighted her down as she sank deeper.

She had escaped the voices. She was free of everything: her mother's disdain; Gran's disappointment; Ryan's heartache; John's consolation; Nic's challenge; and the media's intrusion. Their voices blended together in a loud cacophony until—finally—she was deep enough into the icy water that all she was left with was the rhythm of her heartbeat and the hushed static of water rushing past her ears.

And then, out of the quiet, came the sound of a different voice. But unlike the frigid water, the voice was warm and caring. Even though she was losing her senses to the cold, Shelby stopped moving her arms and legs and floated motionless to listen.

You were loved, so you can go.

Grandpa.

She wanted desperately to stay in the depths and listen to her grandfather's voice again. He was there. Shelby opened her eyes to see bits of ash and crushed bone fragment cascade down from the surface of the lake like a gentle snowfall. Streaks of sunlight pierced through the water, as if reaching for her. A grandfather's outstretched arms, pulling his granddaughter into an embrace as the snow fell lightly upon the orchard.

You were loved, so you can go.

And it was then, as her body began to shake from the cold and her lungs were desperate for a breath, that she knew what had to be done.

With bold arm strokes and strong kicks, she pushed upward toward the surface. She burst out of the water with a splash, gasping for air. And then it occurred to her. She didn't need her mother's acceptance to be whole. She didn't need to forge a life in Bayfield and carry on their business, just to prove her gratitude toward her grandparents. And while she loved John as a friend, she didn't need him to save her. For all of those things, she only needed to rely on herself. Bobbing in the endless waves of Lake Superior, she began to laugh. It started low, and then it grew into a liberating, joyful laugh.

For the first time in her life, Shelby knew exactly what she was meant to do.

"Shelby! What's gotten into you?" Ginny asked, taking hold of Shelby's arm and giving her a shake. "Shelby!"

It was a dream.

"She's really lost it this time," Jackie added. "Who stares off into space and then starts laughing in the middle of an argument?"

Shelby looked at the orange bucket, which was still sitting on the ledge of the boat with all of its contents intact. Her cheeks felt wet, but rather than lake water, she had been cleansed by her own tears. She had escaped into a daydream and re-emerged with a renewed sense of purpose.

"I'd like to know what you think is so funny," Jackie continued.

"Gran, I'm sorry. I don't know what came over me." Shelby took her grandmother's hand. "I don't think it matters if we give Grandpa a perfect send-off, or if we make mistakes."

Jackie shook her head. "What in the heck is she talking about now?"

"You know, Mom. I changed my mind," Shelby said, fixing her eyes on her mother. "I honestly don't care anymore if you're on my side or not. What's important is that you support Gran."

"What?"

"I'm done waiting for the day for you to be a parent. I gave up on that a long time ago."

Jackie raised her arms in exasperation and looked in Ginny's direction. "Mother, are you listening to this?"

"Quiet, Jackie." Ginny put her other hand up to Jackie, and then to Shelby she asked, "You were saying?"

"I know this seems crazy, but I have a feeling we're going to be okay. And I think it's time for us to move on," Shelby said.

Ginny eyes glistened with emotion. Shelby knew her grandmother understood every word that was left unspoken. After giving her flushed cheeks a pat with both hands and clearing her throat, Ginny said in jest, "So, what'll we do about this one?" She raised her eyebrows and pointed her chin toward Jackie.

"If you really want to stay on the farm, you'll have to trade in those fancy shoes of yours for a pair of work boots," Shelby told Jackie. "And you'll need to help work the orchard, and support Gran. If you mistreat her, or try to sell the family business, you're out—even if I have to drag you off the property myself."

Jackie threw her arms out to her sides. "Can she do that?" she asked Ginny.

"She can—and she will." Ginny beamed.

Shelby expected a comeback from her mother. But instead, there was only silence. Jackie looked at her hands, which lay clenched together in her lap. Finally, she said, "You have no idea what it's like."

"What?" Shelby asked carefully.

"To realize your life has been nothing but one long string of lousy decisions." She looked up at her daughter and, with a shaky voice, said the words that Shelby recently read in hidden notes within her diary, but never thought she'd hear aloud. "My parents. My career. Men. I should have done it all better," she said simply. "And you're right, Shelby. Out of everything I've done, the worst has been failing you."

"Jackie," Ginny uttered gently.

With a trembling lower lip, Jackie continued, "And the thing is, coming back here, I realize the only thing I did right was to let Mom and Dad raise you. They helped you to become the woman that I failed to be."

Shelby inhaled through her nose, filling her chest with the cleansing lake air. She then let out a long, deliberate exhale through her mouth. Processing the moment. Feeling strong and renewed. Shelby approached her mother and sat down beside her. "Tell us the truth. Why did you come back?"

Jackie's tired, drawn face looked up at her daughter. "It was time for me to come home," she cried, wringing her hands nervously. "I need to make it right."

"It will take time."

"Yes."

"If you're willing to talk, I am, too." When Shelby placed her arm over her mother's hunched shoulders, Jackie dabbed at her eyes and let out a trembling sigh of relief. "But first, we need to say good-bye."

And to that, Ginny whispered a heartfelt "Amen," cleared her voice, and finished the Frost poem.

> "'. . . I could tell
> *What form my dreaming was about to take.*
> *Magnified apples appear and reappear,*
> *Stem end and blossom end,*
> *And every fleck of russet showing clear.*
> *My instep arch not only keeps the ache,*
> *It keeps the pressure of a ladder-round.*
> *I feel the ladder sway as the boughs bend.*
> *And I keep hearing from the cellar bin*
> *That rumbling sound*

Of load on load of apples coming in.
For I have had too much
Of apple-picking; I am overtired
Of the great harvest I myself desired.
There were ten thousand thousand fruit to touch,
Cherish in hand, lift down, and not let fall.' "

CHAPTER 33

INSPIRATION

A quiet rumble could be heard in the distance as an evening thundercloud moved farther away from Chicago's River North gallery district. As the summer rain continued to patter in the street and on the rooftops, art lovers and friends mingled about a white-walled gallery with exhibit brochures and cocktails in hand. A melody of voices, clinking glasses, and shuffling feet played backup to saxophone jazz that piped in through overhead speakers. At the front of the gallery, heavy raindrops clung to the darkened windows and caught the gleam of a corner streetlight as they crept slowly downward. Late arrivals hurried in through the front door, shaking out their wet umbrellas and wiping their feet at the entrance.

Ryan stood near the windows, speaking with two couples about a photograph of a woman's petite work boots, well worn and tied with red lace, bracing against a massive anchor and a heavy coil of rusting chain links on a ferry deck. "I've never met anyone like her," he said with a laugh, remembering the lively morning he had spent with Nic taking photos on the *Island Queen*. Looking at the larger-than-life print on the wall, he hoped people would second-guess which was stronger—the pile of iron or the gal in the boots.

Twelve hours earlier, while standing at the kitchen counter in his apartment with a cup of coffee and a copy of the morning *Times,* Ryan was relieved to read Josh Stone's preview of the show, *Family Trees—A Bayfield Story.* Ryan had expected Stone to be leery of his artistic ability, and the reviewer didn't disappoint. In fact, Stone made his initial doubts clear in his opening paragraph. "Most children born into the spotlight can make a living out of riding upon their parents' coattails, but offer little in the way of authentic talent," Stone wrote. "Will Chambers unabashedly proved this reviewer wrong."

Stone went on to compare Ryan's work to that of Craig Blacklock, renowned photographer and lifelong supporter of Lake Superior. "Whereas Blacklock captures the patterns, colors, and textures that are found in nature, Chambers drops the natural world into the background and pulls the people who dwell in it into close focus. By paying careful attention to both the scene and the subject, his work beautifully portrays an area of the Upper Midwest that few people have explored," the article read. "Chambers's portraits are filled with such a surprising depth of character that the viewer feels pulled into a story, as told beautifully in a single frame."

While the review had been a relief for Ryan, seeing people's reactions at the show opening that evening was far more rewarding. Ryan continued to move about the room, speaking easily with clutches of people who stood in front of the large-scale photographs displayed throughout the space. He found his friends, Brad and Pete and their wives, admiring a close-up of Gloria's weathered hands weaving a wreath out of ground moss, her fingers berry-stained and etched in dirt-filled creases.

The surgeon who lived in the apartment beneath Ryan's was standing before his piece, *Remember,* with her partner. The women held hands while admiring the photograph of Jeff's nephew, Benjamin, whom he had met on several occasions with Shelby. With the lake as a backdrop, the photograph showed the child holding on to the end of his father's shirt with one hand, and a small red sailboat in the other.

"William, you remember our attorney, Al Jackson," said one of his parents' friends as she threaded her arm around his and led him to the picture of Ginny and Olen driving through an apple grove in a vintage John Deere. While Ryan chatted amicably about the collection, he pointed out a series of orchard photographs that influenced the show's theme.

After wrapping up his conversation with Mr. Jackson, Ryan glanced to his left to see his mother, dressed impeccably in a tailored summer suit, holding her hand delicately over her abdomen as she considered the photograph of Rachelle and the wisp of steam that swirled out of her coffee mug and around her pregnant belly like a protective spirit.

Looking about the room, Ryan realized that the night was about more than branching out on his own. Or about the art. There was tremendous satisfaction for having taken the advice Shelby gave him during one of their talks in the orchard. He had found a way to embrace his life experiences and, in his own way, attempt to make a difference.

But the evening wasn't all about him. It was also about another man whom Shelby loved. The proceeds from the exhibit would go toward a newly formed Olen G. Meyers memorial fund to benefit conservation efforts throughout the Apostle Islands. He had asked for Ginny's approval before moving forward with the idea, and, to his relief, she gave him her blessing. Persuading her to accept a separate financial gift, one to put away in case anything ever happened to her, Shelby, or the farm, wasn't as easy.

"I'd appreciate it if you didn't mention any of this to Shelby," he had said to Ginny over the phone. "You have my word," she said with understanding and gratitude. As he hung up the phone that day, he was relieved to know he had found a way to honor his promise to Olen.

"Great turnout tonight, William," said CM's ruddy-faced programming vice president, who gave Ryan a congratulatory slap on the back. "I like the arrangement you and your father cooked up. It'll be terrific for our community affairs outreach."

"I'm glad to hear you say that, Jerry."

"So you'll be producing a new series on small-town communities that flank our Great Lakes, is that it?"

"Yes, and the proceeds from that programming will go directly into conservation," Ryan said, looking around the room for someone who would be interested in speaking business with the guy. "I thought it would be a great way for CM to give back."

"But did I read the memo correctly—that we're contributing one hundred percent of the—" Jerry began.

"Hang on, Jerry—hold that thought," Ryan interrupted, reaching out to grab hold of the Italian linen suit that brushed past them. "Dad! Just the person I was looking for." When William Sr. turned and saw Ryan, his face lit up in a smile. *I'll be damned. He actually looks proud,* Ryan thought to himself.

"Will—terrific evening," his father said, raising his glass of chardonnay with a nod. "There are a lot of red dots out there. Your pieces seem to be selling quickly."

"I appreciate it, Dad. Thanks," Ryan said, guiding him into the conversation. "Say, I thought you'd like to talk to Jerry for a minute. He has questions about how we structured the financing of our new conservation series."

"Jerry!" his father said, giving the man a welcoming slap on the back.

Pleased to leave the business aspects of his plan to his father, Ryan moved on to speak with others.

"How on earth did you capture this shot of the ice breaking along the shore? It looks so dangerous—and cold!" said a middle-aged woman with a sleek black bob and a boozy slur in her speech. At least twenty years his senior, the woman practically purred. "How do you stay warm on shoots like that?" she gushed while boldly running the long nail of her manicured finger down the side of his arm.

"Lots of layers, I suppose—I'm glad you like it," he said politely before excusing himself and heading directly for the bar. Just as Ryan reached for a glass of wine, however, someone approached him from behind and grasped his shoulder. It was Lance Middleton, the gallery's lanky publicist with facial features that were as sharp as his spiked white hair.

"What a night, man! What a night!" Lance said as he adjusted his fashionable black-rimmed eyeglasses. "But listen, before you grab a drink, there's someone I need you to meet."

"Can it wait? I could use one of these."

"Later—now, come on, follow me. A buyer has been admiring *Inspired*." Lance was referring to Ryan's favorite piece in the show. The one tucked away in the back corner of the gallery. The one he hoped would never sell. "She arrived a short while ago and isn't staying long. Before she commits to the piece, she told me she wants to meet the artist. So it's time to turn on that Chambers charm."

Ryan shoved his hands into his pockets and reluctantly followed Lance back through the crowded space. After reveling in the high of a successful debut, this impending sale made him feel a bit crestfallen. *Let's get this over with quickly,* he thought, putting on a professional face. *It's just a print. I'll always have the original.*

"Who is the buyer?" Ryan asked Lance as they meandered through the crowd.

"A Ms. Bucket," Lance answered, ushering Ryan past a series of photographs of the Meyers orchard. Trees. Apples. Leaves. The images had a dizzying effect as Ryan continued to make his way to the back corner.

"Did you say Bucket?" Ryan asked. His mind raced back to one evening spent in the Bayfield cottage with Shelby. It was a bitterly cold night, a perfect evening to sit on the couch and read by the fire. He had his feet up on the coffee table, while she stretched out on the length of the couch and rested her head on his lap. She had looked up from her book and smiled when Ryan explained how he occasionally used the name Charlie Bucket as an alias, a reference to the young boy in *Charlie and the Chocolate Factory.*

"That's right," Lance said, stopping just before they reached a slender woman standing before *Inspired,* an expansive piece that took up most of the wall space. She wore a dress that was as pale and blue as the water in the photograph. With his hand covering his mouth, Lance leaned over and whispered, "I believe her first name is Carly."

Ryan paid little attention to Lance as he noticed how the woman's brunette hair fell gently over her shoulders. She began to fidget with her dress and then stumbled slightly when her ankle turned in her high-heel sandals. *She's no Cinderella,* he thought, grinning.

"Wait, no—her name's Charley. Ms. Charley Bucket," Lance corrected in a hushed voice. "I'll introduce you."

Ryan shook his head and lifted his hand slightly. "It's okay," he said. "I'll introduce myself." He took a cautious step closer, feeling an anxious twinge in his stomach. *Shelby,* he thought in utter disbelief. *Of course it had to be her.* He needed to breathe. Keep calm. He rubbed his hands together, shaking out his nerves, and looked over Shelby's shoulder at the framed piece of art.

He had taken the photograph along Madeline Island's shoreline nearly a year ago. In it, Shelby was sitting on a rock that jetted out over the lake. As she looked toward the horizon that day, lost in thought, she was unaware that Ryan was sitting in a red kayak, floating in the water just offshore. The moment the photograph was taken, Ryan had felt inspired to move to Bayfield—and the course of his life was irrevocably changed.

Ryan exhaled slowly and then took the last few steps until he was standing beside her, facing the photograph. "Charley Bucket," he said lightheartedly, loving the way she had played with Lance by using his favorite alias.

"Ryan." When she turned to him, he remembered just how much he missed the warmth of her brown eyes. The two of them stood together, in the quiet corner of the gallery, neither one knowing quite what to say. He sensed they were both feeling the intensity of their reunion. Ryan had always thought she was beautiful, even in faded jeans and work boots, but tonight—the sight of her in the dress, her hair done, wearing a hint of lipstick, and the delicate silver and turquoise necklace from her grandfather hanging delicately around her neck—she took his breath away.

"You did it," Shelby said, breaking the silence between them and nervously rubbing her thumb back and forth over the exhibit brochure in her hand. "When I walked through the gallery, I felt like I was home again—the farm, the people, the lake. I'm speechless." It took everything in him not to reach out and touch her. She lifted the brochure and pointed to her grandfather's name. "And then I saw this . . ."

He cleared his throat, looked down at the paper in her hand, and simply said, "He meant a lot to me." A thousand expressions of adoration raced through his head, and yet Ryan held back his words.

"It's incredible." He heard the sadness in her voice. "He would have been honored," Shelby said as she reached her hand toward his, and with apparent second thoughts, pulled it back again.

God, what I wouldn't give to have her back. Ryan's heart raced and his arms ached to hold her. He remembered how he felt on the night of their first kiss as they lay on the sand dunes outside of town, under the glow of the northern lights. He longed to kiss her again, but she was the one who had said good-bye. He swallowed hard. He didn't know why she had come. And so, in his uncertainty, all he could do was ask for the truth.

"It's so good to see you here. You have no idea," he said. "But I'll admit I'm not only surprised. I'm confused. What brought you here?"

She took a hesitant step closer to him, reached again for his hand, and this time easily wove her fingers through his. Beneath her touch, his nerves melted away like snow in the spring. "It's pretty simple, really. Bayfield no longer feels like home . . . without you in it."

And now I'm home, he thought, wrapping his arm around the familiar curve of her waist.

"I love you, Ryan," she said.

He could feel the warmth of her body through the silky fabric of her dress.

"Tell me again."

She happily obliged as he gently eased her closer. He whispered her name, closing his eyes as he brushed a kiss upon her cheek. When she lifted her head toward his, Ryan kissed her lips and felt his heartache fade away.

Words could wait. The apologies. Explanations. Fresh starts. For now, he was carried away in a wave of joy that took him out of the downtown art gallery and back to the tranquility of the lake.

"Hey, Ryan—excuse me," Lance said awkwardly, tapping Ryan on the shoulder before taking a few quick steps back. "Someone from the *Tribune* is here to get a photo?"

Giving Lance little regard, Ryan touched Shelby's chin and tenderly lifted her face back toward his. He didn't care about Lance, the newspaper, or anyone who might overhear him.

"Shelby Meyers, if you'll let me, I want to spend the rest of my life loving you."

"Uh, Ryan?" Lance stepped in to interrupt again, anxiously tapping a scrolled-up pamphlet against his thigh. "Hate to break this up, but . . . the newspaper?"

"Hang on, Lance," Ryan said with a broad smile that matched Shelby's. "I still have some unfinished business with Ms. Bucket." With Shelby wrapped safely in Ryan's arms, he expressed his love with one more kiss. And there, surrounded by images of her home and his hopes, Ryan embraced his inspiration.

ACKNOWLEDGMENTS

Publishing my first novel is a dream that simply would not have come true without the support of so many people. . . .

Joëlle Delbourgo, my literary agent, who opened the world of publishing to me. I'm grateful for your kindness, expertise, and unwavering support.

Martin Biro, my editor, for your enthusiasm for my work and your insightful feedback that has helped strengthen *Family Trees.*

The talented team at Kensington Publishing for everything you have done behind the scenes to help launch this novel.

Anne Greenwood Brown, for sharing your advice, encouragement, and laughter as I pursued each milestone on the way to publication.

Sarah Comber, Beth Djalali, Angela Johnson, and Sarah Quickel, for reading those early drafts and giving your thoughtful input.

My former English teachers, for sharing their love of literature and encouraging me to find my writing voice, especially Marcia Aubineau and Olivia Frey.

The Midwest Writers Group, whose critique session early in this process gave me just the boost I needed.

The Erickson family, whose Bayfield orchard I have enjoyed for years and which served as the inspiration for Meyers Orchard. Thank you for the advice (and the apple cider doughnuts!).

My wonderful circle of friends, who have tirelessly listened to my stories of writing highs and lows as we met over coffee, walks, and dinner parties that lasted well into the evening. *Cheers!*

Most importantly, to those on my own family tree . . .

My husband, David, for believing I could become an author long before I believed it myself. As always, your love inspires me and your support makes everything possible.

My children, Logan, Ethan, and Kate, for filling my life with joy. The three of you make me laugh and love like no one else.

My parents, Mary and Lars Carlson, for sharing your love of Lake Superior, always encouraging my storytelling ways, providing endless support, and for being as excited about this novel as I am.

My brother and sister-in-law, Erik and Libby Carlson, for reviewing drafts and cheering me on from the South.

My grandmother, Elizabeth Biorn, for your smile and grace, and for the advice you wrote along the margins of my manuscript.

Laurel March, Clyde and Debi March, and my extended family, for your incredible support.

Teddy, for keeping my feet warm while I worked. Good dog.

And finally, thanks to *you,* the reader, for picking up this novel by a new author. I hope you enjoy reading Ryan and Shelby's story as much as I enjoyed writing it.

—Kerstin

GREAT BOOKS, GREAT SAVINGS!

When You Visit Our Website:
www.kensingtonbooks.com
You Can Save Money Off The Retail Price
Of Any Book You Purchase!

- **All Your Favorite Kensington Authors**
- **New Releases & Timeless Classics**
- **Overnight Shipping Available**
- **eBooks Available For Many Titles**
- **All Major Credit Cards Accepted**

Visit Us Today To Start Saving!
www.kensingtonbooks.com

All Orders Are Subject To Availability.
Shipping and Handling Charges Apply.
Offers and Prices Subject To Change Without Notice.